WORTH ANY COST

A GAMING THE SYSTEM NOVEL

Brenna Aubrey

SILVER GRIFFON ASSOCIATES
ORANGE, CA, USA

Silver Griffon Associates
P.O. Box 7383
Orange, CA 92863

Publisher's Note: This is a work of fiction. Names, characters, places, and incidents are a product of the author's imagination. Locales and public names are sometimes used for atmospheric purposes. Any resemblance to actual people, living or dead, or to businesses, companies, events, institutions, or locales is completely coincidental.

Trademarked names appear throughout this book. Rather than use a trademark symbol with every occurrence of a trademarked name, names are used in an editorial fashion, with no intention of infringement of the respective owner's trademark.

Book Layout ©2017 BookDesignTemplates.com
Cover Art ©2017 Sarah Hansen, Okay Creations
Copy edited by Jacy Mackin

Worth Any Cost/ Brenna Aubrey. – 1st ed.
First Printing 2017
Printed in the USA
ISBN 978-1-940951-33-1

This one is for the fur-babies, my cuddle-buddies who would much rather I throw toys than type on my keyboard all day.

ACKNOWLEDGEMENTS

As always, I fully acknowledge that I could never produce a book by myself. It takes a team and I've got the best. Thank you to Kate and Sabrina, my first readers, who comb over the manuscript and irk me regularly with their insightful comments while I scratch my head and figure out how I'm going to fix the problems! Thanks to my production team: Sarah Hansen for the gorgeous cover, Jenn Beach, for all the other graphics provided, for Jacy--who stepped in at the last minute with her help when I was in a crisis! A BIG thank you!

Thanks, in addition to... authors Sylvie Fox, Meghan March and Sarah Castile for the answers to my legal questions. And Leigh and Natasha for your wonderful moral support. Thank you Tessa, blurb goddess extraordinaire!

Major gratitude to all the bloggers and reviewers who take time to read and review my books Your work is invaluable to me and I'm so appreciative. Thanks to the bookworms in my Brenna Aubrey Book group for all your encouragement, help and enthusiasm. I know you love these characters as much as I do and you blow me away every day by your awesomeness. I'm so glad to have met each and every one of you.

Lastly, thanks to my family. It's not easy living with a writer and especially when I go into stress mode. Thank you for being so patient while I'm playing the hermit or I'm out of town or completely distracted while physically present because my characters are talking to me in my head. For my wonderful husband and my amazing kids. I'm proud to be part of your family and I love you more than words can express. xoxox

Chapter 1
Adam

RUNNING A COMPANY ON THE OTHER SIDE OF THE Pacific Ocean from headquarters via email, texts and laggy video chats was no easy feat. Even for someone who viewed a smartphone as an artificial appendage. What made it even more difficult was a pronounced lack of sleep.

In fact, I hadn't had a decent night's sleep in almost a week. And I was sure that until I landed in LA in ten hours, I wouldn't have another one. The fast-paced, exhausting tour through Beijing, Shenzhen, and Shanghai ended in Tokyo, with me waiting for the next leg of the long trek home. But Draco Multimedia Entertainment's prospects in Asia already looked wider and brighter. So the trip had not been for nothing.

From my table in the first-class lounge at the Haneda airport in Tokyo, I sent off a flurry of emails and text messages while my hot breakfast grew cold. Jordan Fawkes, my CFO, sat across from me, drowning his eggs in ketchup while complaining there was no salsa, his preferred condiment for eggs. How unfortunate there wasn't some kind of law in Japan against smothering your eggs in condiments.

"China sure was a trip," Jordan said after he chewed and swallowed his eggs, cutting into some sausage. "I gotta take April back there someday so I can enjoy it without doing the eleven-

1

cities-in-ten-days tour on crack. I didn't even get to see the damn Great Wall."

Fighting a grin, I polished off my text message. "Maybe for your honeymoon."

His glare over the rim of his coffee cup made it harder to contain the smile. "Don't drag all of us down with you, Mr. Groom-to-be."

I raised my brows. "Still not sure April's the one?"

He shrugged stiffly. "It's not that at all. I'm in no hurry to make it official. What's the rush? She isn't, either. She's still finishing up graduate school. Why ruin a good thing with marriage?"

Stabbing at my eggs, I fought a grimace, but managed to fake a yawn. "God, you're so predictable."

"So are you...I don't think you've put that phone down since we left Shanghai."

"I have a company to run," I muttered through my teeth after forking a bite in and swallowing. The entire time, my phone buzzed at me.

"Seems like you're just mumbling obscenities and complaining about stack overflow—whatever the hell *that* is."

"It's a very serious IT problem. And if we don't get a handle on it, we're going to have even more problems." I sighed.

Jordan frowned. "Then let Al handle it. He *is* our IT director." I glanced at Jordan out of the corner of my eyes before sitting back and setting the phone aside. "What's that look for? Is he *not* handling it? Do I need to break a few fingers?"

Shrugging, I rubbed the back of my neck. "He's got issues..." What more could I say without breaking the man's confidence? His wife had recently left him, and he'd been slowly falling apart.

He'd asked for understanding, and I'd given it to him. But how to explain that without revealing the private details to my CFO?

Jordan sipped again at his coffee. "Then he needs to sort them out and start working as hard as the rest of us do, dammit."

"It's my purview. I'll handle it," I reassured him.

"If this starts hurting our bottom line, then it's *my* purview, too."

I frowned. "Back off and give me a chance to assess the situation once we get back. I'll keep you posted. Besides, how can you solve the problem when you don't even understand it?"

He shrugged. "I'll leave that to the nerds. Let me know when you want your bank account balanced." Jordan took another sip and swirled the dark liquid in his half-empty cup. Something was on his mind, and I wondered if I should put the poor bastard out of his misery or make him work for whatever he wanted to say. I decided to make him sweat a bit—always fun to keep him on his toes.

"So...getting excited for the wedding?" he asked.

Wow, he was hardly bringing it. I expected more from the charmer who was ninety-nine percent responsible for our company's extremely successful bid to go public.

"Out with it, Jordan. The beating around the bush and small talk is annoying."

His brows twitched. "Sometimes I forget I'm not schmoozing an investor or something." He rubbed his neck self-consciously. "Just thinking about that big board meeting we have coming up."

I swallowed another mouthful of eggs and bit into my bacon. "Yeah? What's got you nervous about that?"

"Well, I got to talking with David not long before we left..."

k the last of my water in an attempt to curb the
__ation from the previous flight. "Ah? What did the *father-in-law* want?" I teased.

April and Jordan might not be married yet, but he was in the unenviable position of being romantically linked with the daughter of the chairman of our board of directors. It was a constant song and dance with her dad, still an uneasy relationship, even a year later. I got the impression that David Weiss still only tolerated Jordan even though Jordan and April were quite happy together.

David was the protective type with his daughter. Couldn't say I blamed him. In the unlikely event I ever had a daughter, heaven help any man who even looked at her funny. Fortunately for Jordan—and for the company—it all seemed to be going well so far, despite the uneasiness.

Jordan grinned and leaned back in his chair. "It wasn't anything to do with April. I think he's finally accepting the fact that he's not getting rid of me without a fight. And that I make his daughter happy—most of the time."

"Then what's got you all keyed up?"

He wiped his nose with a napkin, grumbling about the cold he'd picked up while traveling. Shaking his head, he admitted, "I'm not keyed up. David and I were, uh, talking about someone else."

"Oh?" I picked up my glass and swirled my ice again, impatient for a refill. Checking my watch, I saw that we still had another hour before boarding our connection to LAX.

"Friend of mine who's getting married soon," Jordan said. "We were discussing the merits of prenuptial agreements."

On the way to my mouth, the glass froze midair. Jordan watched me closely as he folded and unfolded the napkin on the table with his free hand.

"You two draw straws for this?" I asked, calmly setting down the drink.

"Rock, paper, scissors."

"Ah. You always did have the shittiest luck." I rubbed my jaw and looked away.

After a few awkward beats of silence, Jordan shifted in his chair and cleared his throat. "Have you...you know... Are you planning to...?"

A tight shrug lifted one shoulder, body stiffening. I had no desire to talk about this with him. "No offense, bro, but it's not really any of your business." My mild words contradicted the strange heat warming under my collar. I'd long since shucked my jacket and tie and would be changing into something more comfortable before getting on the plane.

"Yeah...so that's why I brought up the board meeting." He coughed into a fist.

My brows twitched. "Don't even joke about that. It's *not* going to be discussed at the board meeting." Jordan said nothing. After a minute of silence, my eyes left my plate to look at his face. He was dead serious. "What—there's no way in hell I'm discussing my private life and my personal finances with the board. Don't even go there."

Jordan grimaced. "Adam, you can't fuck around with this stuff. This is business, and we aren't some tiny startup anymore. We're a publicly traded company worth billions." His voice lowered as he glanced around the lounge as if wary of any eavesdroppers. "You, yourself, are worth billions. You need a prenup."

I scowled. "I don't need a prenup. Those are only for people who get divorced."

"And you know for sure you won't? You're prescient and your genius brain powers reach forward even into the future?" he asked drily.

"Maybe they do." I shrugged. It was ridiculous, but I was willing to say *anything* to shut down this subject. The sooner, the better.

Jordan leaned forward, resting his weight on his elbows. "I'm not fucking around, okay? I give you shit because it's fun, and I know you two have been through hell and back. I know how you feel about her and how she feels about you *now*. But—"

"No buts," I growled between clenched teeth. "We aren't getting a divorce."

"You can't predict something like that, and you know that goddamn well. More importantly, you know that California is a community property state. She could—"

"She *won't*," I said. "And asking her to sign a prenup means that I think that she might try." Or worse, that *I* expected the marriage to fail.

"Okay, so…the thing is this. Financially speaking, it's not just a marriage between Adam and Mia. It's you, her, and the company. You aren't simply making decisions for the two of you anymore. If you two divorce, half of your *sizeable* share of Draco becomes hers."

I blew out a breath and rolled my eyes. "That's a risk I'm willing to take."

"It's *not* a risk the board is willing to take." He shook his head. "And they are calling the shots these days."

I blinked. "I have controlling interest in this company. With the officers, we could override any board directive."

Jordan fell silent, now eluding my gaze. I could tell by the uneasy way he shifted in his seat that he avoided pointing out the obvious. He stalled, picking up his empty glass, taking in an ice cube, and crunching it noisily. Finally, he settled back and ran a hand through his hair.

"Enough with the bullshit. You aren't planning to back me on this, are you?" I asked in a dead voice, trying and failing to disguise my mounting irritation.

"It's your fiduciary duty, Adam. To the company."

"What about my duty to *her*?"

He sat back. "The board of directors has no say over your personal life—"

I leaned forward, placing an elbow on the table, tension filling every muscle in that arm. "*Aside* from the fact that they want me to force my future wife to sign papers and attest that she's not a gold digger."

He shifted again, clearly as annoyed by this conversation as I was. "I understand where you are coming from—"

"Do you? Do you *really*?" I leaned forward. "So you're having April sign one of these things when you tie the knot?"

His hand went up. "Whoa, slow down there, buckaroo." He gestured to himself. "No one over *here* is stupid enough to be tying any knots anytime soon."

I replied by flipping him the bird, and he looked away, laughing. "Bro, listen, okay? I don't want you to be blindsided in the BOD meeting. This will give you a chance to mull it over.

They *are* in a position to force the issue, you know. They can remove you as CEO. Steve Jobs—"

Heat burned up my spine, flushing my face. I placed a closed fist on the table between us. "And *you* know goddamn well what happened to Apple when they did that. If our BOD wants to sabotage this company, then let them go right ahead."

Jordan stiffened, making a placating gesture. "No one is threatening anything. I'm doing my duty as your friend and as your CFO to warn you about what could happen in such an event, okay? They could pressure you to do this, and if you refuse, they could claim breach of fiduciary duty." He sighed and raked a hand through his hair. "*Please.* I'm begging you not to let your legendary stubbornness turn this into a clusterfuck."

My fist tightened. "I am *not* going to risk my relationship with Emilia over this. She is more important to me than a hundred boards of directors. This company can go fuck itself if it comes to that."

Jordan's brow creased, and we were given a momentary reprieve from the awkwardness when our waiter finally showed up to refill our water glasses. I looked down at the cold food, now completely uninterested in eating.

Nevertheless, we continued our meal in silence with a thick side of tension. Then Jordan coughed into a fist without taking his eyes off his plate.

"You know, it's really not that bad…if you think of it like an insurance policy."

Chewing my food, I glowered at the table top without responding.

"I know what you're thinking."

The food almost stuck in my throat. "You have no idea what I'm thinking."

He sighed. "Okay, fair enough. I know what *I'd* be thinking in your place, then."

"And what's that?"

He laid his fork down beside his plate to gesture with an empty hand as he spoke. He reminded me of a commentator on an infomercial, blithely trying to sell me something. "That signing a prenup is like planning on getting divorced—planning for the worst. But here's a different way to spin it—"

"Why am I *spinning* it?"

He waved me off. "Down, boy. I'm just saying it's an insurance policy. No one plans on getting divorced when they are young and in love and newly married. I know you're not planning on it. She'd know that, too. But you also don't buy home insurance expecting to lose your house in a fire or an 8.0 earthquake, either. You don't buy car insurance expecting a semi to—"

I held up a hand to stave off the litany. "All right, all right. I get it." Maybe he had a point, but this was different. This was *us*, Emilia and me—*our* relationship, *our* trust, *our* future laid bare to be examined, defined, and documented by lawyers. What would she think if I were to plunk a contract down in front of her and ask her to sign it? She'd be insulted as hell.

And I wouldn't blame her.

While I could tell her that the board was forcing me to do it, why would I? It was worth fighting for. I was going to be her husband, after all. Standing up for her was my job. Protecting her was my job. So, like with any job placed before me, I'd do it—to two hundred percent of my ability.

The trip home was long, and exhausting. I spent the majority of the flight working, handling the pile of work stacked on my plate. But distraction gnawed at me every time I thought of home.

An even bigger pile of work surely waited for me there, but Emilia was the one filling my thoughts. I hadn't spent this much time away from her since we'd gotten engaged. And I missed her, goddamn it. The smell of her hair. The feel of her skin. The sound of her voice—even when she was teasing me about whatever latest joke was going back and forth between us.

After ten days of staring at Jordan's mug, I was done. I wanted Emilia.

Due to a cold he'd caught during our trip, he was now snoring in the pod next to me on the plane. I prayed I hadn't caught his germs. Great souvenir for him to take back to April. She'd be thrilled about that.

We touched down at five a.m. A little after six, my driver dropped me at my front door. Hopefully, Emilia would be sleeping. She was on summer break now, but still working hard in the lab with research and study as she prepared for the start of her second year at medical school. Despite that, she remained a devoted night owl, and it was Saturday morning.

Envisioning her asleep in bed was enough to make me rush upstairs, anxious to catch a catnap to stave off my gnawing fatigue. Fortunately, she wasn't a light sleeper, so she didn't wake up when I entered our room, shedding my clothes as I went. By the time I reached the foot of the bed, I was in my underwear and ready to dive into the sheets.

But I had to pause to take her in…at the sight of her, my chest tightened, and my lungs couldn't draw enough air. Her lithe form curled in on itself. And though she was tall, she appeared small in our huge bed, her long, dark hair splayed across the white pillow. She lay on her side, her back to my side of the bed. *Perfect.*

I slid into bed next to her and curved my body around hers, pulling her flush to me so that we were spooning. With a sigh, she settled against me, and that warm feeling flared in my chest. I buried my nose in her silky hair, and my entire body stirred. If I weren't so exhausted, I would have tried something then. But the pull of twenty hours without sleep was strong. I nodded off instead.

When I woke up hours later, she tiptoed through the room, obviously trying her best to not wake me. Her hair was still messy, her eyes sleepy. The clock read ten minutes after eight. She must have just gotten out of bed.

In that short t-shirt that showed off her stunning legs, she appeared nothing less than delectable. Good enough to eat, and given my raging hard-on, my body agreed. I rolled onto my back and heaved a sigh as she dug out some items from her nightstand drawer.

"Come here," I mumbled.

She jerked her head in my direction, eyes wide. "I'm sorry. Did I wake you up?"

"No. Come here."

"Well, good morning to you, too." She slowly approached the bed. "I was going to hop in the shower and then make a bunch of noise to wake you up so I could attack you. When did you get in?"

"Two hours ago. I got no sleep on the flight." I stretched my arms above my head, yawning.

"Crap, you must be exhausted." She sat down on the edge of the bed, beyond my reach, and grabbed my hand, lacing her fingers with mine. "You should go back to sleep." My fingers closed around hers, trapping them.

"Hell no." I tugged on her hand to pull her toward me. As I did, my arm nudged a hard lump in the bedsheets. I craned my head for a closer look. It was a balled-up shirt nestled among the pillows on her side of the bed.

"What's that?"

She reached for it, blushing, but I was quicker, snatching it up. It was one of my shirts that she'd tucked up into a ball. In fact, it was the shirt I'd worn the day before I left for China.

"This is my shirt..." I shot her a questioning look. She tried to snatch it from me, but I pulled it away. "Were you sleeping with my shirt?"

She blew out a breath and rolled her eyes, laughing. "No...sheesh. Why would I do that? You just leave your laundry lying around." But she didn't meet my gaze, trying to pull her hand out of my grip. I held on for dear life.

"I threw that in my laundry hamper two weeks ago." I fought a shit-eating grin that I knew would only annoy her more. "How did it get here?"

She turned back to me. "Maybe I liked cuddling with the shirt because it smells like you while not being annoying, like its owner."

The grin could no longer be contained. It was unleashed, full force. In response, her mouth twisted, and she narrowed her eyes at me. I feigned innocence. "Wait, what? How am I annoying?"

"Because you're trying to embarrass me for sleeping with your damn shirt."

"I think I have a right to be upset."

She frowned. "Upset? Why? I didn't ruin it."

"No…but I get back from a long trip only to catch you in bed cheating on me with my dirty laundry."

With wide eyes and open-mouthed shock, she leapt for the shirt, tore it out of my hand, and smacked me in the face with it. She expelled a snort of disgust. "You suck."

"That's what you're counting on…" I threw up my arm, trying to fend off her blows. "Provided, of course, that I forgive you for your infidelity."

"Jackass," she said between clenched teeth, but I could tell she tried hard not to laugh. Reaching out, I hooked an arm around her waist and rolled to pin her down. My kiss landed on her face as she wiggled underneath me. It felt so damn good, I could have taken her right there and then. But I managed to control myself—barely.

"So how about getting a whiff of the real thing?" I waggled my eyebrows at her.

"I want to take a shower. Plus, you are on my shit list now for your teasing."

"Your *shit* list?" I faked a frown. "That doesn't sound fun. I'd much rather be on your *Must Give a Blowjob ASAP* list." But instead of letting her up, I rubbed my twenty hours' growth of whiskers against her neck.

"Stop it!" she said breathlessly, squirming in an attempt to escape.

And as good as it felt, I slid to the side to allow her room, since she tended to get claustrophobic. "You're free after you pay the fine."

"There's a fine for cheating on you with your shirt?"

"Yep." I nodded. "Gotta give me a proper welcome-home kiss."

"Hmm." Her eyes rolled up to the ceiling as if she contemplated the pros and cons of such a request. "A hard price to pay."

I grinned. "Better move quickly and pray I don't alter the deal further."

"Darth Adam. I knew you'd show your face sooner or later. I always had suspicions that you might be a secret Sith lord. It explains so much."

"You *will* give me a kiss." I feigned deep concentration.

"I will give you a...*kick*." She jerked her leg toward me as if she was going to kick me and laughed when I reacted.

"Those Jedi mind tricks used to work so much better before Obi-Wan chopped my legs off and left me for dead beside the volcano."

Her eyes widened in mock horror. "You've done the unforgivable! You have invoked the dreaded prequels."

I sighed. "So I have. That must mean I forfeit, then."

She laughed as I slid off her. Then she hooked both arms around my neck, pulling my face to hers.

Our lips met hungrily, eager for each other's taste, touch, smell...and a promise of more, very soon. I'd be making up for lost time with her later. Maybe I'd wait until after breakfast. Probably not, though.

Chapter 2
Mia

KISSING ADAM WAS LIKE STANDING OUTSIDE WHEN THE rain first starts to fall. A shiver runs down my spine in reaction, as if a chilly breeze has risen up. Cold prickles dot every inch of my skin, like the first icy drops sprinkling over me. The air around me thickens, as if full of precipitation. Smells amplify, from the scent of his skin to the fragrance of soap he used—fresh as the world washed by new rain. My senses easily become overwhelmed. Then, much like that rain as the drops beat harder, I start to feel change in everything around me. When he kisses me long enough and the right way, my clothes get too heavy and uncomfortable, as if weighted down by a sudden downpour.

"I'm never going to make it to the shower if you keep kissing me like *that*," I gasped.

He pulled back enough to look into my face, smiling. "Who said you needed to make it to the shower right now? You might have some more...pressing business." And he turned, his erection nudging my hip.

I pushed against his bare chest, shoving him off me. "*I* said it. Besides...I need to make you suffer for all that teasing."

When I sprang from the bed, Adam followed me into the bathroom. I hid a smile so he wouldn't see it in the mirror. He must have known that I wasn't *truly* annoyed with him, but I wasn't about to let him get the upper hand with his taunts, either. Someone had to keep that boy in check.

He had a few more surprises for me, though. I turned on the shower to warm up the water and took off the t-shirt I'd slept in. Out of the corner of my eye, I watched him shed his underwear—the only thing he'd been wearing. When he straightened, he held out the pair of boxer briefs as if to give them to me.

"What? You know where the dirty laundry goes," I said, batting away the underwear he was practically waving in my face.

His cocky grin widened. "I thought you might want to add this to your collection. You could have a whole load ready for the next time I go out of town." My face fell, and it only seemed to amuse him more.

I gritted my teeth and, balling my fists, charged at him. "Ima kick your ass!" He laughed, dodging me easily. "You're nekkid," I growled. "You have your vulnerable bits hanging out. A perfect time for me to strike."

Before I could deliver on my threat, however, he grabbed me. While we both laughed our asses off, he scooped me off my feet with my arms pinned to my sides and walked us into the huge shower.

Our shower was gorgeous. I could spend all day in there if it weren't for the fact that I'd emerge wrinkled as a granny. In fact, this bathroom had spawned habit of taking long showers. One wall was all natural, hewn stone with a double rain-shower head inset into the ceiling above us and brushed nickel jets shooting out from the sides. The shower was recessed into its own corner, where there was no need to have a door over it. Heated wooden slats lined the floor around the drains. Five people could fit in the shower, though at most, it was only the two of us.

"Fucker," I said.

"Yep," he muttered into my ear. "That's *exactly* what's happening right after this shower."

A slice of excitement from that promise glided through my blood as he pinned me against the freezing stone. Naturally, I made a show of protesting too much as he pressed against me, kissing me deeply, reminding me with his body that he had every intention of following through.

I narrowed my eyes at him. "Well, mister, if you want to get lucky, you're going to have to be a lot nicer to me."

He smiled, his face still inches from mine. "Oh, I intend to be nice to you. Very, *very* nice." We kissed again, his tongue exploring my mouth as the hot spray drenched our bodies. "I guarantee you'll be incredibly happy at the end of the day with how nice I am to you."

I tilted my head, grinning up at him. "You don't usually offer a guarantee."

His eyes darkened with mischief and lust and God knew what else. "I should tie you up and have my way with you," he growled.

I hooked my arms around his neck. "*I* guarantee that none of that will be necessary in order to have your way with me."

He reached over to one of the lit shelves inset into one wall and grabbed a bar of soap. But it wasn't his own manly, plain stuff that I loved to smell on his skin. No, he grabbed my frou-frou bar of French *savon*—bright purple and smelling of lavender. And instead of lathering himself, he soaped me up. I bit my bottom lip to keep my mouth from melting into a grin. It must be about *that* time again.

Slowly, methodically, his slippery hands glided over my wet skin, taking extra-special care with my breasts. Desire flamed immediately—stoked from the sparks of watching him strip naked and carry me, warmed by our frisky flirtations, and ignited by our kisses into something much hotter. Who knew such a blistering fire could flare up under a spray of water?

Adam pulled my body against his, my back to his front, as he reached around me and continued to rub those tiny circles with his nimble fingers. I closed my eyes beneath the water, relishing the feel of his hands. It had been almost two weeks since he'd left, damn it, and I was over-the-top lusting for him. Given the feel of his hard body behind me, I could tell he was on the same page. *But* even if I tried to right now, I wouldn't be able to cut this shower short.

Swaying against him, I swallowed as he kissed his way up my neck, his lips pulling my earlobe into his hot mouth. Fire and electricity crackled down every nerve ending. If he pressed me against the wall of the shower and took me here and now, he'd have me coming in minutes.

I had to admit it was the sexiest damn breast exam I'd ever experienced.

He never *said* that was what these were, but they came at regular intervals. The first few times, I'd thought it was the normal prelude to shower sex—a sport we'd been medalists at since the beginning. But though he'd been subtle about it, it hadn't taken me long to figure out the real intention behind his meticulous and specific soapy foreplay.

I bit my tongue and never told him that I'd figured out what he was up to. Having undergone stage two breast cancer, I was attentive to my own regular exams. Adam had even asked me, once, if I did them, and I'd reassured him that I did.

But that answer obviously didn't satisfy. And I couldn't fault him for wanting to be sure. He liked my boobs, and I loved it when he touched my boobs, even like this, turning it into a sexy game with some nice, sizzling foreplay. So why ruin a good thing?

I worried my bottom lip between my teeth, my eyes still closed as he finished up, a smattering of guilt pricking like a needle near the region of my heart. Adam had been left with as much of a scar due to my bout with cancer as the one left on my breast from the surgeon's incision. And I wondered if he would ever truly breathe easy again. If either of us would.

Most of the time we were fine, but there were those brief moments when the tiniest seed of worry could cause a split second of panic before all returned to normal again. Adam was washing my back now and murmuring about all the things he wanted to do to me after we'd dried off. My eyes still closed, I enjoyed envisioning every single one.

But I hadn't gotten my revenge yet. A smart girl never let her man get away with epic mockery. Nope. She got *even*. And that's what *I* was going to do. Minutes later, I thanked him for his attentions and told him he should have of his own relaxing alone time—after I washed his back and did my own arousing version of a scrubdown on his perfect abs.

He enjoyed it—at least, that was what certain body parts of his led me to believe as I slipped from the shower. "Don't dawdle," I ordered in my best come-hither voice, which probably sounded more like a toad with a cold than the effect I was trying to evoke.

Adam promptly poured some shampoo into his palm and started scrubbing his hair, eyes squeezed closed. Gleefully, I seized this moment as my time to act.

The rules are simple when it comes to schooling men—never let them see your weakness. Thus, his joking had been cleverly forgotten—or at least I'd inferred that from his honeyed words about how much he wanted my "sexy body."

But I couldn't pass up the opportunity to strike back. *This* was my chance. I dried off, craning my head to see what he was doing. From the angle of the shower, he couldn't see me go to the linen cupboard and grab every last folded, clean towel from the shelf and leave the bathroom with the entire stack—even taking the ones hanging on the towel warmer.

The next rule was to act *fast*. After all, Adam was highly motivated to get through his shower quickly. And that I did. After stuffing the towels in my closet, I returned to the bathroom. I slipped on my own bathrobe and removed his, along with all hand towels that he might resort to out of desperation.

Satisfied with my results, I settled on the bed, all snug and dry in my robe. Pressing a stack of clean washcloths to my mouth to muffle the laughter, I heard the water turn off. After a few seconds' hesitation, he called from inside the bathroom.

"Hey. Where are all the towels?"

I didn't answer, just laughed some more and smothered my giggles.

The slap of his wet feet on the bare floor sounded as he crossed the bathroom toward the door. He poked his dripping head out of the doorway. "What did you do?" His dark eyebrow arched, hair soaked and plastered to his forehead. A puddle quickly formed around his feet.

I held up one of the tiny washcloths. "You want this, don't you? The hate is swelling in you now."

His mouth quirked. "*Something's* swelling, but it isn't hate." He pushed the hair away from his forehead and cleared the water that had dripped into his eyes. "Somehow I thought getting away with that was too easy."

I smirked. "You should know me better by now. As for drying off…you could always use your dirty underpants."

"*Underpants?* What am I, five?" He clenched his jaw and then grinned. "Don't underestimate the power of the dark side, young Jedi."

I rolled my eyes. "So you're going to try to one-up me? *So* predictable. I'm shaking in my boots."

His dark eyes gleamed as he came closer. Rivulets of water had collected on his tasty abs. It was fascinating to behold.

"And *you* should know *me* better, too." He grinned evilly. "I don't one-up. I one-*hundred*-up." Then he shook his head inches from my face. Droplets of water sprayed everywhere. I let out a screech and pulled back. "You are looking too dry over there, little girl. Let me help you with that."

And he promptly pinned me, dripping wet, to the bed and started rubbing his drenched face in mine. "You're gonna soak the bed!" I screeched.

"Collateral damage," he replied. He reached down and pulled the belt on my robe, opening it. Then he shifted, sandwiching me between his wet body and the bed.

I squirmed and wiggled, and he only seemed to like it more. He shook his head again. My hand smacked his hard chest. "You're such a boy."

He grinned. "I'm *all* boy," he said, pressing his erection against me.

"I won't take this lying down," I muttered.

"You don't have to take it lying down." He laughed. "There's always up against the door or the shower wall. Or you can take it bent over the back of the couch or a dozen other different ways. Whatever way you take it...you *are* taking it."

"You've got a smartass answer for everything, don't you?"

"It's one of the reasons you love me."

"Uh huh." I made a face at him. "I just keep you around for the mind-blowing sex."

"Speaking of which...I'm hungry. Time for breakfast." He punctuated his statement with a hard nip on my neck, and desire snaked through my body, insidious in its betrayal. I was going to lose this battle—happily so—*but* the war would rage on.

"You're a pain," I muttered even as I closed my eyes, relishing the sensations as his mouth moved lower, over my chest.

"So you've said. I'm also a lot of fun."

I laughed. "You are."

"And I'm irresistible."

"Hmm."

"Even when I'm soaking wet."

I bit my lip. "Let's not push it."

He pulled back so I could see the devilish grin, the lust in his dark eyes. "Oh, hell yes I'm going to push it over and over again. And you're gonna love it. Just like you always do."

Thrill and anticipation clenched in my deepest center. I licked my lips, ready to drop the pretense. My legs opened and hooked around his hips, locking them tight around him.

"Show me what you got, big boy."

But he still had surprises—as always, full to the brim with those. "How about breakfast in bed?"

And with one swift, powerful motion, he unhooked my legs and pushed them apart before settling his head and shoulders right between them. *Oh, hell yes.* This was happening. My thighs flexed and touched his cold, wet hair. I let out a yelp. "Jeez, your hair is cold."

"Don't move your legs, then." He shifted, and suddenly his hot mouth connected with the most sensitive bundle of nerves, and my body instantly arched.

Yeah. Right. A searing, liquid lust so intense it scalded my blood commanded my complete attention. Enslaved me with every movement of his mouth.

When he wrapped his lips around my clit and started sucking, I nearly lost my mind. I *did* lose control. He *was* irresistible—even when soaking wet. And I proved that in a few short minutes when I screamed his name.

But he wouldn't budge from that spot until he'd wrung out every last drop of pleasure from me like spilled water from a soaked rag. And I felt very much like that rag—all wrung out—once he lifted his head. But *he* wasn't done.

Good God…what this man did to me. If he were around more, I'd probably be dead of exhaustion from all the sex. But *damn*, what a way to go.

In spite of that thought, I *did* want him around more. And not only for the phenomenal sex.

I lay there, boneless, buzzing with my afterglow as Adam moved to the nightstand to grab a condom and put it on. I watched, my eyes glued to his fantastic butt. I'd missed that butt.

But *damn,* he was getting cocky, and I still needed to put him in his place.

He was back with me again, though I knew not for long. He didn't have a lot of free time in the next few months, and I couldn't travel with him because of my rigorous academic schedule. We seized these moments the minute they appeared, savored them, and hung on for dear life lest they slip through our fingers like water.

That didn't mean he still couldn't afford to be schooled every once in a while. And Adam had a tendency toward overconfidence that needed to be watched closely—and taken down when it got out of hand. Nevertheless, my next practical joke didn't go over as well as the previous one... When he returned to the bed, he didn't buy for a second that I had fallen asleep, despite my best attempts to feign it. And thank God he hadn't, because oh, what fun it was.

***

The next day, when I'd much rather be spending more time with Adam, I had to go through the motions of meeting an old friend at a tea shop, of all places. My eyes drifted toward my best friend Heath where he sat across from me. The table was dainty, covered with delicate doilies. And Heath was a huge, blond Viking warrior in jeans come to sip tea with me and our mutual friend. Heath dwarfed everything around him, looking as out of place here as I felt. It hadn't been my idea to meet here...it had been Camille's.

Camille, our friend from high school, had recently contacted us because she'd be spending some time in OC. She wanted to see us, since we'd all parted ways after graduation, only sharing pictures and posts over social media.

"I miss Tucson." She sighed, pushing her long, mousy brown hair over her shoulder with a perfectly manicured hand. Camille was impossibly thin and impeccably dressed in a frilly frock that would have looked right at home in Sunday school. With a silver spoon, she added honey and lemon to her cup of tea and pressed the cup to her mouth, red with lipstick. "But there are no jobs there, much as I'd have loved to stay. Still, I'm managing to keep in contact with all my sisters. I'll be going back for homecoming in a couple months."

My brow twitched. She'd only left the University of Arizona after graduation in June—having been a year behind us in school and then on the five-year plan. During her time at college, Camille had joined a sorority. My impression was that she'd transformed from misfit, who used to hang out in high school with the likes of Heath and me, to popular Delta Delta Gamma girl.

Heath snickered as he finished off his breakfast pastry. He seemed in good spirits, which was not usually the case, since his boyfriend had left for an indefinite stay in his homeland of Ireland. When I caught Heath's gaze and Camille wasn't looking, I blew on my tea to cool it. The frilly teahouse had been her choice and watching Heath blunder about in here was something close to comedy. He flagged down the server to ask for a second bear claw.

"So, Mia, what have *you* been up to?"

"Studying, mostly."

Her brows shot up. "No charity events? Evening galas? Fundraisers and all that exciting stuff the one percenters do?"

I blinked. I was a one percenter now? "Only all that stuff med school students with no social lives do."

Camille shrugged. "I'm surprised you haven't quit med school, but obviously, you're doing what you love. That's great. I wish I were in the position to do what I loved, like run my own art gallery. I'd love that. But Mom and Dad want me to show that I'm productive, so to the job market I must bend. There's not much out there for an art history degree."

Camille had spent the first half-hour of our get-together complaining about how her parents had refused to pay for graduate school until she could hold down a responsible job for a year. Not too long ago, I would have killed to have that problem.

She bent forward and added milk to her tea. "I wish I could be like Heath and work for myself. Or, you know, just marry a billionaire." She giggled as she gestured to my engagement ring.

I resisted the urge to pull my hand off the table and sit back. I was almost used to it now—*almost.* Adam and I had been engaged for over a year, and everyone outside my close circle saw our relationship as my winning lottery ticket. Few viewed Adam as a man beyond his staggering bank account. One acquaintance, after a few drinks to loosen him up, had even attempted to pry the value of Adam's total assets out of me.

I'd responded with the truth—I had no idea how much he was worth in dollars. And I'd made sure to add a deliberately saccharine *but he's priceless to me* with a cutesy smile and the hopes that he'd soon begin gagging from the treacle.

Nobody seemed to believe that I didn't really know. After that lovely experience, I'd come up with a list of sarcastic responses to use in the likely event that his net worth was broached again.

• *It's too hard to count it all while I'm swimming around in all that gold.*

• *I don't know. He hides it all in the Batcave underneath our house where he parks his Batmobile.*

• *I don't know, but if he starts making me call him Daddy Warbucks in bed, I'm out.*

• *I don't know. I haven't weighed him lately, nor have I been able to discern his karat number.*

• *Every time I try to check out his bank balance online, the screen locks up.*

"That reminds me." She leaned toward me. "I wanted to ask you a favor."

I leaned back, mind racing. *Uh oh. Shit.* Should I get up and go to the bathroom? Maybe interrupt with one of my prepared snarky rebuttals? Instead, I said nothing, waiting for her to continue.

"Since I was elected as president of my sorority's alumni committee, I've been tasked to raise money for new front room furniture. It's been on the sisters' wish list for a few years now, and I'd love to finally get the money together. Contributions are tax deductible. I'm sure your fiancé needs a *ton* of deductions."

I took in a deep breath through my nose and let it out through my mouth, feeling my face burn hot with irritation. "I, uh…um…" *Damn.* Why was my mind blanking on the list of smart, snappy comebacks?

Before I could shut her down, Heath deftly changed the subject, and she started talking about high school gossip. Who had seen whom, who had graduated from college, and who had dropped out. Who was still up in the Anza/Idyllwild area and who, like us, had managed to escape the high desert small-town community from which we'd all sprung.

"Oh. You'll never guess who I ran into, Mia. Julian Kerr." My stomach turned. I didn't give two shits about any of the high school football players—who'd been worshipped as gods in our small town. I kept a straight face and hoped the subject changed again soon. "He's working at his parents' store. I guess Hollywood didn't work out for him."

I frowned, sipping more tea. Heath's head jerked to me. Our eyes met, and mine darted away.

"He's a loser," Heath said. He'd opened his mouth to say more—hopefully to change the subject—when Camille rode over him, obviously drooling with the opportunity to share her next tidbit.

"Yeah, well, he might be, but he had some awesome gossip that I think might interest Mia. He told me that Zach Downs got arrested last month in Mexico." She seemed satisfied when my cup clattered loudly back on its saucer and I sat back. I could feel myself pale at the mention of the name. *That* jerk. The asshole I'd dated in high school. I swallowed, and Camille was already continuing with her story. "They nabbed him at the airport for possession of a whole kilo of cocaine he was trying to bring home with him. He's in prison down there, and his family is frantically trying to crowdfund legal fees in order to get him out."

Sucking in an involuntary breath, I coughed ferociously. Blood pounded in my veins, but not because I'd accidentally tried to aspirate my own saliva. And not simply from hearing the name, either.

I was reliving that moment last spring when I'd run into the asshole again—for the first time since high school. My attempt to suppress a shiver was unsuccessful. Heath was all too aware of it, too, frowning at me in concern. I shot a self-conscious glance at Camille. She knew that Zach had been my high school boyfriend, of course, but she didn't know *everything*. She didn't know why we'd broken up or why I'd spent the last few months of my sophomore year at home. Everyone thought I'd caught a bad case of the chicken pox.

They had no idea that Zach had sexually assaulted me and beaten me up badly enough to leave marks that took months to fully heal. Or that I'd stayed home from school because even the thought of running into him on campus gave me panic attacks that prevented me from breathing.

I begged off, leaving that annoying tea date early by feigning a splitting headache. I gathered my stuff, gave Camille a rushed goodbye, and ran to my car. Heath caught up with me there.

"Hey. You okay?"

I fiddled with opening my car door and throwing my bag inside. "I will be. Just a shock to hear his name, that's all."

He reached out and put a hand on my upper arm. "That's *not* all. I heard you ran into him up in Anza earlier this year."

I hesitated, nodding. There were no accusations in his tone, no demand to know why I hadn't told him. But I should have figured on my mom letting him know. I suppressed a sigh.

"Adam and I went up to help her get the B&B ready for the season. We were in Bartons, and his mom, Beth, was there." I shuddered, and Heath rubbed my arm to reassure me.

Retelling this story felt almost as if I was standing in the middle of that grocery aisle again, facing off with the mother of my ex. I shook my head. "She was all coos and smiles. Everyone wants to act like they are my long-lost best friend now, even Beth. Remember how much she hated me when she thought I was going to press charges against her baby for assault? She had the nerve to act like nothing had ever happened, and even wanted to *introduce* him to Adam."

Heath's jaw tightened, along with his hold on my arm. My stomach roiled at the memory as I remembered the panic, the pure fear, the heartbeat pounding in my ears at the thought of them meeting. Knowing that I would never in a thousand years be able to keep my cool around Zach and that Adam would pick up on it immediately—and ask questions—I did what I'd done just now: made my quick excuses, grabbed Adam, and bolted.

"Zach was in the store, too?"

I shut my eyes. "In the next aisle over. She called out to him, and I was trying to get the fuck out of there. But as soon I rounded the corner, I ran right smack into him—literally."

In the present, my stomach sloshed with panic. I took a deep breath, forcibly reminding myself that I was *safe.*

When I'd smelled that same cologne he used to wear in high school—that heavy-handed stuff he practically bathed in—that was all it took. Gibbering panic had set in—my heart racing, adrenaline pumping, fight-or-flight mode kicking in. I'd almost peed my pants.

"That fucker tried to stop me, to say hello as if nothing had ever happened." I was practically grinding my teeth as I said it.

Heath shook his head, clearly puzzled. "I never took him for *that* much of an idiot."

I ran my hand over my eyes, tried to control the shaking. "Everyone sees stars in their eyes now. I'm the girl who's about to marry a billionaire. Ever since that *Forbes* magazine feature article on Adam that mentioned my name. I'm supposed to forget everything about the past and help them *all*."

Heath drew back, revolted. "Jesus. That's disgusting. Did Adam notice your reaction to Zach?"

I dropped my hand from my eyes and tilted my head to look at Heath. "What do *you* think?"

Heath's brow went up. "Yeah, not much gets by him."

"I dragged him out of the store, and we drove down to Temecula to get groceries there instead." I shook my head. "I wished to hell I'd done that in the first place."

"What did Adam say when you told him why you were so freaked out?"

I bit my lip, but looked away without answering.

"Mia...shit. You *didn't* tell him?"

"No. I didn't want him to freak out and go back in there and punch the guy. You *know* he would have tried. And as for that dickhead...the way everyone sees dollar signs when they see Adam or me, I wouldn't put it past that asshole to pick a fight so he could sue Adam and his deep pockets. To say nothing of Adam going to jail. No, he doesn't need to fight my battles."

Except there was a sinking suspicion about the timing of the news Camille had delivered to me. After all this time, Zach getting thrown in a Mexican prison mere months after that encounter...

Had Adam somehow been involved in that? *But how?*

Heath blew out a breath. "So Adam didn't say anything?"

"He wanted to, but I never let him. I talked so much during the drive that he never got a word in edgewise. Whenever he'd try to broach it, I'd change the subject."

Heath's brow crumpled, and he appeared at a loss. Ugh. Sometimes life was too confusing. And all the thoughts stirring around in my head like a stew? I had no idea what to make of them.

Heath and I said our goodbyes soon after, and I got in my car.

During the drive home, I couldn't stop thinking about that encounter in the grocery store. This new development—Zach going to jail for drugs—seemed like an eerie coincidence. I knew that Adam had dug for info after the grocery store incident. The next day, I'd caught him in my childhood bedroom at the ranch looking through my old high school yearbooks. They'd been buried in the top shelf of my closet. He'd been in there a few times before to look around, but that day in particular, he'd shown an inordinate amount of interest in the books. Had he continued to dig deeper, after that?

When I arrived at our house at noon, Adam wasn't home yet. Since I'd had the tea date already set with Heath and Camille, he'd ducked into work for the morning to check on things. But he'd promised he wouldn't be long. While I waited for him, I finished up some work in my new study, which Adam had converted from a guest bedroom across the hall from his home office.

I heard him come in and went down to meet him in the kitchen, where he'd grabbed a bottle of water. Throwing my arms around him from behind, I stood on tiptoes to kiss him on the neck. "What should we do today?"

"Let's take the Duffy boat over to the Fun Zone," he answered without even a pause. "I owe you a rematch in Skee-Ball."

I grinned cheekily, resting my chin on his shoulder. "You mean...you crave further humiliation."

He shrugged. "Maybe I have a bit of a masochistic streak going on." He turned around and returned the hug, pulling me up against him. "How was tea? I bet Heath was about as dainty in there as a WWE wrestler."

I blew out a breath. "Poor guy. At least it got him out of the house, though. He's been less than social since Connor went back to Ireland."

With a smile, he took my hand, and we went out to the slip where the electric Duffy boat bobbed, dwarfed by the much larger yacht. I sat lost in thought as we motored across the back bay to the Balboa Peninsula, home of the Fun Zone. Across the inlet, the pier and boardwalk rimmed the water, gleaming in the temperate sunlight.

We strolled along the boardwalk, stopping, of course, to play our rematch game—which I duly won in defense of my champion Skee-Baller status.

And I taunted him with the childhood chant "Brick Wall Waterfall."

"Peanut butter, Captain Crunch. I got something you can't touch." I danced in front of him, doing the little girl's taunt while he laughed at me. "Reese's Pieces, 7 Up. Mess with me, I'll mess you up." I held out one hand to stop him in his tracks, while putting the other thumb and forefinger in the shape of an L on my forehead. "Loser, loser. Double loser. Whatever. As if. Kiss this. You just got dissed!"

He took it like a champ, appearing happy that I was talking again. But we fell into easy silence when we grabbed a quick meal, and on the way back to the boat, I munched on a Balboa Bar—the famous sprinkled dipped ice cream on a stick, reliving my childhood in so many ways.

"Don't you drip that ice cream all over my boat," he muttered as we climbed in.

It was definitely time for more taunting. I turned to him, mouthing the thing suggestively—pulling it in and out of my mouth, giving it long licks while I moaned my enjoyment of the sweet dairy treat. He watched me, eyes widening in disbelief before he nearly fell to the floor in laughter.

"Wow, I never thought I'd say this, but I'm almost getting turned on watching you give your ice cream a blowjob."

I responded by smacking my lips and finishing up the ice cream as we took the long way home all the way around Balboa Island, which wasn't that big. But since the Duffy was slow, it took some time.

"You've been quiet this afternoon," he finally said when we were halfway around.

I shrugged, looking out over the water, studying the play of late afternoon light sparkling off the surface. "Not much to say. I'm not really in a talking mood. Just happy you're home.."

He frowned, steering around some moored boats, complete with decks full of sleeping sea lions lazing in the sun. "Any particular reason?"

I darted a look at him before turning back to the scenery, admiring the lavish homes that equaled the one in which we lived, and others on the level of ostentation. "When I was at tea, my friend from high school, Camille, shared some hometown gossip with me."

His brows rose. "Ah. Has there been some excitement up in good ol' Anza?"

I turned back to him and shifted on my bench. "Yeah. Someone I knew in high school got arrested in Mexico and thrown into prison for drug possession."

I tried to gauge his reaction. Did I notice a brief, stony glaze cover those dark eyes? A slight flexing of his jaw? Or was that all my imagination?

"Huh. Was it a friend?"

"No, definitely *not*," I said. "It was that jerk I dated my sophomore year."

His eyebrow twitched, and there was a long pause. I turned to see that we approached Bay Island, headed right toward our slip. The water slapped up on the sides of the yacht off our private beach.

Adam deftly maneuvered in, and I hopped out of the boat before he could respond. Bring this up? Or push it aside? What should I do?

Was it really essential that he even know? These questions swirled round and round, and I wasn't sure how I felt about hearing the answers. Did I care whether he was involved or that the guy was getting his comeuppance?

Once inside, I went to the fridge and pulled out the bottle of red wine we'd opened last night with dinner. When he entered the kitchen, I held it up to him and he shook his head, so I pulled out the cork with a thunk and poured a glass for myself.

Adam observed this silently, eyes narrowing slightly as I immediately scooped up the glass and sipped at it. The air between us grew a little thicker, a little heavier. I swallowed and waited.

"Wanna talk about it? You're not upset about that news, are you?"

I took a breath and let it go. "No." I sipped again. "I'm fucking overjoyed by it and struggling with how guilty that makes me feel."

He put a hand on the smooth granite counter and leaned against his arm, never taking his eyes from me. I couldn't return his gaze, looking at the muscles bulge in his strong forearm instead. "Why would you feel guilty, Emilia? I guarantee that shit-stain never spent a day in his life feeling guilty about what he did to you."

I nodded, still avoiding his eyes and the question burning on the tip of my tongue. The space between us filled with those unasked questions, those unvoiced answers. My heartbeat flooded the silence with relentless thumps. Then I downed the rest of the glass in one gulp. "My brain is mush. Can we veg out with a movie?"

He smiled, but that forehead still buckled with concern, the dark eyes heavy. "After watching the way you ate that ice cream, I'd be *very* happy with some Netflix and chill." He grinned, flaunting that devastatingly handsome smile.

I smirked at him. "You should be so lucky, punk."

Setting the wine glass in the sink, I enjoyed the warm glow and happy flush the grape had brought me—*grateful* for it, in fact. Adam swept up behind me to encircle my waist with his arms, and my heart surged, beating quickly as he landed a brief, warm kiss on the side of my neck.

I leaned back against his hard chest, and this feeling—*this feeling...*

It congealed behind my eyes, causing tingles. It thickened in my throat. Cradled in his strong arms, I decided then and there...it didn't matter. Nothing mattered but this feeling. How *he* made me feel—*safe, secure, at peace.*

By the time we moved downstairs to the audiovisual room in the basement, all the emotion had clumped together into a full-blown lump in my throat, around which I could barely breathe—preventing speech.

When he settled into his recliner and watched me where I stood, he deliberately scooted to the side and held out his hand for me to come sit with him. I squeezed in beside him. We were a perfect fit, and he settled his arm around the back of my waist, pulling me even closer. My head lowered against his solid shoulder, and he reached for the remote, beginning to cue up a movie.

I leaned over, straining upward to kiss him—though it landed somewhere between his jaw and the top of his neck. He turned to me, features blank, but still those eyes, so full, so heavy. Was there something there or was I reading into it?

Worry? Attentiveness? *Guilt?*

Should I tell him what I was feeling?

"What was that for?"

"It was just for being you." I melted into his side as his arm tightened. "For making me feel safe. All the time. And for knowing when I need to feel that safety."

He leaned forward to kiss me on the forehead. "Does this have anything to do with that news you got today?"

So he *did* want to know how I was feeling about it. I took a deep breath and let it go. "I don't need to know if you were involved with what happened. Don't tell me, please."

Another long silence where I tucked my head close to him and he didn't reply, smoothing a hand over my back. Then...

"But...if you *were* involved...I'm good with that."

We sat like that for long minutes, holding each other close. That was all I needed to say—nothing else mattered beyond that. And nothing more needed to be said.

Whether he'd had something to do with Zach going to jail, I didn't care to know. And I'd consciously chosen *not* to find out.

We spent a pleasant hour watching the first half of *Deadpool* before I couldn't stand it anymore. Just as Deadpool was trying to reconnect with his lost love, and failing, I pulled Adam's clothes off and attacked him on the recliner. We never even shut off the movie. For the record, recliner sex is fun. Two thumbs up, and I'd do it again in a heartbeat.

Chapter 3
Adam

EMILIA DOZED AGAINST MY CHEST AS THE CREDITS rolled, Deadpool lecturing viewers in his bathrobe, Ferris Bueller style. I kissed the top of her head, taking a long drag of the vanilla scent of her hair, my eyes closing at that familiar, visceral pull in my gut. I swallowed, hoping it was the wine and hot sex that had worn her out and not the stressful news of that bastard from her past.

So she suspected my involvement in that. And though I wouldn't have hesitated to come clean to her, I was relieved that she didn't require it. I'd known the risk when I made the decision to act. She might have become upset—even angry—over my interference, but it was too important that she feel safe.

I shifted her weight against me so I could get to my phone and check email, trying not to think about what would have happened if she'd reacted unfavorably.

How in the hell could I *not* interfere, though? I was with her in that grocery store. She'd bailed out so fast she'd been a blur—after having gone white as a sheet. That fear. It had killed me to see it paralyze her. And in that moment, I made a note to remember the last name of the woman she'd introduced me to in a stammering, shaky voice.

All of that was enough to get me suspicious. But that night...

That night I'd woken up to her sitting on the edge of the bed hyperventilating, claiming she'd had a nightmare. When I'd finally coaxed her down beside me, I held her shaking body tightly to mine. She slept with a death grip around me the entire night. I'd lain awake for hours, fearful that moving would disturb her. I'd listened helplessly to the occasional distressing whimpers she made in her sleep.

I'd burned with hatred for the bastard who'd done that to her, simply from that two-minute encounter. Witnessing the power of terror he held over her still was enough to put me on a vendetta mission.

It was my job to protect her. To keep her safe. And as long as this shit stain was free to approach her whenever he wanted, her perception of safety did not exist.

For a week after the fact, she'd fought insomnia, growing more and more exhausted. By the time we'd returned home, we'd needed a vacation to recover from that traumatic getaway.

I'd investigated. How could I not? I'd looked through her yearbook to avoid having to interrogate her mom. Once I had the guy's name, I'd confirmed it with Heath. Then I'd contacted Jordan, who always had his shady network handy (that same shady network that'd gotten me into trouble with Emilia once before). Without asking for details, Jordan hooked me up with a PI.

Emilia sleepily shifted against me as she slowly blinked awake.

And I'd decided to act, even with the chance of her finding out and being upset. After witnessing what that chance encounter had done to her, I'd been ready to take the risk.

From the PI, I'd gotten all the details of this piece of shit's life since college. An injury his sophomore year had shot his pro football hopes, and he'd lost his scholarship. He'd finished community college and worked as a real estate broker in LA. And he had a nasty drug habit to support.

Emilia smiled at me through sleepy eyes, quietly apologizing for nodding off. I kissed her hand. "Nothing to apologize for," I replied.

It had been easy, really, to set the trap. Arrange for him to "win" a luxury week-long trip to Cancun, assume his natural habits would take over and he wouldn't be as careful as he should be. Then have a helpful anonymous tipster alert the authorities to closely inspect him on his way back into the country.

Admittedly, that plan had left several things up to chance, and I recognized it, ready to come up with a plan B had it been necessary. But luckily, it hadn't.

My arms tightened around her involuntarily. So the asshole had gotten away with raping a woman in high school—and though I'd never tell Emilia this, several complaints had been filed against him during college, too, eventually dropped. A serial victimizer who managed to get away with it. But sooner or later, I could hope that it all evened out. Karma and all that. With some help from the vengeful fiancé.

***

Monday was almost over, and it had not gone well.

I glanced at the dusky sky outside the window of my office, dropping into my leather desk chair. It groaned in protest. It was getting late. Too damn late. I'd already texted Emilia to tell her that I wouldn't be home for dinner or even our semi-usual sunset walk. Her response had been affable but terse, minus her usual dose of snark. What she'd left unwritten spoke more loudly than what she had. I'd probably be in the dog house when I got home.

I traced a thumb over my lips, thinking. Her irritation was understandable. I'd been coming home later and later since Asia, and the balance that we'd been so good about establishing had been upset.

But right now, after the board meeting I'd sat through, I was in no mood to walk through the front door, trying to fake that nothing was bothering me. Were I back in my not-so-good ole single days, I would have calmed the rage by working out in our campus gym then showering in my private bathroom. Then I'd finish by staying in the office to work until dawn, exhausted, catching a quick nap on the pull-down bed before starting the next day. But she wouldn't stand for that. And, at this point in my life, I was glad of it.

Nevertheless, after an insufferable board of directors meeting twenty minutes before, I'd have to wait until I calmed down enough to see any color besides red. Or trust myself not to punch holes in the walls. Because this asshole board had stabbed me in the back. And honestly, I was still reeling.

It had just gotten personal.

A knock on my door came almost exactly a half-hour after the BOD meeting had adjourned. At that time, I'd hurriedly excused myself—pretty much the only way I was going to keep my cool. I hadn't been very successful. Doubtless, others noticed that I was angry and seconds from losing it on everyone around me.

I called for whoever it was—probably Jordan—to come in. Not only did I get him, but also David Weiss, our chairman of the board, as a bonus. *Great.* I could be rude to Jordan, and he'd take it like the punching bag he deserved to become. But with David around, I wouldn't be able to pull the gloves off. I respected David too much to drop the number of F-bombs and general threats required to get through Jordan's thick skull.

I stood, stuffed my hands in my pockets, and walked to the window, staring out at the purpling sky.

"Hey, Adam," David said. Jordan, wisely, kept his mouth shut. "Just wanted to, ah, stop by and check up on how you are doing."

"I'm doing the same as I was thirty minutes ago in the meeting," I replied in a flat voice.

David paused. "Well, that didn't seem to go over well. So that's why I'm here."

I turned back to him where he stood near the door. David was a man in his mid-fifties, someone I'd known and admired for a decade. He'd been the one to recruit me for my first job— persuading me to quit college and go work for him at Sony years ago. And when the time had come to start my own company, he'd given me his blessing on that, too.

I folded my arms over my chest. "You're going to try to talk me out of going to war with the board."

He grimaced. "That would be unwise."

I balled my hands into fists, gritted my teeth, but did not reply. There was no way either of them would understand.

"Adam—" Jordan began.

"I've already heard everything you've had to say on this subject in Tokyo," I said.

"Try to analyze this logically."

I turned on him, fists now dropped to my sides. "Tell me that you're going to make April sign one of these when it's your turn," I snarled.

Jordan's brow twitched, and he shot a self-conscious glance at David. I knew he wouldn't give me his sarcastic one-liner about not being stupid enough to get married. Not in front of his girlfriend's father, he wouldn't. Yeah, I was putting him in a shit-tastic position by throwing that at him in front of David, but right now, I was too pissed to care.

Jordan cleared his throat, and the look in his eyes spoke darkly of budding resentment. "When the time comes, yes, I'll ask her to sign one."

"Really...and you think she'd be okay with that?"

Jordan flushed, and David moved deeper into the office and sank into one of the available seats. "*I* do," he answered for Jordan.

I blew out a breath and ran my fingers through my hair. "But *she* has assets to protect, too, right?" Jordan and David shared a long look, but didn't answer. "I see what this shit is about. It's because Mia is poor."

David leaned forward. "Adam, trust me, I've been through this. It's not a walk in the park by any means. I've been married twice—prenups both times—and—"

I gestured in a cutting motion to him, and his mouth snapped shut, his eyes widening in surprise at my rudeness. Despite my earlier misgivings about being candid in front of David, I had zero fucks to give for his hurt feelings. "Neither one of you knows what it's like to be poor. *I* do. Until I was in my teens, there were days where we went without food or even knowing where we were going to sleep that night. Mia's never had to live like that, but I refuse to put her in a position—"

"No one's asking you to impoverish her, Adam." David shifted in his seat to cross an ankle over his knee. "Jordan is right. You're being entirely too emotional about this."

That was a low blow. I turned back to the window. "Yeah, God forbid I be *emotional* about my future, about my goddamn marriage. God forbid I want to protect the feelings of the woman I love."

"Maybe you should talk to her about it," Jordan said quietly. I heard him sink into the chair beside David. "Just in the context of what the board has asked you."

I scrubbed a hand over my face, wanting them both gone as quickly as possible.

Putting that paper in front of her to sign would be saying that I considered myself above her. That *my* money was more important than *her* feelings. That we were *not* equal, when my feelings and perception were very much the opposite of that.

I could imagine the look on her face, in her eyes, if I asked her to do this. To witness a spark of what made her *her* die just a little. To know that the trust she'd assumed I had in her was merely an illusion.

And the knowledge that if she didn't sign the paper, we couldn't get married…that the board was now coercing *me* to require her to do this. Or she'd never be my wife. That rankled most of all. That they were ripping control of this situation—of the financial welfare of *our marriage*—away from me and insulting my future wife in the process.

The board threatened to make me choose between my job and Emilia, like some medieval drama featuring star-crossed lovers avoiding an arranged marriage. *I* was the CEO of this company. A *billionaire* before the age of thirty. I knew how to run my own life, goddammit. Why did I feel like I had less control over my future than ever?

My shoulders stiffened. "I'm not going to let a board of directors micro-manage my private life," I finally muttered.

"Adam, can you sit down with us for a minute?" David's voice sounded strained now. I recognized the tone. Every deadline I'd almost missed. Every envelope I'd tried to push all those years ago when he was my boss. Those sounded exactly like this. "Can we talk this out? It's really not as bad as you think."

I turned and went back to my seat, sank slowly down into it, and then glanced at my watch. "I'm only doing this for ten minutes. You two aren't going to convince me that I'm wrong."

And they didn't.

I'd stand up for her with my last breath. Protecting her was my job. I wouldn't subject her to this.

When they left my office a quarter hour later, the tension was thick. I packed up my shit, heartily slamming drawers and doors as I did so. I knew the two of them were going to go somewhere and talk about how pigheaded I was.

I didn't give a rat's ass. I'd handle this my way. I'd steer my own ship. My own life.

Chapter 4
Mia

"BREATHE IN. NOW EXHALE SLOWLY," KAT murmured calmly.

I stared up from where I lay on the floor, past my thigh—which was curled awkwardly above me—at Kat. This was *not* natural.

"Bodies were not meant to bend this way," I muttered tightly as I inhaled like she instructed.

Her hand supported my lower back as, ass in the air, my legs were thrown over my head, feet resting on the ground somewhere behind my shoulders.

"Adam is going to love how bendy yoga will make you. It's *great* for sex. Now lock your fingers together behind you. See how your arms help your stability? This pose is called the Easy Plow."

"Jesus, it even sounds like a sex position."

She smirked. "Why do you think I got into yoga in the first place? Show him this pose and he'll be plowing you in minutes."

I interrupted my calm breathing to laugh at her. "Stop it. I'm going to fall over and injure something important."

"Keep breathing."

I complied, feeling the stretch in my lower back, all along my hamstrings and calves. Around me, the steady rhythm of the weight machines and the relentless pounding of footsteps on the treadmill kept time. We had staked out a corner of the Draco campus gym for this private yoga lesson. I'd made the mistake of telling Kat that I wanted to start yoga, but hadn't yet due to self-consciousness. She'd volunteered to get me started.

The girl always surprised me with her hidden skills. And typically, they were somehow tied to sex.

"Speaking of sex. When are we finding you Mr. Right Now?" I asked.

She grinned. "I don't need Mr. Right Now. I only need Mr. Makes-Me-Come. You throw me your bouquet at the wedding and I'm kicking your ass so hard there will be *no* sex—easy plow or otherwise—on your honeymoon. Don't even think about it."

"Ugh. Don't even mention the wedding or this yoga session is going to do the opposite of calming me."

Kat's brow rose. "Oh yeah? That bad?"

I inhaled and exhaled like she'd showed me before responding. "It's just...we can't agree on what we are doing."

"Well, you need to have that discussion with him soon. You're getting married on New Year's Eve, right? That's only months away."

I blew out another long breath. "Again, I thought this yoga session was to *decrease* stress?"

"Yo, Cranberry!" someone called from the other side of the gym. "What are you doing in here?"

Kat's head whipped up, and her eyes narrowed. With a grimace, she flipped the bird at whoever it was. "Staying in shape. Something you're obviously not familiar with, Jedi boy. I'm shocked you even knew there was a gym in the building."

"Have you checked the leaderboard lately?" he asked, voice fading as he walked away from us. Clearly, he'd been passing through and had taken the opportunity to taunt Kat.

Kat watched him go and then began muttering. "Jerkwad."

"Who was that?"

"The bane of my existence."

"*Oh*...Lucas from play testing again?"

Technically, he was her boss, but the hierarchy over there was kind of murky and confusing. Those gameplay testers were as competitive as test pilots. And Lucas and Kat had some kind of frenemies-intense rivalry going on that I, despite being a gamer girl myself, didn't fully understand.

"What was the leaderboard thing all about?" I asked. "Is that something new? And can I get the hell out of this pose yet? I'm starting to feel like a human pretzel."

Kat gently helped extricate me from the Easy Plow— seriously, I would not be showing Adam that pose *any*time soon, despite Kat's promise of great sex. Our sex life was already fantastic, thank you very much. I sat up slowly, careful not to pull any muscles. The blood rushed from my head, and I blinked, waiting for the lightheaded feeling to fade.

"Ah, he means the Twitch TV leaderboard. He's jealous as fuck because I've got more subscribers than he does. Forget about him. I can help you with some meditation next."

I cocked a brow at her. "Why don't you two just bang and get it over with?" I asked, repeating something she'd often said about another couple we knew that had bickered like Time Lords and Daleks before they'd gotten together.

Her brow arched up at me. "I don't shit where I eat. Never screw someone you work with."

"Ah." Luckily, that wasn't an official rule, or there'd be a lot of people fired around here.

Kat led me through some meditation, and then we sat on the mat while I consumed water by the bottleful and blotted my sweaty head with a soft white towel. "Well, thanks for that. I *really* needed a study break. But even thirty minutes away from the books these days gets me twitchy."

Kat unscrewed her bottle cap and threw me a long look. "Well, we should take a few more minutes, at least. I need to talk to you about Heath."

I hadn't seen Heath in almost a month, since our tea shop meeting with Camille. We hadn't managed to connect much since then. I'd only started back at school a week ago, and already the second year of medical school—called M2—was promising to kick my butt. And Heath had grown quieter and more subdued, during the few months since Connor had left.

But Kat, as his roommate, had more current info. So I asked, "How's he doing?"

"He was doing okay till we all got the news that Connor's dad had died."

I nodded, remembering the stoic email we'd all received from Ireland. "Poor Connor. We sent his family a basket. It's so sad. I think they were expecting him to make a full recovery."

Kat fiddled with her water bottle. "Yeah, well, now Connor is saying he needs to stay longer, help out his family."

"Understandable." I shrugged. "I'm sure this has put quite a burden on them all. And Connor being the eldest—"

Kat's lips thinned. "They had an argument about it. Heath was shouting at him over Skype."

That seemed unusually insensitive of Heath. I frowned. "What's this *really* about?"

"Heath thinks Connor's not coming back. That he's returned to Ireland for good because his family needs him."

I bit my lip and chewed on it. "And why does Heath think that?"

Kat shook her head and took another sip of water, the plastic of her bottle crackling as she tightened her grip on it. Her lips whitened, too. "He's not doing so hot, Mia. He's either spending hours on the game or he's drinking. He's behind on all his web design deadlines, or so I suspect. I think he's starting to fall apart."

Ugh. Worry gripped me, but at the same time, my eyes drifted over to my book bag and the massive stack of notes, highlighted articles, and papers I knew were inside. I had so much to do to prepare for the Step 1 Medical Board exam that all M2 students had to pass. My gut tightened—shades of my MCAT failure as an undergrad had come back to haunt me…and then some.

And a wedding to plan.

And a ghost fiancé to connect with somewhere in that mix.

I'd come over to his workplace today to spend time with him and instead hadn't even caught a glimpse of the elusive CEO beast. He ran—sometimes literally—from meeting to meeting. And at night, half the time he wasn't home, either out on the road on some trip or managing a crisis that apparently only *he* could oversee.

I licked my lips and fidgeted. "I'll talk to Heath, but…" I shrugged, suddenly awash with hopelessness. "I have no idea what I can do for him or even how."

More crackling from her now-empty bottle. I reached out and gently took it from her grip. The sound was driving me up a tree. Kat cleared her throat. "I think that making the effort will help a lot. I've tried, but...you know damn well that I'm not as close to him as you are. Not by a long shot."

I smiled at her. "I'm thankful that you're there. Imagine how much worse this could be if he were dealing with this completely alone. Problem is he's going to be all belligerent if I show up after not getting together with him in weeks and suddenly ask him to spill his troubles to me."

She rocked from side to side on the mat as if trying to get comfortable. "Why don't I invite you over for movie night or something? Then I could, uh, get a phone call and disappear into my room."

I blinked, shifting my gaze to my friend. "Wow, you're good at this stuff."

She nodded, a grin tugging at the corners of her mouth. "Better keep your eye on me."

"I fully intend to."

We chatted some more, firming up plans for the Heath ambush, and also discussed other things...her Twitch TV following and her rivalry with Lucas Walker.

I bit my tongue, noting how her fists tensed when she talked. I knew Lucas—barely—and remembered that he was good looking. And Kat had not dated a single soul since coming to California from Canada when I was sick the year before. She'd dropped everything—her entire life, her *job*, everything—to come south and be with me.

But she rarely talked about home or her family, and it worried me sometimes.

I finally did catch a glimpse of the elusive fiancé—on his way out the door to the dinner meeting he'd told me about.

"Hey! Not even a drive-by smooch?" I called, chasing after him as he strode toward his car. He slowed his gait—but, notably, did not stop—and held out his hand, which I grabbed.

"Sorry. I'm already late." His fingers closed around mine—too tightly.

"Why aren't you and Jordan driving there together? Looks like he's late, too." I nodded to Jordan's massive SUV parked beside Adam's Tesla.

"Eh, screw him," he muttered, and before I could ask, he threw an arm around my waist and pulled me into a kiss—again, harder than normal. I reached up to push against his shoulder to ease him off a bit and almost gasped at the tension in his entire frame. He was wound so tight he seemed about to break.

When I pulled away, he was already halfway into his car. A glance over my shoulder revealed Jordan coming out of the front doors at a half-run. His eyes narrowed when they landed on Adam's back. Were these two not getting along? What the hell?

"Don't forget you live with someone, and I'm trying to keep my bedtime at a decent hour. I'm not waiting up till midnight for you."

He started the car. It whirred to life. Even though I drove one very similar to this, I still couldn't get used to how quiet they were. "I'll be home before you go to bed."

"How much before?" I folded my arms across my chest.

"Enough before," he said with a smirk and a gleam in his eyes before he hid them behind his sexy Aviator sunglasses. Then he backed out of his space, and I shifted my weight, jutting out my hip and feigning a scowl as I watched him go. Of course, he'd get home in time for bedtime sex. He only missed that when he was out of the country.

Jordan had paused by his car to watch Adam drive off, his eyes still narrowed. I turned around and looked at him.

"Hey, Jordan."

He nodded at me as he threw his briefcase into his car.

"Everything okay?"

"Just fine. See ya, Mia."

"Tell April—" But he'd already jumped in, slammed the door and started the car, waving to me as he pulled out.

Weirder and weirder.

Adam made it home in time—barely. I'd drifted to sleep slumped over my textbooks in my study, and he carried me to bed. When I sleepily responded that he was too late for bedtime sex, he apologized and said he'd make amends and devote the entire weekend to me.

It was enough to convince me to rescind my punishment. When it came to Adam, I was an easy lay.

So the weekend was mine. And he kept his word. Mostly.

He did spend some time attached to his evil phone, however. Even when we went for dinner at Peter and my mom's house—this time on Saturday night instead of Sunday, because Mom wanted some alone time with the two of us. Adam and I were anticipating some kind of premarital counseling session or something.

But hey, she made moussaka, one of my favorite dishes to ever come out of her oven, and our chef, while very talented, rarely did Greek, so who was I to argue? I'd sit through some well-meaning advice if it meant I could scarf down Mom's awesome food.

"Damn, that was good," I said, picking up the last bits of custard and meat from my plate. It had been eons since Mom had made moussaka. In fact, the last time was the night she told me about her cancer biopsy. I frowned at that thought. The dish was labor intensive—multiple layers, each taking lots of chopping, mincing, and sautéing to execute. She hadn't made it in years...

But she'd made it tonight. Had this somehow morphed into the "bad news" meal? Were Peter and Mom going to get a divorce or, worse, have a baby or something?

I studied her suspiciously. She kept darting nervous glances at Peter, who would look at me. And if he noticed me watching them, he'd clear his throat and ask a question or change the subject.

Adam, as usual, engaged in a love affair with his phone. Mostly it would beep at him. He'd check it and then stick it back in his pocket.

Finally, I turned to him. "Any interest in turning that off?"

He smirked at me. "Not really?"

"What if I threaten to give you a wedgie?"

"It would be amusing to see you try."

"Turn off the phone, or when you least expect it...expect it."

His dark brows climbed his forehead. "Resorting to threats?"

"It's not a threat—it's a promise." I rubbed my hands together. "Atomic wedgie time."

"He's six feet tall and one and a half times your weight. How are you going to give him a wedgie?" my mom asked.

I shrugged. "I'll figure out a way."

Adam gave one last glance at his phone. "I'd better shut it off. I'm really scared right now." He feigned biting his fingernails in fear as he pointedly turned off the device.

I snickered. Usually a joke or two like that was all it took to remind him that he was being irritating with his goddamn phone. I used to get madder at him, but I'd come to the conclusion long ago that most of the time, when he was in work mode, he didn't even realize he was being rude.

That was what spouses were for, right? To when you were screwing up?

I winked at him and pointed to the last bit of moussaka on his plate with my fork. "You going to eat that?"

In a split second, he speared the morsel with his fork and popped it into his mouth. "Yep," he said after he'd swallowed then winked right back at me.

"Balls," I muttered.

Both Peter and Mom started laughing.

"Never going to be a dull moment at your house, that's for sure," Peter said after the laughter had died down.

Adam's eyes were glowing with amusement when he looked over at me. Tucking a strand of hair behind my ear, he grinned and chucked my cheek. "Nope, the word *dull* can never be applied to us. That's true." His hand opened. and he smoothed it across my cheek.

I turned my head and kissed his palm before he dropped it. Our gazes locked with promises of more kisses later, when we were alone. If he stayed off his damn phone long enough, that was.

Whatever this server data center project was he was working on lately, I'd be damned relieved once it was over. His work stress level was ridiculous. I was going to need to work up the courage to have "the talk" with him. Hopefully, he wouldn't start rolling his eyes and tuning me out whenever I brought up the phrase *work-life balance.*

"Well, since we're all in a good mood...I need to pass something along to you, Mia." Mom reached over to her purse on the adjacent table, pulled an envelope out, and slid it across the table to me.

It had my full name typed on it and was a legal-sized manila envelope. "Are you serving me papers, Mother? Am I about to be sued?"

Mom's long, thin fingers tapped the surface of the dinner table nervously. "No...not suing you. I'll save that for later when I seek a refund for all the ballet lessons I footed. They never paid off."

"*Ballet?* As in a little pink tutu?" Adam said, turning to me with a huge grin.

I held up a hand to block out his commentary. "I'll deal with *you* later. Now...back to the woman who birthed me." I tapped the envelope with my finger. "What is this?"

Mom's mouth thinned. She'd likely been hoping I'd open it straight away so she wouldn't have to explain. She nodded to it. "It's, uh, from Glen Dempsey."

I ripped my hand from the envelope as if it had morphed into a poisonous scorpion.

Mom expelled a breath. "Oh, come on, Mia."

Adam's eyes flicked from my mother to me and back again. "Who is Glen Dempsey?"

Mom waited quietly while I sorted through a complex but brief progression of emotions—shock, dismay, surprise, anger, curiosity. About two minutes into that process, while I sat fidgeting and frowning at the envelope, Mom finally answered Adam's question.

"Glen is Mia's half-brother."

Adam did not respond, but returned his gaze intently to me. When I looked up, he cocked his head at me. "I thought you didn't know your half-siblings."

I shook my head. "I don't. I have no idea what this guy wants. And I don't much care."

Mom admitted, "It's my fault. I, um, contacted his father."

I was sure my face showed the shock and disgust I was feeling at the thought of what it must have taken for my mother to do that. To reach out after twenty-four years and make contact with the man who'd lied to her, used her, and then dropped her like a hot rock when she was barely more than a teenager herself.

"Why... Just, why would you do that?"

"Because you got really sick and I realized I didn't know half of your medical history. So I asked him for medical and genetic records."

I took a deep breath and then released it. Well, it made sense. My mom had shown a lot of initiative—and courage—to make the contact.

"So I presume this is his information?"

"Not exactly...he wouldn't comply to my request."

I raised my brow, unwilling to think too long or hard about that information, but aware of the vague sting at his rejection. Yet again. It didn't matter how long ago I'd come to peace with it, it still hurt. What a piece of shit.

Mom cleared her throat and continued. "Somehow Glen got hold of my letter and contacted me, volunteering to provide his own information if that would help."

Suddenly, Adam's hand was on mine, and his fingers closed tightly. "You okay?"

I shrugged. "Sure. Why wouldn't I be? Newsflash, my father's an asshole. I already knew that."

Mom sighed heavily. "It's probably because the communication came from *me*. I'm sure he's avoided anything with my name on it for legal reasons. I, ah, signed a non-communication agreement with him when he gave me the settlement over you. Don't take it personally."

I blinked. "Oh, I take it personally, Mother. How could I not? But I also know it's not through any fault of mine that he reacts the way he does." I picked up the envelope and went to tuck it inside my bag. "Thanks for the medical info."

"When he gave it to me, Glen told me he wrote you a letter inside." I froze and met Mom's gaze. Her voice died out as she continued. "A personal note…"

"You met him?"

Mom nodded. "Yes. He asked to meet me. We had lunch, and it was very pleasant. He asked to meet you, too."

My jaw loosened, and I gave the envelope an extra-forceful push into the tote bag I'd brought. "Interesting." It was the only thing that popped into my head to say at that moment.

"He's a good man, Mia. I think it would do you—"

I held my hand up. "No, please. No lectures. I'm fine, and I'll continue to be fine, and I don't need to meet the asshole himself—*or* his children or his nephews or cousins or anyone else related to him. As long as I have the medical information I need, I'm good."

Mom wanted to say more—I knew she did—but her mouth snapped closed, and her gaze dropped from mine as she nodded vigorously.

Later, when we were in the driveway saying goodbye before getting in the car to go home, she held me tight around my neck and said quietly into my ear, "I would never make you do something you didn't want to do. I hope you know that. But...I love you, and I'm sorry."

I shook my head. "You have nothing to be sorry for."

She nodded. "I do...I do. I'm sorry I didn't make better choices."

I kissed her on the cheek and reassured her again, but...there was something in her words. And when I examined my feelings deep down, I did acknowledge the resentment—even if just a tiny tinge of it—I felt toward her. If she'd made a better choice, I could have grown up with a dad like Peter...

But when I went down that path, it got weird. Because if Peter *had* been my dad, then Adam and I would have been first cousins. And, well, that was squicky, and I didn't want to go there.

Eventually, I'd muster up the desire and courage to look at the report—maybe even read the letter. But for now, it wasn't important.

Chapter 5
Adam

EMILIA WAS SILENT ON THE WAY HOME, AND I KNEW IT was because of that bomb her mother had dropped on her during dinner. It usually took Emilia time to process things like that, and it was best to leave her alone to work through her thoughts. So I skipped the small talk as we drove. She reached out and took my hand, sliding over to lean her head on my shoulder. I kissed the top of her head and kept driving.

When we got home, I kept my phone off and asked her what she wanted to do until we went to bed. To my surprise and delight, she suggested we pull out our laptops and play Dragon Epoch together. We'd create brand-new characters on a different server to avoid getting chastised by our friends, who'd take offense at us logging on and playing without them.

I rolled a dark-haired woman named DirtyTshirtLuvr, complete with brand-new and shiny chain mail bikini. In retaliation, Emilia created a human male named *Wedgie*. And we laughed and did every stupid thing we could think of—like attempting quests way beyond our level and jumping off high places and going splat, leaving as many virtual corpses on the ground as we could. She joked about pulling trains using AoE spells and kiting mobs, but I wouldn't let her. The innocent newbies around us didn't deserve that.

"You're no fun. I could start a guild war." She pouted, the effect spoiled when she started laughing.

"Yeah, you could, but *no*," I replied. "I'll ban you."

She narrowed her eyes. "Ban me from DE at your own risk. You won't like what I ban *you* from, wedgie boy."

"Very funny," I said, finally closing my laptop and studying the glow of the computer screen across her beautiful features. "I'm not scared."

Her dark eyebrow arched. "And why is that?"

"Because you would never ban yourself, and I know you like those certain activities as much as I do." I winked.

Minutes later, we were upstairs in our bedroom, and I collapsed on the bed. I'd been figuring out how to circle back around to our awkward dinner conversation with her mom. Hence, I went for it.

"So how are you feeling about that news your mom dropped on you tonight?"

She shrugged out of her sweater then unbuttoned her jeans, dropped them onto the floor, and stepped out of them. My eyes glided down the long stretch of bare leg, and that familiar pressure of arousal rose up. In a few minutes, those mouthwatering legs would be wrapped around me, and every part of my body enthusiastically readied for it.

"Take a picture—it lasts longer." She smirked then stuck her tongue out at me.

"If you didn't want me perving on you, you would have gone and changed in your closet. If you're changing out here, that means you want me to watch you."

She reached around and unhooked her bra. The straps retracted, but she didn't pull it off. Turning around, she demurely gazed at me over her shoulder, slowly sliding one side off her arm and then the other. "I don't want to inflame your lust any further…"

"Yeah, you do." I grinned, rolling onto my side and propping my head up on my bent arm to continue enjoying her show. To be extra obnoxious, I smacked my lips together. "My *underpants* are starting to feel tight."

She laughed as she wiggled out of her panties. "Someone wants a bonus tonight? After that fun little nooner?"

"The nooner was the bonus. Tonight's the regular."

She wrinkled her nose at me. "I think you're getting spoiled. You might have to work for it tonight to convince me."

"Maybe I'll finally follow through on that threat to tie you up."

She turned around, fully naked now. "Or maybe I'll walk around here and torment you for a while and not give in."

"Not give in? That never happens." I ran my eyes over her from head to toe. She was gorgeous…her body curving in all the right places. Delectable, smooth skin. Even her nipples were perky, all ready for my tongue to taste them. *Perfect.*

"Come here." I relished the feel of the blood pressure rising in my veins. Though I'd never in a million years admit it to her, I loved when she teased like this.

She mock-frowned. "That wasn't very convincing."

"Come here, you tease. I'll make you feel good."

"I'm sorry…I didn't mean to inflame your desires. It was completely accidental." Her eyes gleamed with amusement.

"You inflame my desires just by breathing," I said.

She crawled across the bed toward me, shoulders flexing like a cat's. But I was the one who sprang without warning, flipping her onto her back and pinning her down. "Surprise. Desires inflamed beyond control."

"I guess we'll have to do something about that. Even though you don't deserve the bonus."

"I told you, this one is the regular."

She grimaced at me. "You always were a cheater." Then she grabbed my head and pulled it down in a fierce kiss. And we were lost in each other. And yeah, my original question about the news at dinner had been completely derailed. I'm a guy, after all. Where sex with a beautiful woman was involved, I was easily diverted.

Then I tried again a while later—afterward—as I cradled her naked body against mine. She pressed her back to my chest. "Okay, that part about making me feel good. That was completely accurate." She sighed.

I kissed her neck, basking in my own afterglow. "Good."

She laid her head down, using my bicep as her pillow. "I'm gonna fall asleep in ten seconds flat."

"Before you do..."

"Mmm?"

"Just want to make sure you're okay with your mom's news at dinner. You haven't said anything about it."

She was quiet for some time—enough that I almost thought she wouldn't answer. I was debating whether to ask her again when, finally, she took a deep breath and rolled over to face me.

"I don't know what to think about all that. It kind of...came out of nowhere."

I reached up and pushed a strand of long, dark hair out of her face, tucking it behind her ear. "Well, you should think about it—

about reading that letter, anyway. There's no harm in that, is there?"

"Sometimes, there is harm in knowledge." She took in a deep breath and then let it go. "For example, I was always comfortable with the formless idea that my father is an asshole. But to hear that he blew my mother off—when I was sick. *Really* sick. That's...the reality of it."

"But it's not your father. It's your brother."

"Who's to say he isn't a chip off the old block?"

I shrugged. "That's a chance you have to take, but your mom seemed to like him a lot."

She expelled a breath that was almost a light laugh. "My mom...I'm not sure I trust her judgment in this matter."

"What?" I asked, puzzled. "You're still judging her based on a mistake she made twenty-five years ago?"

She shook her head. "No, no. I don't mean that. I mean her own guilt might be driving her to accept him when he's not a nice person. I think she feels guilty that I grew up without a family. She wants me to have one so badly that she'd recommend this guy. He is, after all, half of him."

"But so are you."

She made a face at me. "You're only talking honestly because you already got sex tonight. No need to butter me up anymore."

I kissed her nose. "I think it might be good for you to read the letter. I don't think there could be harm in that. I'll read it first to screen it if you want."

She reached out and traced an idle doodle with her index finger across my chest. It tickled. "Maybe. I'll think about it."

I kissed her again. "Okay. Don't forget we have that meeting with the wedding planner tomorrow."

"Sure...she's coming to your office?"

"Yeah. I had a full schedule, so that was the only way we could fit it in, over lunch."

She nodded. "I'm falling asleep now. You better be doing the same, or I'm gonna turn into a nagging wife before my time."

I smiled. "Damn, I don't want that. I'll read, then. Go to sleep."

Once she was out—and I checked thoroughly—I got up to go work in my office until the small hours of the morning, ensuring I left Kim's big envelope on the middle of Emilia's desk.

I'd been doing that lately, happy with the stealth factor that evaded Emilia's concerns.

Tonight, I was up for hours, continuing my research on how to fight this prenup. I learned that the board could not legally coerce me to sign the contract or require my spouse to sign. That was the good news. The law was on *my* side.

The bad news? They were perfectly within their power to follow through on their threat to have me removed as CEO of the company for breach of fiduciary duty, if it came to that.

I began building a list of legal references and lawyers to consult. I was going to do this. For her. For us both.

But that involved being up late at night, composing emails, researching and reading legal documents, and verifying legal restrictions. It was exhausting, but it was working. I was managing those feelings of helplessness and rage for the most part.

And I was planning to execute my next move all while running a company, planning a wedding, and fending off a persistent board of directors. No big deal.

***

"*Adam.*" A shout echoed across the floor of the R&D warehouse days later as I sat huddled with several devs and art team leaders in a pick-up scrum meeting.

I knew the voice. Ignoring it, I kept talking. "Because we're way off our sprint goals—"

"Adam." The voice was closer now. His footsteps echoed across the polished cement floor of the warehouse. Everyone who was crowded around me looked up at Jordan, wrapped up in his own thundercloud, headed my way.

"—emerging requirements have shifted," I continued. "That means tighter deadlines." They answered with groans all around. "I'm sorry, guys, but—"

Jordan was now standing on the outer rim of the group, hands on his hips, scowling. "I need to talk to you for a minute."

"As soon as I'm done here," I replied flatly.

His jaw worked, but he said nothing. *Good.* The leadership team was taking notes, and the few members of the art department—my cousin among them—were whispering to each other. I ignored Jordan's obvious posturing and continued with the scrum, taking my time.

I never even so much as glanced Jordan's way. Once I'd finished and dismissed them, Jordan proceeded to chase people away with a curt "Excuse us, please."

The group broke off into small clusters that either returned to their desks or hovered around the edges of the big warehouse, out of earshot, in order to discuss how to form up and work the problem. Jordan pulled out his phone, which he promptly shoved in my face. It showed the same attachment the entire board had received in the email not even half an hour before.

"Susan sent me this agenda for tonight's BOD meeting, and it says you're bringing a 'guest' by the name of J.B. Kensington. For real?"

I nodded. "That's correct."

He glanced around us to make sure others weren't close enough to overhear. I leaned back on my stool, arms folded across my chest, completely unconcerned about the storm I saw about to break on my long-suffering CFO's head.

He tucked the phone into a front pocket. "A fucking shark lawyer, Adam? Have you completely lost your mind?"

I narrowed my eyes, but otherwise did not move as I stared him down. "And what the hell did you expect? The board calls an unannounced meeting on me to discuss this—matter. You cornered me. How did you think I'd react?"

"That's the problem. You're *reacting* instead of acting. Look," he said between his teeth, "you need to knock it off. Believe me, I've already been doing the research on your behalf. If the board gets agitated, they *will* press this issue. You're playing a dangerous game."

My arms tensed where they were folded across my chest. "I know all about games. This isn't a game."

"It's bullshit posturing, and you're above it—or you *usually* are. Lawyering up for a board meeting is over the top." The expression on his face was a cross between disgust and exasperation. It only angered me more. Heat burned under my collar. "You remember that warning I gave you about your stubbornness? Well, it's rearing its ugly head now. And things don't appear optimistic."

"Is that a threat?" I stood up, suddenly agitated with him looming over me while I was sitting down, and, yeah, taken with the need to intimidate him. Would have worked better if we weren't almost exactly the same height.

My movements must have been more sudden than I'd planned, because several of the people still standing around jerked their heads in our direction. When I stared at them, they discreetly glanced away.

Jordan was shaking his head in disbelief. "Don't do that. I'm not here to threaten you. I told you, I've got your back..."

My fists flexed at my sides, and I forced myself to relax them. "Those are nice words to say, but you *don't*."

"It's *business*, Adam. That's my job—to protect your business interests."

"*And* your own."

He blinked. "To protect *this company's* business interests."

"*My* company's business interests."

His jaw set. "I think the board of directors would disagree with calling it that."

"*Fuck* the board of directors. Yet another thing that you've talked me into that I now regret."

He seemed to fight wanting to roll his eyes. "I'm going to ignore that."

I raised my brow, shifting my posture. It was ridiculous, but I could feel my chest puffing out. Jordan's eyes narrowed, taking in my body language. I knew he was carefully assessing it. He bit his bottom lip and cast a quick glance up into my face.

"If you *did* have my back, I wouldn't be fighting with those assholes about my private married life and personal finances that are none of their goddamn business. *My* company. *My* life. Get the fuck out of it!" By this time, I was shouting.

Jordan's eyes cut to mine. "You're unbelievable."

"A *friend* would have used his influence with the board to put a stop to this," I said. "Instead, you've put your own personal feelings ahead of doing what is right and throwing your *friend* under a bus."

He held his hands out, palms up. "Who's throwing who under a bus? Christ Almighty, Adam." He gestured stiffly with his right hand. "Pull your head out of your ass."

That heat from under my collar exploded like a supernova. In a flash, I was in his face, grasping his shirt. "My head isn't up my ass, fuck you very much."

And there we were in that warehouse, our faces inches from each other and a whole lot of testosterone in the air. My blood gushed in my veins, heart hammering. And I was *this close* to swinging on Jordan. My best friend.

That was when I sensed the presence of a third person. Hands on each of us, pushing us away from each other. Someone, luckily, as big as we both were. My cousin, speaking as a voice of reason.

"Back off each other. *Now*," Liam ordered in his typical monotone, a surprisingly authoritative ring to it. The tension washed from my body as if a spell had been broken.

I released Jordan's shirt immediately and stepped away. When I finally became aware again of our surroundings, the few people who were left in the warehouse all seemed to be hightailing it out of there as fast as they could. Soon, the entire place was empty except for the three of us.

Jordan was flushed, breathing hard with a WTF expression on his face. Honestly, if I could see myself in the mirror, I'd probably see that same look reflected back at me. Jesus. What the hell was wrong with me?

Liam had moved between the two of us. "If you two really want to handle this the old-fashioned way, then take up swords and don armor. We'll hold a duel at the European martial arts studio. But you definitely shouldn't be challenging each other in front of employees."

Fuck. I ran a hand through my hair, eyes glued to the ground. Jordan shifted where he stood, as if trying to see around Liam.

"I'm not swinging a sword at him," Jordan muttered. "But I wish he'd listen to some *friendly* advice. I can't help him if he chooses to antagonize the board."

I closed my eyes and massaged them through my lids. "Understood." Resisting the urge to reach out and pat Liam on the shoulder, because he didn't like anyone touching him without a warning. "Thanks, man."

"Don't thank me. Thank him for not hitting you," Liam said. "He has a powerful left hook."

Jordan laughed. After an awkward-as-hell pause, I finally sucked it up. "Jordan. I'm sorry, man."

"You're wound a little tight. Any man facing the impending doom of marriage would be, I'm sure."

I flipped him the bird, and we both laughed. That wordless gesture signaled that things were going to be okay with us. Eventually.

Liam glanced from me to Jordan, obviously confused. Jordan stepped back and said he needed to go take a walk to unwind. I could have used one, too. I expected Liam to leave and go about his business, but he watched me with open curiosity instead.

I met his gaze, and he didn't jerk his eyes away as he usually did. He'd been getting much better about eye contact, in fact, though it obviously still wasn't his favorite thing. I suspected it was Jenna's influence in his life.

"Why are you and Jordan fighting?"

I sighed and rubbed my forehead. "It's a long story. Boardroom stuff."

"Oh. Well, I meant what I said about you two fighting it out with swords if you need to. I can get my sword master to set it up."

I blew out a breath and turned to walk out of the warehouse. Liam fell into step beside me. "Thanks for the offer. I think we're good." I *hoped* we were good, anyway. That spat had solved exactly nothing.

"Is that how you and Jenna resolve your disputes?" I teased. "Sword fighting?"

"No, of course not." He shook his head. "When we argue, we each present our side. Somehow, she's the one who always ends up in the right, or I end up conceding. Then we have sexual intercourse afterward. So I end up not caring who won and who lost."

I laughed. Someone had discovered the joy of make-up sex.

Later that day, not long before the board meeting, I met with my new lawyer in my office—and made no secret of it. But I didn't bring him with me to the meeting.

The agenda itself was clear and succinct. They were putting down an ultimatum that I was expecting. But they were going to allow me time to respond.

That may or may not have been a good thing.

Chapter 6
Mia

"**T**HERE YOU ARE." APRIL ANSWERED HER DOOR WITH A big grin. "Long time no see. It's not like you're busy or anything."

I stepped forward to give her a hug. "Yeah, all that partying and drinking I'm doing." I made a face. "And my wild social life and love affair with medical textbooks."

"Sounds like my life, only with econ textbooks. We're living the dream, aren't we? *The Billionaire Girlfriends Club.* They should start a reality show about us." She motioned me into the home she shared with Jordan—a gorgeous beach house that sat right on the Wedge in Newport Beach and, conveniently for me, only a mile and a half down the road from our house.

"Come in. I have your stack of magazines. Not like you could have ordered a ton on your own."

I shrugged. "The wedding planner offered. But I hate killing trees, and I wasn't crazy about practically anything she showed me. Someone must have sent her the wrong memo, because she thinks the prince of the United Arab Emirates is getting married or something. I need a handle on a more normal-looking wedding."

Her dark brown eyebrows arched perfectly over clear blue eyes. She really was stunning. And sweet. And smart. Jordan had done a lot of stupid things in his short life, but April was the clever choice that made up for most of it.

"Sid, my old roomie, passed these along to me. I think she was trying to hint that she doesn't approve of Jordan and me living in sin. Kids these days!" She rolled her eyes dramatically. "Anyway, these were her sister's. She had a lovely wedding recently, so there might be some good ideas in there." Then her eyes gleamed with mischief. "I *may* be keeping those around just to fuck with Jordan, too. It's kinda fun to start paging through *Brides* magazine when he's annoying me."

"I like how you think. Keep that man in line." Glancing over at the stack she indicated, I sighed. "I need wedding ideas, stat."

"It's getting kind of close to the wire, isn't it? Doesn't the resort have a planner? Why not go with what they normally offer? *And*, by the way, thank you for that. I cannot *wait* to go to St. Lucia for New Year's. Best choice ever. I've always loved a destination wedding."

I plopped down on her couch and plucked a magazine from the stack waiting for me on the end table. Idly thumbing through it, I shrugged. "I've never been super big on weddings, you know? I have simple tastes. I'm glad we're having it in St. Lucia. I *love* the resort, and we have some special memories there, but...I have to confess, I was relieved when he suggested it, mostly because I knew it would limit the guest list."

"You have your dress picked out, at least?"

I smiled. "Yeah. It's gorgeous. Wanna see? I have the final fitting in a few weeks." I pulled out my phone and showed her a shot that I had snapped in the mirror.

"Holy shit. It's stunning. I love the silver accents on the white." She looked at me and then the picture several times, her mouth growing round. "Oh em gee. I'm so jealous right now. I can't wait to see Adam's face when you walk down the aisle in this."

"He is being a lot more...detail-oriented...about the whole thing than I am."

April cocked her head at me as she handed me my phone. "That's a funny kind of reverse. Usually the guy wants nothing to do with it at all."

"Yeah. It's weird. He wasn't this focused on it until recently. Like, in the last few weeks, he's gotten kind of...obsessive about it. Says he wants me to have the perfect wedding. I keep trying to tell him it's a party, and as long as we all have fun, who cares what kind of the flowers there are or how tall the cake is. Know what I mean? I want good memories."

She frowned. "You guys aren't arguing about it, are you? I don't mean to pry. I..." She shook her head.

"No, it's okay. I know it's common to argue about weddings."

She nodded. "I was going to say, you two do remarkably well for how busy you both are. It would just be criminal if on top of all that you had the perfect relationship, too. I guess there always has to be bumps in the road. I honestly don't know how you two make it work so well. You're studying all day and all weekend long, and he's off on business trips or working eighteen-hour days."

"We have our little tricks. We steal a lot of moments. Lots of text flirting."

"Ohh. *Sexting.* Jordan loves that." She laughed.

I grimaced. Figured he would. And I could have lived a lifetime without knowing that about him.

"Adam actually forbids sexting because of the security risk. But flirting's okay. We also do video calls when he's out of town. We're always in touch."

April made a face. "How boring. I guess computer nerds are paranoid about that kind of stuff."

Probably with good reason.

"We do fine most of the time. Lately, though, he's been a total stress case, and I don't think it's *all* about the wedding."

She blinked at me. "I wonder if it's something going on at work, because Jordan is the same way."

I sat back a moment, closing the magazine and remembering the few times that Jordan had been brought up, Adam had stiffly changed the subject or made a cryptic—and not often kind—remark. And that weird display a few weeks before, when Adam had stormed off to a dinner meeting without even caring Jordan was coming, too. "Are they not getting along, do you think?"

Her eyes widened. "Adam and Jordan? I—" She looked off into the distance as if thinking. "They haven't gotten together outside of work in quite some time. They don't run together anymore. I figured it's because of all the new projects they've got going now that they are flush with stock market cash."

"Work stress probably has a lot to do with it but...I don't know. I'm getting a weird vibe from both of them."

"I can ask my dad if he's noticed anything when I see him next weekend. Only problem is that Dad is notoriously close-mouthed about work. But since it's about Jordan, I might be able to wheedle something out of him."

I propped my elbow on the back of the couch, resting my chin in my hand. "Maybe we both need to suck it up and ask the men themselves."

"I think I'd rather eat a peanut butter and mustard sandwich."

I grinned. "I'd rather gargle with hot sauce."

"I'd rather take his surfboard out at high tide after a tropical storm."

And the conversation ended there, with us laughing and thinking of things we'd rather do than get between two man-babies having an emo standoff.

After that, we moved on to more important matters...like how I would be wearing my hair. What shoes and jewelry would best compliment the gown?

All that girly stuff.

Later I tossed that stack of magazines into the passenger seat of my car and went to study at the university library for most of the afternoon before landing over at Heath and Kat's place after dinnertime.

Heath greeted me, stone-faced and silent, as Kat squeezed her way out the door, deserting me almost immediately. Minutes later, she sent me a text. *Sorry, I can't even with him right now. I think he really needs to talk to you alone.*

From that small bit, I surmised they weren't seeing eye to eye.

Was it in the air or something?

I frowned as Heath led me wordlessly over to his computer and logged it into Dragon Epoch.

"You need to see this," he said when I asked him what he was doing.

Fragged, his mercenary, was located in the newbie zone—that same old city gate where most characters in Yondareth begin their adventuring life.

"Check out this new character next to General SylvenWood."

"The Town Crier?" I bent over his shoulder to get a better look at the monitor. "What the hell is that? Is this for a special holiday event or something?"

"No, wait. Check out what happens when you hail him.." Heath maneuvered his character to stand before the Town Crier.

Fragged says, "Hail, Town Crier."
Town Criers says, "The high lord of all the land is about to be wed. His lucky bride? The princess Emma."

Huh… I read the screen again and then turned back to Heath. "How'd you find this?"

"It hasn't been advertised yet. It wasn't as hard to uncover as the goddamn secret quest we did last year. I have a feeling it's been implemented and won't be publicized till the next official update. Check this out—once I follow the dialogue chain, he offers me a quest."

Town Crier has offered Fragged: Lord Sisyphus's Wedding Quest.

I straightened. "Wait, Lord Sisyphus. That's Adam's public game persona."

Heath turned to watch me closely. "Yeah, and he's getting married, right? To 'Princess Emma'…"

My mouth dropped in shock. "He put a special wedding quest into the game? He didn't even tell me about this. Do you think he meant it as a surprise?"

Heath shrugged exaggeratedly. "No idea. He's full of them...surprises, I mean."

I mock-glared at him. "Is that some kind of warning?"

Heath shook his head emphatically. "Oh no, you don't. No Bridezilla McColdFeet that he can blame on me. I mean...he's secretive."

I folded my arms over my chest. "Since when is that news? I still have no idea where we are going on our honeymoon."

"How do you know what to pack for? Bikini or ski suit or city walking shoes?"

"He's having our shopper take care of it and pack for both of us." I rolled my eyes, and he muttered something about first-world problems.

"He's *really* into the wedding." Heath rubbed his jaw, thinking. "Kind of playing the bride part, huh? Damn. I still say it's a waste and a shame that he's not into men."

I stretched my back, the muscles tired and sore. "He likes boobies too much." I patted my chest. "*Mine*, to be specific."

Heath held up a hand in front of his face. "Didn't need the visual. Thanks."

"So? Are you going to pop us some popcorn? This *is* movie night, right?"

"As milady commands." He bowed. I followed him into the kitchen, and he plopped a bag of popcorn into the microwave while I grabbed a bottle of beer out of the fridge for him and a mineral water for me.

I was settled on the couch, remote in hand, when he showed up with the bowl of salty, buttery goodness. I began scrolling through the options listed. "So what are we in the mood for? Classic rerun? Marvel blockbuster? Romcom?"

Heath snorted at the last choice. "As if."

"How about the latest Jack Eversea action flick? He's *so* hot."

"Watched it last week."

"Oh, okay." I bit my lip and sent him a look out of the corner of my eye. "Well, here's a travel documentary on Dublin."

Heath stiffened next to me, but didn't say anything. *Ugh...real smooth move, Mia. About as subtle as a hand grenade in a frilly doily tea shop.*

I chanced a glance at him, and when I caught his eye, he said, "Something with lots of car chases and explosions."

I shook my head and tsked. "Such a boy."

But I didn't scroll away from that Dublin travel show. We both sat and stared at the screen. "Have you...heard from him lately?"

Heath grabbed an impossibly huge fist of popcorn and shoved it in his face, crunching loudly. I waited.

Finally, once he'd swallowed down the mess, he shoved the bowl at my chest, and I took it. "No," he muttered.

"He's busy." I shrugged. "I'm sure if you Skyped—"

"His mother's house has shitty Internet, and he can't seem to find the privacy he requires to Skype me from an Internet café. He's not out of the closet in Ireland, and I'm sure the world will end if anyone in his circle finds out he's been carrying on with an American man." Heath's voice was dry, emotionless, edged dark and as bitter as pure unsweetened chocolate.

"Not everyone is as brave as you are, Heath. It took a giant pair of balls to risk what you did—given how your parents are. And you were only sixteen when you came out."

Heath took a long pull from his beer, but didn't say anything.

"You should go to Ireland."

"No," he answered quickly.

"Why not?"

"If he can't even bring himself to Skype me in private, how the hell do you think he's going to handle me showing up at his door? With his *very Catholic* mother hovering over his shoulder and his six younger siblings all crowded around him? I'm not going to force his hand, Mia. I'm not going to force anyone to go through what I went through when I came out. And I'm most definitely *not* going to force someone out of the closet."

I shook my head. "Of course not. But can't you just be his friend? Go to Ireland and be there for him while he mourns the loss of his dad and gets his family back on their feet again?"

Heath's jaw tensed, and he looked at me out of the corner of his eye. "If he wanted me there, he'd ask."

I turned to him, plunking the bowl of popcorn onto the couch between us. "Heath, he wants you there. I know he does."

"Oh?" His entire body tensed. "You have an in with Connor that I don't know about?"

Shifting to face him, I took a deep breath. "I called him last week, yeah. Wanted to give him my condolences. We sent a basket, and I followed up to see how he and his family are doing. He's *my* friend, too. And he asked about you. In detail."

Heath scowled. "Then why are you asking *me* how he's doing? You have more recent news than I do."

"He misses you."

Silence.

"And you miss him."

He muttered something and rubbed the back of his neck. "And your point is?"

"Heath! Don't be a stubborn idiot. Take it from someone who almost lost the man I love because *I* was a stubborn idiot. You were a firsthand witness to that catastrophe. Please learn from my mistake and don't repeat it with Connor. Go to Ireland. I know you have the time off."

"I'm saving those vacation days for your wedding."

Oh. Shit.

I sucked in a breath and let it go. "You have my permission to skip my wedding."

He looked at me like I was insane, folding his thick arms over his broad chest. "Oh really?"

I swallowed a sudden lump in my throat. The thought of him not being there when we got married made me almost nauseated and want to spontaneously burst into tears. But...it was a sacrifice I could gladly make for his happiness. "Yes, really. We'll take lots of pictures. I can video-chat you right after. It's okay."

"*No.* It's not. I'm not missing your wedding. At the very least, I have to make sure you get there in one piece and fucking get married already. It's taken you two long enough."

"Heath." I shook his shoulder. "You need to go get Connor."

"I can't *get* him if he doesn't want to be gotten." That powerful shoulder turned to rock under my hand. "He's staying in Ireland."

I blinked. "Temporarily—"

"No. He's looking for a job. Didn't he tell you? He needs to make money to help out with the family. He's got young siblings still."

"That's…" I shook my head. "That's so sad."

"He doesn't seem sad." He shrugged off my hand. "He probably wasn't that into me."

I shook my head. "I was there at the airport when you said goodbye. He *sobbed*, Heath. Don't say he's not that into you. That's bullshit. When I talked to him last week—"

Without warning, Heath's huge hand swatted down, batting the bowl of popcorn off the couch to bounce off the wall below where the TV hung. Popcorn scattered everywhere—the floor, bouncing off the wall, raining down on the coffee table.

Heath was on his feet, shouting, "Goddamn it, Mia! Don't fucking preach to me. You messed up your own life and made it a shit show. You got *lucky* and everything's fixed. *Now* you think we all can follow suit?"

I sucked in a breath, sitting back, breathless, as if he'd punched me in the stomach. It took a moment of stunned silence and vigorous blinking through my own hurt to remember that Heath was wounded and he was striking out at me because he could. Because I was a safe punching bag. And he had nowhere else to vent.

"I—I want you to be happy, Heath. That's all I want." My voice faded into a whisper, eyes stinging with the beginning of unshed tears. And, as abruptly as his anger had appeared, it evaporated.

He collapsed on the couch beside me and grabbed me to him, crying. "I'm sorry. Fuck. I'm so sorry."

I returned the hug, almost suffocated by his embrace. Heath was a mountain of a man. That brief display of violence would have caused fear in me from any other source besides my self-adopted brother. I knew I was safe with him. Always.

He was rocking back and forth, his hug tightening, pulling me along with him like a rag doll. "God, I suck. I'm so sorry," he kept repeating.

Now his voice was breaking and his head was on my shoulder, his chest vibrating with violent sobs. And inexplicably, I started to cry, too. It wasn't every day that you felt your best friend fall apart in your arms, his heart shattered into tiny bits.

I'd done this before, helped pick up the pieces. And though Heath liked to imagine himself a tough guy, when he loved, he loved with his whole heart. He put everything out there uninhibitedly to be stepped on and crushed. Without fear of consequences. And though that made for more painful breakups, I knew that if I'd been the same way with Adam in the beginning, we may not have encountered some of the huge problems we did later.

Fortunately, as Heath said, I was lucky. V*ery* lucky. Adam and I had a second chance, and we were learning every day how to make this one stick forever. But that didn't mean that Heath and Connor couldn't have their own brand of luck, too.

I held him tight and didn't speak for long minutes—probably longer than a half-hour or so, while he sobbed on my shoulder. I didn't shush him, didn't rock him, didn't coo like he was a baby.

I was there for him. A silent presence. I cried with him. I relived those moments when my own heart had broken. I *empathized.*

Adam and I had never had to worry about things like family, religion, beliefs, or someone hating us simply because of who we loved. I couldn't even imagine what that would be like.

Heath's parents hadn't spoken to him in almost a decade. Connor had to keep his identity deeply in the closet, never fully being able to reveal who he was to the people he loved most in the world. And I couldn't help but think about how cruel that was.

Heath was right. I was lucky. And I had no business giving him love advice from my position of never having to worry about those other things. People would never oppose my and Adam's right to love each other and get married.

So that night, as we held each other, I tried my hardest to be a good friend.

And hoped. Hoped that someday he'd get to be happy, too, with the man that he loved.

We never did get to the movie. After a long talk, a cleanup job, and another bowl of popcorn, we pulled out the Munchkin cards and played that instead. It was great for a much-needed laugh.

By the time I made it home, it was after nine and—miracle of miracles—my significant other had made it home before me. However, he was on his laptop in his home office, likely still working.

And he was exhausted. He couldn't even hide it from me. He'd changed out of work clothes—looking delicious, as usual, in a pair of gray sweat pants and a black t-shirt (a gift from me) that read *I'm a programmer: To save time, let's just assume that I am never wrong.* I swooped up behind him, threw my arms around his neck, and smooched his prickly cheek.

He leaned back, hooking a hand behind my neck to bring me in for a kiss on the lips. "How was movie night with Heath?"

I straightened, throwing a significant glance at his laptop. "You still working?"

Adam ran a quick hand through his hair, as if smoothing it out. He was trying to eliminate the telltale signs of him having pulled at it or fiddled with it—a habit for him born of frustration.

"Still dealing with all that IT stuff? The IT guy still not coming through for you?" I asked before he could formulate an answer.

He nodded. "I'm really disappointed in Alan. I keep waiting for him to get his shit together, and he's not rising to the occasion. I get that his personal life is in the toilet, but there's only so long that I can wait on that."

"Bet when you sat down to write your first program, you never imagined yourself being more a manager of people than a plain ol' computer geek."

He heaved a sigh. "Sometimes I really wish I could go back to those days. Just me and my PC and my source lines of code in C."

"*But*...in those days, you hoped to build your dream game and have millions of people enjoy it. And now here it is, reality."

"Yeah. But one man can't do it all."

"Not even *you*." I leaned away to get a better look into his face. He appeared pale, drawn. There were circles under his gorgeous, dark eyes. I smoothed my hand across the whiskered cheek. "That's why you surround yourself with kick-ass, awesome people and jettison the losers. If they don't share your vision, let them go. Like, sadly, you may have to do with Alan. But if they rock, hold them close. Like...Jordan, for example."

His jaw tensed under my hand, and those dark eyes hardened like black ice. Nevertheless, I wasn't sure which mention brought about that reaction—his IT director or Jordan? Maybe both. To ease the tension, I away, tilting my head to see his computer screen. He reached over and closed it. It locked with a final click, and I stared at him, raising a brow.

"Business BS. I really do need to stop for the night."

"Yeah. Or you'll never sleep. You'll toss and turn for a few hours like you did last night. And the night before. Then you'll finally give up and sneak out of bed at about three or four a.m., hoping I won't notice."

He grimaced. "Guilty."

"You aren't sleeping. You're working as hard as ever. You're starting to look raggedy."

His brows rose, and he appeared indignant. "*Raggedy?*"

"Yes." I nodded. "You've got a lot of pressure on you. And with this wedding—"

His eyes narrowed. "We are *not* delaying the wedding date."

"I didn't say we should. I *am* worried about you, though. About your health."

He laughed, leaning back in his chair and patting his lap. "I'm perfectly healthy. Want me to prove it to you right now?"

I grinned. "Now, now." I gently sank onto his lap, settling in to get comfortable as his arms encircled my waist, and he kissed my cheek. "Just don't take good health for granted."

"I don't," he murmured. He didn't have to say the rest. After what we'd been through the year before, it didn't need to be spoken between us. We'd learned the hard way that good health wasn't something that anyone should assume they had until it was too late.

"Let's go to bed." I kissed him. "I'll give you a massage or we can sit in the hot tub if you want. Nice and relaxing. You need a good night's sleep for once."

He smiled. "The hot tub sounds good. I think I can be persuaded if you promise to wear that black and white bikini."

I winked at him. "Maybe I'll go commando."

He bit his lip. "Even better."

Minutes later, we were in the hot tub off the main deck of our house. We kept the lights off, since that deck looked out on the back bay. In the dark, it was sufficiently private, and we enjoyed the silence, watching the lights on the water while the hot water bubbled around us.

He scooted me next to him and put an arm around my waist, relaxing with a satisfied sigh as my bare skin pressed against his.

"So…was it supposed to be a surprise?" I finally asked one of my burning questions.

"What?"

"The new quest."

He was quiet for a moment, resting his head against a cushion on the deck behind him. "There are new quests with every game update. You're going to have to be more specific."

"Lord Sisyphus's Wedding Quest."

He laughed. "That's actually a good idea."

"So was it yours?"

"*Was?*" He lifted his head toward me, brow furrowing. "I'm confused."

"The quest is in the game already. Heath found it and showed it to me."

He frowned. "Huh. Maybe I missed that memo."

"You mean you're not the one to okay every single new quest that's implemented?" I teased.

"And you think I'm busy *now?*" He laughed.

"Did someone sneak it in as a surprise, then?" I leaned my cheek against his warm shoulder.

"I have no idea. Honest to God. Someone must be playing a joke."

"Well, the wording of the quest describes the imminent marriage of Lord Sisyphus and 'Princess Emma.'"

He turned to me and grinned, his head sinking back onto the pillow, his arm tightening around my waist. "Lord Sisyphus is a lucky sonuvabitch. Princess Emma is hot, but she's sassy and smart, too. With a heavy dose of sarcasm. And did I mention she's hot? Especially when she's sitting next to me, naked."

But even with that come-on, I wasn't about to let this go. It wasn't every day I could get him talking about in-game quests. "So what do *you* think the quest is about?"

He shrugged. "How he hires a wedding planner? How his fiancée is apathetic to all his grand schemes and plans to write her name in the sky?

"Pfft," I said. "Very funny. I'm not *apathetic* just because I don't quite share your *enthusiasm*."

He paused for a long moment, appearing to be thinking. "I'll see what I can find out by asking around at the office tomorrow."

"Okay. I'm very excited. Can't you tell?" I turned and nibbled on his collarbone.

He smiled, kissing my forehead.

I was suddenly reminded of my earlier conversation with April. "So…"

He turned to me when I hesitated. Should I ask him about Jordan and work right now when he seemed to *finally* be relaxing? I blinked. If I wanted him to unwind enough to get a good night's sleep, bringing it up now seemed counterproductive.

I made a note to ask him tomorrow instead.

"So?" he repeated, as if prompting me to continue.

"So, uh, is this helping you relax?" I adlibbed.

"Yeah…it is." He took a deep breath and then let it go as if to convince me that he was successfully unwinding.

"Good. I thought it might. Maybe all we need is to get you on a relaxing routine at night."

"You know what else would be super helpful to get me to fall asleep, though?"

I raised my brows. "A massage?"

"An orgasm."

I laughed. "You are so fucking predictable."

He tugged on me, pulling me into his lap so that I was straddling him. "You like it that way."

I kissed him again. "I do."

And I *did*…that stability, the predictability, was my home. Adam was my constant, my lodestar. He was the solid rock beneath my ever-shifting sea. And he wasn't quite himself these days. I knew that. He'd taken too much on himself, and I could tell that we needed to have *that* conversation, too. But not tonight.

Not tonight.

Chapter 7
Adam

WITH THE WEEKEND FINALLY HERE, I WAS STUCK at home as a promise to Emilia that I'd at least take one day—*twenty-four whole hours,* as she put it—away from work. Which meant no phone calls, no texts, no emails, no laptop.

In keeping with the spirit of that promise, I set aside the day for wedding plans instead. She'd try to talk me out of it and divert to some idea of having fun. I'd satisfy her with a trip to the beach or a nice dinner out, later.

But the morning would be all wedding, all the time, whether she protested or not.

Ironically, it was *me* who caught *her* working when I popped my head into her study after I was done with my morning workout. "Is that a textbook I see?"

She slammed it shut, lowering her legs from where they rested on her desk. "Pleasure reading. Purely for my own enjoyment, I assure you."

I padded across the floor, bare toes crushing the soft, loopy carpeting beneath my feet. Snatching up the book she'd been reading, I peered at her. "And how are you enjoying *Rapid Interpretation of EKGs?*"

She grimaced at me—like she normally did when I called her on her antics. "Uhh. It's *fascinating*. Can't put it down. Can't wait to see how it ends."

I raised a skeptical brow, and she began to laugh.

"Know what else is fascinating?" I said with a meaningful grin. "Our wedding plans."

Her smile drooped, but she didn't say anything.

I held out my hand. "Come with me, young lady."

When she locked her fingers around mine, I tugged her out of her chair. She followed me across the hall into my office. "I'd be more excited if you were taking me into the bedroom for a booty call."

"Later."

"Pfft."

"I wanted to know your thoughts on colors." Pulling out the wedding planner's notebook, I turned to her.

"Colors?" Her expression clouded. "Let's do something simple. It's the whole reason we decided to fly people to St. Lucia in the first place, remember? We have the hotel all to ourselves for our party." She turned pleading eyes on me—big, brown, beautiful pleading eyes that usually got her exactly what she wanted. *Usually.* "Wouldn't it be *so* much better to have the wedding planner connect with the events coordinator there? Since both of us are *so* busy. Those two can get it all done. We show up and have a blast. Simple as that."

Frustration rose up inside me, and I clenched my jaw, trying to be patient. "It's our *wedding*, Emilia."

She drew away, running a hand idly up and down my arm. "Okay. I'll be good."

I smirked at her. "I don't believe *that* for a second."

"Well..." She gave me a flirtatious wink. "Win-win for you, then. You like it when I'm bad."

"I do...*but* not right now. We have to make some important decisions." I pointed to the chair beside the one I was sinking into. "Sit."

"The most important things are that we share with our family and friends, we have fun, and we come home husband and wife. Right?"

I fumbled through the binder for the correct page. "It should be the perfect day. It will set the tone for the rest of our life together."

And she didn't know this yet, but the ceremony and party afterward were going to make up for all the other bullshit surrounding this wedding. I would make sure of that. If we ended up having to sign that piece-of-shit document after all my struggles against it, I was determined that a spectacular wedding would ease that difficulty.

She sighed, crossing her legs and slouching in the seat beside me like the impatient student at the back of the classroom. "It's a *party*. People are going to eat, dance, and get drunk. Take a lot of funny pictures. Then you and I are going to say some very sweet things to each other, dance, force-feed each other cake, and drink champagne before going up to our room alone to screw like bunnies."

I threw her sharp look, and her brows rose halfway up her forehead. This was the disapproving glance I gave an underperforming employee or a friend who was being annoying or over the top (cough—*Jordan*—cough). The woman with whom I planned to share the rest of my life didn't typically receive it.

She blinked, appearing puzzled at my reaction. When I remained silent, she stammered, "I—I was—I was thinking. Wouldn't it be fun to randomly show up at the airport with only our passports and the clothes we're wearing? We could pick any destination and fly off there…a few weeks later, we return rested, tanned, and married. Wouldn't that be cool?"

Tense silence hung in the air between us, and she frowned while I simmered with irritation at her words.

I finally set aside the notebook and folded my arms across my chest. "So your mom would be okay with that? And my family? You, yourself, said that the most important thing is that we share this day with our family and friends. You actually think they'd be fine with missing that moment in our lives?" I clenched my jaw so that my head hurt. "Or maybe it's not as important to you?"

She flushed. "Of course it's important to me. And—" She took a deep breath and let it go, as if trying to curb her anger before it flared up. Not unlike what was happening with me. "I'm sorry. I was spitballing. I didn't mean to make you mad." Her eyes flicked away from mine to focus on the notebook I'd set aside. "It is *very* important to me. But the wedding planning kind of stresses me out."

"That's why I'm handling it," I said quietly.

She nodded, silent. I relaxed my arms and picked up the notebook again.

She leaned toward me and put her hand on my leg. "You okay?"

Yeah, I was stiff. These days, tension was a constant. Her eyes opened wide, and she licked her lips.

"It's the most important day of our lives." My tone of voice cut like a knife. Even I could hear it. She visibly swallowed.

"There will be *a lot* of important days in our lives." She tilted her head.

Resentment boiled up, making my skin hot. "So you don't care?"

She pulled away. "Of course I care." She shifted in her seat, watching me closely. "But I'd be thrilled beyond words to become your wife at the courthouse or some cheesy chapel in Vegas, too."

She was trying, but her words were doing nothing to stave off my irritation. "Okay, so...you're down for Vegas, then? Wedding performed by Elvis? I hear they have drive-up chapels."

She made a face. "You know what I mean...or maybe you don't. I only mean that getting married to you will be the reward in and of itself." She reached out for my hand, but I pulled it back. "I'm excited, and that's all I need. You. Me. Some champagne. A person to perform the ceremony. Our loved ones. All the other stuff is extraneous."

"All the other stuff makes great memories. And pictures, too..."

She wilted into her chair. "Whatever you decide on will be wonderful."

"So if I decide I'd love to have you walk down the aisle in a chain mail bikini?"

She glared. "You'd *better* not."

I finally let out a laugh. Her mouth quirked as she watched me. She seemed to be studying me, as if she'd noticed something for the first time.

"What?" I asked.

She shook her head and shrugged. "Nothing. I had no idea you were so into weddings. I mean, you never seemed to be all that interested in the details of the weddings we've attended together."

"I want this day to be worthy of you."

Her forehead smoothed suddenly, and she bit her lip. "That...that's the sweetest thing ever. So thoughtful." She leaned forward and wrapped her arms around my neck, pulling me to her. I returned the hug, landing a light kiss on her neck, relishing the vanilla smell of her skin.

I closed my eyes, reaffirming that vow. It *would* be worthy of her. It would be my way to show her what she really meant to me, shitty contract or not. If I had to give in to that, then *this* was something I could control. And hopefully, this epic wedding would help her forget all this other crap—paperwork and contracts that had no place in a wedding and a marriage.

Every time I thought of it, it made my blood boil.

"So tell me what we're deciding today," she said after a long pause and a significant look at the binder.

I snatched up a pen to take notes. "I need to know what color palette you like best and how many bridesmaids."

"Bridesmaids?" She glanced up at me, as if afraid to give me an answer I'd disapprove of. "I was only going to ask one person."

"Kat?" I pulled out a pencil and pad of paper, ready to take notes.

She fidgeted. "No. Um. Heath."

I paused, running that through my mind before turning to write it down on the wedding planner's to-do list. Emilia bent toward me to get a closer peek at the list.

"How do you have time for all this? Is this what you've been working on at night when you get out of bed?"

I grinned. "You think I'm cheating on you with the wedding planner's notebook?"

"I think you're trying to do her job for her. We are paying her good money."

I shook my head. "She's doing her job just fine. But she needs this info from us, and you aren't replying to her emails."

She shook her head and glanced away. "Sorry. But...you are looking a little tired and a lot stressed—"

"I'm *fine*," I snapped then took a deep breath and ordered myself to calm down. "No offense, but Heath is going to be one ugly-ass maid of honor."

"He's the *dude* of honor. Or maybe we can call him the bride's bro." She laughed uncertainly, as if nervous from my outburst. "Think how cute it will be to see Heath and Jordan walk down the aisle together. And cuddling together in all the pictures."

My mouth twisted. "I haven't asked Jordan to be best man."

She did a double take. "Oh? Why not? Who are you going to have? William?"

I shrugged. My cousin was an option, but it wasn't a job he'd enjoy. He'd do it, though, if I asked him. Shuffling through the pages in the binder, I searched for a way to change the subject while still getting all the info I needed for the wedding plans.

My hand touched on the envelope full of color palettes. *Perfect.* "The next thing on the list is colors." I pulled them out of the envelope and laid them on the desk in front of her.

I honestly didn't give a shit which one she chose. As long as she chose *something.* Something she loved.

She tore her eyes away from me mid-scrutiny and stared at the color palettes. I pointed to the first card. "This is all jewel tones, four different colors. She says that's nice and dramatic for a holiday wedding. Or we have something more seasonable—light blue and silver or red and white. Then there's the all-metallic palette."

She rubbed her neck, and I swear she almost shrugged. If she had, I would have lost it. But she didn't. Then she pointed to the last card. "I like the silver and gold. That's pretty together, and it looks nice for a New Year's Eve wedding, too. Festive."

I let out a sigh. *Good.* She was finally being cooperative. "I liked that one best, too."

"Great, then let's go with that one. We all done?"

"Yeah..."

Her grin widened as she stood up. "Okay. I'm going to force you to have fun now. You're going to be in San Jose for half a week. You owe me fun before you leave and I have to go days without seeing you."

Emilia grabbed my hands and pulled me out of my chair.

"*Fun.*" I sneered, just to mess with her as I followed her out of the room and down the hall.

"Yeah, you seem quite allergic these days." She turned around and walked backward in front of me so she could face me, still holding my hands, as we headed toward the stairs.

I shook my head. "Makes me break out in a horrible rash."

"Unless the *fun* is sex." She laughed. "Then you're not allergic at all."

I stopped, breaking our forward momentum. "Sex? That's a great idea...I wish I'd thought of it." I towed her along with me toward the bedroom.

"You're always thinking of it." She tugged back, laughing.

I pushed forward, swooping up, and pinning her against the wall. Holding her head in place firmly, I kissed her hard. "How'd you know?"

She laughed and pushed me away. "Later. Consider it your reward for going out and spending the day doing something *fun* with me."

I followed her down the stairs, aware that though she'd said those words laughingly, there was a spark of truth in them. She thought I required a reward for leaving work and spending time with her. A normal day of aimless fun.

And she'd never once snapped at me, never acted irritated. I winced from the guilt, grimacing at what that must be leading her to think. And I vowed to do better.

Chapter 8
Mia

ADAM WAS DUE TO RETURN HOME TONIGHT. HE'D ONLY been gone three nights and four days. Not as long as some trips, but still. It never failed that we'd fall into a routine of normalcy, and just as quickly, he'd have to pick up and go away. Sometimes to the East Coast, but more often, lately, up to Silicon Valley. The pluses were that it was a short flight and still in the same time zone as me.

Of course, he'd squish two weeks' worth of work into that four-day stay in Northern California. He ran from meeting to meeting to facility tour to yet another meeting. And if he did catch a meal that wasn't filled with power lunch meetings or dinner networking, I was in class or lab or study group. We hardly found a moment to Skype or call, apart from the group emails to our wedding planner.

But as I'd told April, we always found a way to stay connected, in spite of how crazy things got.

So this week, we rocked it with text messages.

In some ways, it was like the old days, when we'd first met over chat on Dragon Epoch. I'd send him a text...sometimes about any old random thing. And he might respond immediately, or he might respond hours later.

A normal conversation that would take minutes at home over morning coffee or a wee spot of pillow talk could span a day or more.

Me: *I've been thinking about pet names. When we're married, we should have pet names for each other.*
Him: *What? Really? Like Honey Boo?*
Me: *Not that one.*

And his mobile phone, the instrument with which he conducted business constantly, the device that often distracted him in my presence, became the very vehicle he'd use across the miles to flirt with and tease me.

The irony was not lost on me.

Him: *Wifey? Little woman?*
Me: *Only if you want me to remove your man parts. Painfully.*
Him: *Ouch. Okay... Your Majesty? Love Bug? Sweet Bumps?*
Me: *Sweet Bumps? For real?*
Him: *Okay, maybe not. But they -are- sweet. Your bumps, I mean.*
Me: *Definitely not Sweet Bumps.*

To accept this man into my life, to *love* this man, was to take him in with his flaws and foibles as well as those qualities that made him the closest match to perfect for me. So, with no other choice, I turned my enemy—his phone—into my ally.

I sent him a headless shot of those very sweet bumps he'd been extolling.

He reprimanded me, as he usually did, whenever I sent him a naughty photo.

"Security lapses, *blah blah.* Not safe. *Blah blah.*"

My fiancé was a computer nerd. I'd take the risks because if I wasn't safe sending *him* dirty pictures, who *was* safe?

His answer—predictably—was no one.

He got back to the subject at hand a few hours later when I was in class.

Him: *How about I call you Goddess?*
Me: *Getting warmer.*
Him: *What will you call me? I suggest Iron Man. I would answer to Iron Man.*
Me: *Hmmm...*
Him: *Or RoboCock.*

My mouth was full of tea when that text chimed on my phone, hours later, during my study time. I almost sprayed the full contents of my mouth all over my phone screen *and* my open textbook.

Typical Adam. He'd probably sent that in the middle of some boring think tank meeting.

Me: *Dude, No way am I calling you that.*
Him: *No?*
Me: *Nope...that one, you've got to earn.*
Him: *That's what our honeymoon is for.*

A snappy answer to everything. No wonder we suited each other so well. Which reminded me of *another* ongoing object of conversation between us. The honeymoon.

Me: *And we are going...where?*

Him: *It's still a surprise.*

Me: *You and your secrety secrets. You're sadistic.*

Him: *I definitely could be. I'm a billionaire with a troubled past. Isn't that the perfect recipe for sadistic?*

I almost forgot to take his rolled-up t-shirt out of bed before he returned home. Every day, our housekeeper quietly made up the bed and tucked the shirt underneath my pillow. This made it all ready for cuddling purposes the following night. But damned if I was going to let Adam find it again. He didn't need any more ammunition to tease me with. He did perfectly fine without it.

That afternoon, when I got home from my virology module lab, I plopped down at my desk and stacked my notebooks on the corner. As I'd done every day since Adam had placed Glen Dempsey's large manila envelope there, I stared at it, wondering if this was the day I'd finally open it up and see what was inside. Would it hurt to look and see what kind of information my half-brother had gathered for me?

I wouldn't even have to read the personal letter, would I?

Fingers tapped against the sleek marble desktop. The chair squeaked as I fidgeted in it, speculating for the ten thousandth time about what was in there. What was I afraid of?

Ovary up, Mia. Time to be a big girl.

I sat up straight, snatched the envelope, and tore it open before I could fret for another second. The contents of the envelope made it fairly thick. I pulled them out and laid them in a neat stack beside my textbooks. I immediately took the letter, which lay at the top, and turned it facedown before poring over the rest of the stack in order.

It contained not only Glen's full medical chart, but also that of my father, Gerard. And there were also notes about my two half-sisters.

Under the law, Glen was free to share his own medical information with me. But how had he gotten Gerard's? I pondered that question only until I noticed Gerard's signature on the consent form for release of the medical chart. Glen's father—*our* father—must have finally consented to give it to me. What had changed his mind? When Mom had informed him of my cancer, he hadn't budged.

I frowned, scanning through the papers. For his age of sixty, Gerard was a fairly healthy man, with some history of diabetes and heart disease from his father's side of the family.

When I got to the bottom of the stack, I was stunned to see the results of full genetic testing on Glen—and that of his sisters—along with handwritten notes about what came from their mother and what from their father.

It was a massive amount of information that had probably taken him a great deal of time to collect, collate, and annotate. I knew Gerard's hadn't put this information was in my hands.

I was absorbing it all, tapping the stack of papers idly with the eraser tip of my pencil, when I heard the front door open and close downstairs. I set the papers down, laying them carefully so that I wouldn't lose my place. Then I sprang out of my chair.

Adam took the stairs at his normal breakneck speed, two at a time, and I met him in the hallway outside our bedroom. He dropped his luggage and pulled me into his arms.

"Sweet Bumps," he said after a long, lingering kiss.

I lost it, laughing. "Don't even start with me, Drake."

"I made you laugh, didn't I?" He scanned my face, as if taking in every inch for the very first time—from my forehead to my chin, from my left ear to my right. I pulled him into another fierce kiss. God. I'd *missed* him. "*And* she rewards me with another kiss. It's good to be the king."

"I thought you were Iron Man?"

"You can call me anything you want, just don't call me late to bed—*or* dinner."

I grinned—I couldn't help it. Adam had discovered the secret to keeping me head over heels in love—make me laugh every single day. "Speaking of which, Chef left dinner in the oven. You hungry?"

"Let's do it."

We caught up over plates of organic spaghetti squash in creamy pesto sauce with asparagus tips. I told him about the prep work I needed to do for my practicum the next day, and he told me about the latest drama with his IT department and its failing director, Alan. And all the crises he'd had to avert from four hundred miles away. "Are you going to fire him?" I asked, sipping from my glass of sweet red wine.

He shrugged. "Alan has been with me since the beginning. Almost as long as Jordan. His life is a disaster, and that can happen to anyone. *But* I've decided to give him a timeline and some ultimatums. If he doesn't meet his deadlines, yes, he's gone."

"Isn't that up to the board of directors to decide, though? Can you make that type of decision without them?"

His features darkened, and he glanced away, taking his last bites and cleaning his plate. I frowned at him. Something was up.

The way he clenched his jaw, the slight flush at his collar. He looked *angry*.

I pretended not to notice. I'd wheedle the truth out of him later, sure enough. "Well, I guess you could fire him. You fired Jordan, after all…"

"Did not. He quit when I refused to fire him."

"Meh. Jordan's a pain." I grinned. "Shoulda tried harder."

We both laughed.

"Guess what?" I asked, once my glass was empty.

His eyes were on the glass in my hand as he laid aside his fork and knife. "Hmm. Let's see…you want another glass of wine?"

"No."

"You are feeling super horny after *that* glass of wine?" His dark eyes danced with humor and, maybe, a little hope.

I stuck my tongue out at him. "You wish."

He smirked. "So what am I guessing, then?"

"I finally cracked open that envelope of Glen's."

He raised his eyebrows in surprise, and I recounted what was in it.

"And his letter? What did it say?"

"I haven't read it yet." I shook my head. "I was contemplating it when you walked in the door."

"Well, you should read it."

"Not now…you've been gone for four days."

He covered my hand with his, twining his larger fingers through mine. "It's not going to take you that long to read it. Aren't you the least bit curious about him?" He leaned toward me almost as if imploring me—as if my mom wasn't the only person sad that I had very little family. "Especially after looking at all the info he collected for you?"

I smiled. "Okay. You've finally talked some sense into me…"

We put our dishes away, and he followed me up the stairs and into my study. He plunked down on the couch under the window. I grabbed the letter off the desk and then plopped down beside him. He settled an arm along the back of the couch, and I leaned into his shoulder.

"You ready?" he asked.

"Yeah…give me a sec."

He rested his head against the cushion and stared up at the ceiling to allow me privacy while I read the letter. With not the steadiest of hands, I held it up and read.

Hi Mia,

This is probably the most awkward letter I've ever written, especially considering it should have started with the sentence: 'I'm your brother. Nice to meet you via this letter." I'm not sure what is going through your mind right now, but I've had a chance to speak with your mother about you, so I think I can guess.

First, let me say, most importantly, that I am not my father. And I strongly feel that he has not done right by you, and this knowledge saddens me. But this note is not about him. I'd be glad to answer any questions you may have about him should you ever decide to meet with me in person. But he is not the reason I'm writing to you, beyond the fact that we are related to each other through him.

I have a sincere desire to meet you and a concern for your welfare. I know that you are in remission from cancer. I can't even imagine what going through that must have been like, but I can empathize, especially at your young age. I'm pained to learn of all the challenges you've had to overcome.

In the interest of keeping this brief, let me close with this... I would love to get to know you better, but I also realize that you may not be ready for this step in your life. That is completely understandable. You may reach out at any time you want to. Don't do it because your mom wants you to or because I'd like you to. Do it for yourself only.

I wish you nothing but happiness, great health, and success in all of your endeavors.

From your older brother,
Glen Dempsey

With a long sigh, I handed the letter to Adam, and he read it at his typical breakneck speed.

When he was done, he looked up, black eyes revealing nothing. "So what do you think?"

I shrugged. "First impression? He seems like a nice guy."

He tilted his head, watching me while also indicating in his subtle way that he agreed with my conclusion.

"And it seems like he really wants to meet me."

"Yeah. Are you going to?"

I shrugged. "I guess I have to decide if I really want to. Maybe?"

Adam nodded and handed the letter to me.

I skimmed it again. "I could email him for now...to thank him for the files and the trouble he took to get all that together. Thanks to that, I probably know more about my father's medical background than most people who grew up knowing their father."

"Yes, the biological sperm donor is no longer a mystery." Then his voice died out into a long pause. He cleared his throat and shifted on the couch to face me. "Did you…did you find any cancer history on his side?"

He asked the question so quietly. So calmly. With a practiced nonchalance that I knew was his typical mask behind which he hid a certain level of anxiety—in particular, about this subject.

"No cancer that I could see."

He nodded, face still blank. "Anything else to worry about?"

"Only the same things that afflict much of the American population. Diabetes. Heart disease, all that fun stuff."

He frowned briefly before getting up and moving to the folder on the desk. "Mind if I have a look?"

"It's *fascinating* reading," I said drily.

He shrugged self-consciously. "I'll have it back to you shortly."

I wondered what he was going to do with it—beside commit it to his photographic memory. As I sat down at my laptop to compose a quick email to Glen, I thought about Adam's sober behavior when it came to my health history.

Of course, it made sense. Sometimes when we referred to that dark year—the year I'd gotten cancer and then barely survived cancer's even lovelier cure—it was in hushed tones. And we almost never discussed the terrible loss we'd endured in order to get that far.

It had taken its toll on both of us. And in some ways, we had our own form of post-traumatic stress disorder from it. Thus, the regular but thinly disguised breast exams in the shower and the subtle but not-so-subtle questions about how I was feeling. The fact that his assistant had been instructed to make my doctor's appointments on the first day a follow-up appointment was due. Thanks to Maggie, I never missed an appointment.

As usual, Adam was taking control or grasping to the illusion that he had some modicum of it where this issue was concerned. But we both knew damn well that we didn't have control. We could be diligent and vigilant. But there were no guarantees. And the heavy, sick feeling in the pit of my stomach told me that my health issues had caused this uneasiness in him. But when you loved someone, you took all of their baggage on. And some of my baggage was health related. So be it. *In sickness and in health...*

I gazed out the door where Adam had disappeared with the papers. And I opened my laptop and composed an email response to Glenn Dempsey.

***

"Is there such a thing as a Groomzilla?" I asked the young women sitting at the table with me—April, Jenna, Alex, and Kat. We had met at a nearby hotel for Sunday brunch to discuss the details of my bridal shower that they insisted on organizing for me. The girls had all dressed in Sunday best, far outshining the bride, who hadn't read the memo and showed up in jeans, a sweater, and heels instead. My bad.

"Yeah. Groomzillas are the opposite of Bridezillas," Alex said. "My big brother was like that when he got married—a typical big Mexican Catholic wedding. Groomzillas act chill and don't want to hear anything about the details of the wedding and then veto things days before and make it all about them."

I frowned. "Oh." I pushed tropical fruit sprinkled with shredded coconut around on the plate in front of me. That definitely didn't sound like whatever it was Adam had. In the days since he'd returned from his trip, I'd been privy to a flurry of emails that were cc'd to me. They whizzed back and forth between Adam and our wedding planner as they worked out the most minute details.

I read most of the emails when I could keep up. Seriously, *when* did he have the time for them? I'd fallen behind on reading the news and then all had grown silent. I'd assumed that meant they'd finalized those details and we were all set—until I overheard Adam on the phone talking to her and referring to the most recent emails, emails which I'd most definitely not seen. With no small amount of shock, I realized then that I'd been kicked off the email loop and Adam only consulted me on things he couldn't do without me. Like deciding on the dude of honor's outfit, for example.

"Your hubby-to-be has a type A personality," April pointed out, sipping from her tall, skinny mimosa glass.

"No shit, Sherlock," snorted Kat as she signaled for the waitress to bring her *third* mimosa. "Calling Adam type A is like saying water is wet."

April shrugged. "I mean that it's natural that he'd take this over. Think of it like he's the CEO of your wedding. And you're the chairman of the board of directors."

I raised my brow, feeling a bit woozy from my one and only Bloody Mary. "So that makes me the boss, right?"

April grinned widely. "Of course. He probably realizes you've got a lot going on with your big medical board test and wants to make it easier on you. Consider yourself lucky. Jordan won't even say the M-word in my presence. Not that he has to worry about me jumping on it. That boy. Sometimes…" She shook her head.

"Sometimes you want to punch him in the face?" I laughed. "Me, too." April's smile faltered, and she studied my empty cocktail glass. I pointed to it, following her lead. "Totally the alcohol talking. I don't *really* want to punch Jordan in the face." *Most of the time, anyway.*

"Don't hurt his face, Mia. It's too pretty." Her smile returned.

A few minutes later, I excused myself to go to the bathroom and caught April's eye with a nod.

"When you're finished in there, we are totally going to talk about the bridal shower," Jenna said. "*Totally.* Soon as the mimosas wear off."

April followed me to the ladies' room and turned to me expectantly once we got in there.

"Did you find out if there's anything going on between Jordan and Adam?" I asked.

April grimaced. "Yeah, Jordan's being tightlipped. But there is definitely something. Whenever Adam's name comes up, he gets all tense and starts swearing."

My brows shot up. "That's almost the same reaction on the other end. I think I'm going to bite the bullet and ask him tonight. I was ninety-nine percent sure he was going to ask Jordan to be his best man, but he hasn't and was evasive about it when I asked him. I'll report back if I hear something. These crazy kids need to kiss and make up."

April looked off to the side, giggling and then, suddenly, blushing furiously.

I frowned at her. "What?"

"I was picturing them kissing and making up. It was...um, kinda hot." We both laughed.

Once we returned to the table, I was grilled about my wedding dress. I passed around the same fitting picture I'd shown April weeks before. Kat had already seen it, too.

"I'd *love* one of those new ombre-style wedding gowns with all the dark colors around the skirt," Jenna chimed. "I'd get it in shades of green—or purple."

"*I'd* love to do something with those 3-D lace floral appliqués and the tiny crystal beads. Have you seen those? They are to *die for*," April cooed.

"Shall I let William and Jordan know that you two have your gowns all picked out?" I snarked, glancing up from my phone after having sent off a text. "I'm sure they'd *love* to hear it."

April's big eyes grew impossibly bigger, and Jenna gave me a smartass smirk.

"Oh, I know...I'll make sure to get *two* bouquets, and now I know exactly who to throw them to. Won't *that* make your men freak out?"

"Speaking of freaking out...have you told Adam you want to keep your maiden name yet?" Kat asked, nibbling on a piece of smoked salmon on toast.

Before I could answer, Alex piped up. "You're going to keep your maiden name? You can't do *that*. Unless you want to add his name, too. That's okay. But you want to have the same last name as your kids, right?"

I let go of a shaky breath, with no desire to go *there*, especially with Alex. I wasn't going to base such a decision such an uncertainty. "I've lived my entire life with this last name. I've accomplished some wonderful things with this last name. It's the last name on my college degree. Why would I get rid of it? Besides, I've always envisioned myself as one day being called Dr.

Strong, you know? Dr. Drake sounds weird. We won't even *discuss* Strong-Drake with a hyphen... That one is off the table."

Jenna laughed. "Yeah, that one sounds a bit ridiculous."

I cocked an eyebrow at her. "Drake's gonna be *your* last name, too, someday, so don't diss it."

She blushed furiously. "Back to *you* and *your* weddin*g*..."

"You know what a lot of women in business do?" April offered, her fork poised in the air like a lecture pointer. "They take both names legally and use their maiden name for business and their married name socially. So you *could* be Dr. Strong at work and Mrs. Drake when accepting invitations to social galas and the like."

Because we knew I'd be attending *so* many of those in between lectures, labs, and exams. But it *was* a good idea. "That's a perfect solution. I will be bringing that up with Mr. Type A himself tonight."

April smiled wide at me, clearly happy to have been useful.

We finally got down to business and talked about the shower. Since we weren't going to have a massive local affair for the wedding, the shower would stand in for a nice luncheon with great food and live entertainment at a beachside restaurant. The girls all happily took to the planning of it. More power to them.

Finally, we made our way home. Or rather, a driver took us. Someone had made a good call and organized that, considering all the breakfast cocktails.

A fun time was had by all. Now to stop procrastinating and get to the bottom of this Jordan and Adam business.

Chapter 9
Adam

"JORDAN WOULD LIKE TO MEET WITH YOU SOMETIME today," my assistant, Maggie, stated during our usual late morning check-in.

I rubbed my head, fearing the beginning of a migraine. I felt like shit, and I knew that lack of sleep was catching up with me. But after my morning workout, that general crappy feeling was joined by a sharp pain in my shoulder. *Great.* I must have pulled a muscle or agitated an old injury.

And it was Monday. And I had the week from hell laid out in front of me—including yet another board meeting. My lawyer had not delivered good news where that was concerned, but I was not giving up, pursuing multiple opinions.

I planned on bringing him to my next meeting regardless. It was time to ready for battle. I'd even made a note to pull out my favorite book and reread it. *The Art of War* may not have served me well when applied to personal relationships, but it was absolutely applicable to business.

And since I expected an ultimatum soon, it was time. *He will win who, prepared himself, waits to take the enemy unprepared.*

"I don't have time." I sighed.

"He's getting testy. He complained that you canceled on him twice already."

"Please inform him that the position of CEO of this company is rather time-consuming," I snarled.

She shook her head. "How about you send him an email?"

"And what do I pay *you* for?" I asked with a lopsided smile.

She sighed heavily, punctuated with her own smile. "Fine. *I'll* send him the email. But he listens better when it comes from you."

Maggie and Jordan didn't see eye to eye very often, so I assumed it would be no sweat to her to put him off. If he was getting bitchy about it...not my problem.

"Make sure and mention that I'm doing a review of IT performance again today. That should keep him away."

"Can I at least mollify him with a slot tomorrow or *anytime* later this week?"

Only if you warn me so I can cancel it beforehand. I almost said it. Instead, I nodded to placate *her*—which I cared more about doing than appeasing Jordan.

"Friday afternoon," I stated. "*Late* afternoon." That should send him the message. I had no fucks to give him.

This issue, along with the ongoing drama in IT with my slacker director, was enough to be migraine-inducing. But, of course, the onslaught of wedding plans continued. Work was turning into drudgery. I generally loved my job—a lot—but nowadays, everything was starting to feel empty and pointless.

This sucked. And every day sucked harder.

Maggie was watching me with narrowed eyes. "Are you feeling okay? You don't look so good."

My breath escaped with a hiss. "I'm fine. We're done here, right?" I reached over and opened my laptop.

"Yeah, we're done. Apparently, I have some emails to write." She got up to go then turned back toward me before leaving the office. "Drink some water, Adam, and maybe catch a nap? You don't want to get sick…"

I waved her off, already engrossed in my laptop.

Later that day, I found myself in play testing, remembering that I hadn't gotten to the bottom of that surprise quest. Emilia had asked me about it again last night. The devs were on a deadline, and I usually stayed away from their neck of the woods during that time. They got punchy when they saw me lurking around and found it hard to concentrate on their work.

But the play testers knew about every quest in the game, thus, I could easily get to the bottom of this mystery here.

Except that when I walked into their section—nicknamed the Den—it was half empty.

"What—" I scanned the room, noting the half-dozen empty stations that were normally filled with heavily caffeinated game testers.

A tall, skinny kid—Lucas, my lead play tester—jumped out of his seat and trotted up with a smile. "Hey, Adam. What brings you to our cavernous wasteland?"

"Hey, man. I was in the neighborhood, actually. How's it going?" I reached out and bumped a fist with him. "Everybody out on a taco run today? I thought that was on Fridays."

A few people sat at their consoles wearing headphones and testing software and equipment. Since they were busy, none of them had noticed me enter, though I recognized the bright red hair of Katya—our friend and, for the past year, my employee.

"Most of the group is on that field trip to the new backup server facility," Lucas explained. "It's on the calendar for today. Wasn't that your idea?"

Nodding, I rubbed my forehead, noting the beginning of what was going to be an ass-kicking headache. "Yeah, forgot that was today."

He paused, waiting while I tried to clear my head then rubbed at the pain in my shoulder. Jesus, I was a goddamn mess. Maybe I'd give in and take a sleeping pill tonight. The two- and three-hour nights were finally catching up to me.

After a long and awkward pause where I imitated some cranky grandpa with my aches and pains, he asked, "Anything I can help you with?"

"Yes. There's a new quest in the game, and I don't recall any discussion on the implementation."

He hesitated. "The devs would be able to help with that."

"I'm well aware, but as you guys run through every quest, you would know, too."

Lucas nodded toward his workstation, and I followed him over to the table where he'd been working. He sat and logged into the database. "Is it live?"

"Yeah, apparently, or at least the first part of it is."

"What's it called?"

"Lord Sisyphus's Wedding Quest."

Lucas frowned, hesitated, and then shot a curious glance up at me. He straightened without having typed anything into the database. "Oh, *that* one."

"You know it?"

"I tested it," he admitted, standing from his chair like he wanted nothing more than to bolt from the room.

"*And...?* Can you give me the background on it? Who implemented, when it was implemented? Its status?"

Lucas shot me a careful look. "It, uh, came down in a batch of orders from development marked important, so I took charge of it and ran all the testing on it."

"And where did it come from?"

He shrugged. "Where they all come from. Development."

It didn't take a rocket scientist—or a computer programmer—to realize that he was being deliberately evasive. I folded my arms over my chest. "Is one of the devs pulling a joke on me with this? What does the quest do?"

Lucas's eyes widened. "Uh. I'm—I'm not supposed to reveal that information."

I blinked. "*What?*"

Behind me, I heard someone stand up from their console and slowly walk toward us. I was too busy skewering young Lucas with an icy glare.

Naturally, he appeared increasingly less comfortable. "Yeah, that—um—that came with the order. Confidential."

Despite my aching head and the general frustration of the day, I smiled. "Come on, enough with the BS, man. You can tell me."

"Hey, guys," Kat interrupted us. "'Sup, Adam?" She landed a faux punch right on the painful shoulder. Suppressing a wince, even though it hurt like hell, I nodded to her. Then I returned my attention to Lucas.

"Actually, you're the *last* person I can tell. I was told the quest was put in there for you," Lucas supplied.

"*For* me?"

Kat darted glances between the two of us, and I hoped she was wise enough to stay out of the conversation.

Lucas continued, "Maybe it's a wedding present from the devs to you. I tested it myself last week. It's a fun one. You should try it."

I rolled my eyes, putting my hands on my hips. "And when would I have time for *that?*"

"I'm sorry, Adam. I have it on my work order."

"I'm your boss," I reminded in a deadpan voice. You could have heard a pin drop. Kat shifted on her feet, watching Lucas with an expression that was somewhere between concern and amusement. I folded my arms across my chest, still scrutinizing him. "I'm your boss's boss."

Lucas visibly paled then cleared his throat. "I think if you—"

"I'm your boss's boss's boss," I overrode him.

"Adam, you're going over the top," Kat cut in.

I turned my glare on her. "I'm *your* boss, too."

She, however, was not deterred. "But *I'm* best friends with *your* boss—a.k.a. the future wife—so I pwn you." Despite my irritation, I had to admit her usage of the gamer term was well played. Then her nose crinkled up. "You're *so* cranky today."

I stared at her, my irritation suddenly dissipating, or maybe I was too tired to maintain it. Plus, it was a stupid thing to alienate an employee over—a dumb quest and a mystery. Especially if I was meant to figure it out myself.

Kat and I both started laughing at the exact same time.

Lucas appeared as if he might faint with relief. "This is the awkwardest situation ever." His eyes flitted between us nervously.

My mouth quirked. "If I fired you, I wouldn't be your boss anymore..."

His eyes went round and he paled. It'd be a shame for him to soil himself because of my joke, so I laughed and put my hand on his shoulder. "Just messing with you, man."

"You better be. Don't make us rat you out to HR," Kat said. Lucas and Kat exchanged a long gaze, and in that moment, even I noticed some unspoken message pass between them. I had no idea what it was. They appeared to be fairly good friends. Maybe it was an inside joke.

Once we sobered up, she continued, "You look exhausted. Maybe you need a nap. Or go relax and do the quest. If Jedi Boy says it's good, then it probably is."

Lucas's face fell, and his eyes narrowed at Kat, but she didn't seem to notice.

"All right, I'm out, then." I was halfway to the doorway when I turned to face him. "Oh, and Lucas...may the Force be with you." I gave him a thumbs-up and an obnoxious wink.

Due to his name, Lucas Walker—*never* Luke, he often emphasized—despised Star Wars references. And the more he despised them, the more he was tormented with them. As I was his boss, his boss's boss, and his boss's boss's boss, he didn't dare have a comeback for me.

But Kat cackled loudly, which was my best reward. "You owe me one, junior," she said to him when I was almost out of earshot.

With a grin that almost helped me forget that the rest of me was falling apart, I left play testing and returned to my office in time for a scheduled phone conference, which I barely lasted through.

Maybe Emilia was right. Maybe the abuse I'd been wreaking on my body lately was catching up with me. I made a special note to try to get to bed early tonight. Her shock alone from that might even be worth it.

Chapter 10
Mia

I T WAS ANOTHER LATE DAY WITH MY VIROLOGY LAB AND then my infectious diseases study group. Good god, M2 was a barrel of fun.

And though I wouldn't be home until well after nine, I knew I'd likely beat the significant other there by hours. He always stayed late at the office after being out of town.

As my medical school schedule had ramped up, he'd taken it as an unspoken cue to go back to his workaholic ways. Our time together suffered greatly as a consequence.

On my way to the bedroom, I stopped by my study to dump my books and check my email. A reply from my brother awaited me. It still seemed weird to use that term—*my brother*. I read through it immediately, but hesitated before replying.

He wanted to meet. Part of me really wanted to, and the other part was way too scared.

Maybe if Adam came with me. Or my mom.

Or both.

It was ridiculous, because he was only a man. What was I scared of? I'd have to think it through, and I was way too tired tonight. I flipped on the light and almost jumped out of my skin when I noticed Adam in bed. *Asleep.*

What the...?

I checked the clock—a few minutes after ten p.m. He never went to bed this early. What was up?

Quickly, I flipped the lights off again before they would wake him. Then I spent the next half-hour tiptoeing around the room, bumping into things in the dark and swearing under my breath as I got ready for bed.

Finally, feeling as exhausted as he probably did, I skipped my usual bedtime studying to snuggle up beside him and fall asleep early, too. Adam had gone to bed without a shirt on, only sleeping in his underwear. If I wasn't half dead myself, I might have been tempted to wake him up for a booty call.

Instead, I rolled over and was out like a light. Only to be awakened a few hours later by his tossing and turning. He was still fast asleep, but he'd kicked the sheet and blanket off and was shivering.

Half-asleep myself, I reached over, grabbed the sheet from where it was tangled in with his legs, and dragged it up over him again. My hand brushed his arm, and I froze.

He was burning up.

Like *feverishly* hot.

I placed the back of my hand against his forehead, and he jerked away, moaning, still fast asleep.

"Adam," I said quietly, and he didn't move. So I got out of bed and headed straight for the medicine cabinet in the bathroom, where I grabbed the fancy ear thermometer. I doubted there was even one of these in the house before *I* had gotten sick. As a typical bachelor with uncommonly good health, Adam had likely never thought to equip his home with first-aid supplies. Naturally, I had taken care of that for him.

I ran the digital thermometer through a quick test to see if the batteries were working, then returned to the bedroom.

Adam was now on his side, still shivering. "Adam, I need to take your temp."

His only reply was incoherent mumbling, so I bent over and stuck the damn thermometer in his ear. He batted my hand away—and not gently. I took hold of his shoulder and shook him, once again noting the heat coming off his skin.

"Adam, *wake up.*"

Slowly, his eyes cracked open. When he saw me standing over him with a medical device in my hand, he shot straight up to a sitting position.

"What?" he barked.

"You're burning up." I indicated the thermometer in my hand. "I need to take your temperature."

He rubbed his forehead. "I'm fine."

But even with that short outburst, I observed how his voice sounded different, hoarse, a little thick. As if his throat was bothering him.

"You have a virus or something. I'm not making this up. You're feverish. Let me stick this in your ear."

He took the thermometer and moved it—and my hand—as far away from his head as he could. "*You* don't stick things in *me.* It's supposed to be the other way around."

"Don't be a smartass." I let out a long-suffering sigh and replaced the thermometer near his face. It just figured that Adam would be a patient from hell. How could I even imagine otherwise?

"Adam, you were shivering, and your teeth were chattering. Now, unless you want me to stand over you like this all night till you fall asleep again, let me take your goddamn temperature."

"Okay, okay," he said. "As long as you promise to leave me alone if it's normal." I bent down and pushed it into his ear. "*Ouch*. I still need that eardrum."

"Don't be a baby."

A few seconds later, the thermometer beeped. Pulling it out, I read the digital screen—only to almost drop it again in shock. "Holy shit!"

"What?"

"Your temperature is 103.4. That's *way* too high. You've got a virus or an infection."

He groaned loudly. "I don't have time to have a virus."

"You don't have any say in the matter."

He reclined against his pillow, his hair damp from perspiration. "Jesus. I feel like shit."

"And you have all day, haven't you? That's why you were in bed so early. I should have known then." I set the thermometer on his night table. "Stay here. I'll be right back."

"I can guarantee that I'm not going anywhere." With eyes closed, he rubbed his forehead.

I went to the medicine cabinet and grabbed the bottle of acetaminophen and, from an upstairs cupboard, a bottle of water.

Adam wasn't in the bed when I returned, but soon appeared from the bathroom.

"Did you vomit?"

"No. I peed."

I shoved two pills and the bottle at him. "Here. Take this now. And if your temp is not down in thirty minutes, we are taking a trip to the ER."

He scowled, took the pills and the bottle, and downed them. "I'm not going to the ER."

"You are if I say you are." I pointed to the bed. "You are running a very dangerous temp. Now, do you feel like taking a tepid shower, or can I run a wet towel over you?"

With a groan, he sank on the bed, rubbing at his neck. "Neither. And that's saying a lot that I'm turning down an offer of a sponge bath from you. Even if you were wearing a naughty nurse's costume."

"Is your neck stiff?"

"No, but I'm achy. It's a flu."

"I'm the med student here, not you." Crawling onto the bed from my side, I sat beside him. "Any pain in your stomach or abdomen?" I pressed his shoulder so that he was lying flat on the bed.

"Well, *you're* starting to become a bit of a pain."

Reaching over, I began to lightly palpitate his stomach and abdomen. I hit upon a swollen spot, and he let out a slight grunt.

"Your voice sounds weird. Do you have a sore throat?"

"Sore throat, headache, body aches, the whole package— *Ow.*" He jerked away when I reached up to check the glands in his neck.

"Hmm. Tender."

"*Tender?* That fucking *hurt.*"

"I barely touched you. Your glands feel like golf balls. You've been vaccinated for parotitis?"

"Paro-what-is?" he said, sounding exhausted again.

"Mumps," I answered.

"Yeah, I had all the shots when I was a kid."

"Then it's probably mononucleosis." I pulled the sheet over him. "But that can't be diagnosed without a blood test."

He slumped against his pillow. "I'm gonna take a nap."

I bent down and kissed his hot cheek. "I'm sticking this thing back in your ear in twenty minutes. Fair warning."

He mumbled something incomprehensible in reply, already half-asleep.

When I rechecked, his temp had dropped a full degree. With relief, I set the alarm on my phone for three and a half hours, when he could have more medicine. I needn't have bothered. I stayed awake to make sure he was covered whenever he started shivering, but was uncovered whenever he seemed hot. Instead of sleeping, I sat and read a textbook on my tablet, keeping a watchful eye on my not-so-patient patient.

In the morning, he only felt worse, and yet—insanely, but unsurprisingly—he wanted to go to work. I threatened to bar the door with my entire body or attach myself physically to his right leg so he'd have to drag me along. And in his state, he wouldn't have been able to put up a fight even if he tried.

What *really* clued me in that he was feeling crappy, though, was that he *didn't* argue when I challenged him.

It did take me a few days to get him to go to the doctor, however. And each day, he got grumpier and grumpier, but also sicker and sicker.

After my one and only class of the day, I came home late morning, went into his closet, and pulled out some clothes. At his bedside, I stood over him with his clothing choice. He appeared only semi-conscious, with three days' growth of beard and an ashen complexion.

"C'mon, sicko. Time to get dressed."

He brightened, sitting up. "I do feel better today. I think I might go in for a few hours." He sat up and put a hand to his head.

"Head still hurt?"

"Yeah."

"And your temp is still high despite popping pills like crazy. Keeping any food down?"

"Ugh." He blinked and pushed his legs over the side of the bed. Figured that the promise of work would have him fighting being half dead in order to get his ass out of bed. Too bad for him we wouldn't be going to work. I wasn't going to break that news to him until he was dressed and ready to go.

"So no food at all? You're drinking the water I leave by the bed, though, so that's good."

He grimaced. "It makes me have to get up and pee all the time."

"You need your fluids."

He stood up, fastening his khakis. "If I wasn't feeling like I'd been dropped off a five-story building, your Dom-doctor routine would be making me *so* hot right now."

"You like playing doctor?" I wrapped my arms around his waist. "How about a really mind-blowing BJ when you feel better?"

He paused. "A BJ for getting better? Wow, I like this hospital already."

I smiled. "Good, because you're going there. Right now."

He froze. "I'm going to work."

"The fuck you are." I put my hands on my hips, standing in front of him. "Have you *seen* yourself in a mirror? Do you want your employees to scream and run in terror when they see you coming? Zombie boss. Rise of the undead CEO?"

He blinked, appearing to have to think about it, as if he wasn't quite capable of complex thought in his state.

"You're going to the doctor, Adam."

"But *you're* a doctor."

I shook my head. "Not quite yet. I'm going to take you over to the medical center at the school."

"You can't abduct me and take me where I don't want to go. We're not married *yet.*"

I stared him down, eyes narrowing. "I can be as stubborn as you, Adam Drake. *Stubborner.*"

He hesitated, but I gave him no time to contemplate an escape plan. Tugging his hand, I towed him behind me. "Come on. Let's go."

There was no further argument. *Men.* So pigheaded, even when practically at death's door.

We drove to Orange, to the facility where I'd received the majority of my cancer treatment and where I now trained to become a doctor. When we arrived, the phlebotomist took Adam's blood before he was assigned an examining room. Adam sat in his underwear, refusing to put on the paper gown they'd offered him. He was scowling, his arms folded across his chest. I turned my face toward the wall, pretending to admire the reproduced artwork while, in truth, avoiding laughing at his pouting.

He was cute when he was playing the part of the reluctant patient.

Once I composed myself, I turned to him. "Well, this is a switch...you on the examining table, me the healthy one."

"Yeah. Hilarious," he replied. He'd opened his mouth to say more when the doctor knocked on the door and entered. Odds were it would be a physician that I knew, but I was pleasantly surprised that it was one of my current instructors, Dr. Sharma.

She was surprised to see me there, as evidenced by wide eyes and raised brows. "Mia. Hello," she said, glancing down again at her tablet, which probably displayed Adam's chart. Adam darted a glance between us. It seemed almost...nervous.

I quietly asked him, "Want me to step outside?" He shook his head. "Dr. Sharma is one of my instructors." To her, I said, "Adam is my fiancé. He's been spiking a high temp over the past three days. Swollen lymph nodes. Body aches. Nausea. Migraine headaches, but he presents those regularly anyway."

The doctor glanced down at the tablet. Then she approached him. "Your monospot test results are positive."

He cursed under his breath and looked away. I moved up to rub him on his back. "It's okay. You need to rest and take care of yourself."

"Well, I'll do an ultrasound to check the internal swelling, but basically, yes, you have a viral infection. No physical exertion and no work until I release you to do so."

Adam sat up straight at the mention of no work. "How long? A week? Two?"

She unhooked the wand from the ultrasound machine and held it up. "Let me see what's going on inside, and I'll give you a better estimate. Lie back now."

She squeezed some gel onto Adam's perfect abs, and he sucked in a breath.

"Sorry for the cold," Dr. Sharma apologized, and Adam rolled his eyes skyward while I fought laughter.

She moved the wand over his abdomen before angling the screen toward me. Dr. Sharma, it seemed, never passed up a teaching opportunity.

"What do you see?" she asked me.

As I bent for a closer inspection, I could feel Adam staring at me balefully, clearly unamused. Jeez, he was crabby.

I squinted at the screen. "Wow."

"What *wow*?" Adam snarled.

"Uh huh." The doctor nodded.

I turned to Adam. "Your spleen is extremely swollen." I pointed to his left side at the bottom of his ribcage. "You can even see it distending your abdomen. It's probably why your shoulder was hurting so badly the other night."

"My *spleen*? Is that a real thing?"

Dr. Sharma laughed. "It's a risk with mono. Certain tissues can become inflamed—like your glands. Organs, too—the spleen, the liver. You've got an acute case. Have you been working particularly hard lately? Stress? Lack of sleep?"

I darted a glance at Adam, who lay silently staring up at the ceiling, his jaw set and his mouth a firm line. "All of the above," I answered. "Adam is, um…a compulsive worker."

Dr. Sharma pulled the plastic off the wand and tucked it back onto the ultrasound machine. "Well, you now have doctor's orders to slow down."

"How slow?" Adam asked.

"Bed rest for at least two weeks." She typed something into the chart. "You're only up to use the bathroom. As much sleep and fluids as possible. Eat when you feel up to it. Then I want to see you. After that, no working for at least two more."

Adam shook his head. "*Four weeks?* Not possible. I run a company."

Dr. Sharma opened her mouth to answer and then closed it, darting me a pointed look instead. Another teaching moment, apparently. "Adam. If you don't do this, your health could—and probably will be—permanently impaired."

"Hmmph," he grunted. "What about our wedding? It's just over two months away."

"Odds are you aren't going to feel much like working anyway—at least for the next few weeks." I grabbed a towel and wiped the ultrasound gel off his stomach. "I'll work with the wedding planner. You need to rest or you'll prolong this. Then you'll be sick when we're supposed to get married, so I guess we'll probably have to push the wedding date back."

That got his attention. His narrow-eyed stare said it all. *Over my dead body.*

Dr. Sharma intervened. "From the look of your spleen, you have a great deal of inflammation inside. This can cause permanent damage to your organs and tissues if you are not very careful with your recovery."

"Fuck." This time he didn't mutter.

"Also," she continued, "no heavy exercise for at least six weeks, and no sexual activity."

"You sure know how to hit a man when he's down," Adam replied, and I burst out laughing.

I took his hand, which was still really warm. "Let's get you home and recuperated."

"You took all the fun out of everything," he complained after Dr. Sharma had left and he got dressed.

"Listen, buster. I'm here to make sure you follow orders. I don't want my new groom passing out at the altar."

"No sex?" He made a face. "That was a *really* low blow."

I goggled at him. "Do you even *feel* like it right now?"

"Not really," he admitted. "But I *will*. And soon."

"Oh, c'mon. You'll live. Lots of couples abstain until marriage."

He shook his head. "Fuck that."

"Don't be salty."

"Isn't mono the kissing disease? I kiss you all the time. Why aren't *you* sick, too?"

"I've already had it, when I was in middle school. It's not common to get it more than once, but it's rarely as bad as the first time, though. Just in case, I won't be kissing you on the lips for a while."

I ushered him out of the office and drove him home—though he was annoyed about that, too. He usually did the driving when we were together, but he clearly wasn't up to it, given the headache and nausea.

The poor guy was a mess. And if he felt half as bad as he looked, then he was going to be out of commission for a while. But *damn*, he was cranky when he was sick. And it occurred to me that I'd never seen him sick before, not even with a cold. The man had the immune system of an alligator.

"None of that is possible, you know," he stated as I drove.

"None of what?" I glanced at him as I exited the freeway onto Newport Blvd.

"The no work, no exercise. *Especially* the no sex."

"Adam, you have to be serious about this. And be vigilant and proactive about your recuperation. Or no wedding. I'm *not* kidding." He heaved a huge sigh. "Right now, you don't feel like doing any of that anyway. When you start feeling better, but are still unwell—*that* will be the true test."

"Yeah, I'll die of boredom. That will be *so* much better."

I shrugged. "This is your body's way of telling you to slow down and stop abusing it."

"Sex is not body abuse," he growled between gritted teeth.

"Why are you pissed at me? I'm perfectly healthy, and now I have to go without, too. You don't see *me* bitching about it."

He gazed at me out of the corner of his eye, like he'd come up with some sly idea and was very happy with himself. "We can do *other* stuff, right?"

I bit my bottom lip, but didn't answer.

His jaw dropped. "*No?*"

"Not unless you don't mind, um...not finishing."

"*What?* You mean no orgasm?"

"Yeah. Anything strenuous like that, even an orgasm, can put strain on your spleen—at least while it's super swollen like that."

"Do I really even *need* my spleen?" he whined. I pulled the car into the structure and parked it carefully beside his.

I laughed, opened the car door, and got out. I waited for him to follow suit before I continued. "It filters your blood and purifies it. Removes microbes and old or damaged blood cells. And it keeps your epic immune system going."

Adam followed me down to the gate that opened the bridge to Bay Island, where we lived. "Well, my epic immune system didn't do such a great job this time."

I slid my arm around his waist as we walked across the bridge toward our house. "Sigh...stop with the pity party, please? When I—"

He held up a hand. "Don't you dare pull the cancer card on me."

I grinned wide. "It trumps everything."

"Meh," he said, scrubbing a hand across his face. He didn't even object when we grabbed a golf cart at the end of the bridge to drive the short distance to our house. That right there told me he was still feeling like crap.

"I think you need to take a nice, long nap, and then I'll make you something to eat."

He cringed. "No food."

"Oh no." I shook my head. "You were constantly shoving toast in my face when I was getting chemo. You are at least going to have toast."

"Ugh. What is this, illness revenge?"

I shook my head, laughing. "It's payback."

"Very funny."

Later, I watched him sleep, making sure to monitor his temperature—still elevated, but below 101, an acceptable level. I let him sleep as long as he wanted and made sure he always had fresh fluids on the nightstand to drink. Then I slipped into bed beside him, propping myself up on pillows so I could keep an eye on him while I studied.

Right now, he was too sick to be more than a grumpy nuisance. But I knew I had to be prepared for when he was feeling better. Because he was going to be his usual stubborn self and try to ignore doctor's orders. At least I had the wedding to hold over his head to make sure he behaved himself.

That might get ugly, but if I stuck to my guns, I'd have a healthy bridegroom to take to my exotic, faraway, and probably over-the-top wedding.

Chapter 11
Adam

IN THE SAME WEEK THAT I GOT SICK AS HELL, I FIRED MY IT director *and* got an ultimatum from the board of directors. I had six months to sign a prenuptial or postnuptial agreement with my legal spouse or face evaluation by a committee. If found in breach of fiduciary duty, I would be dismissed as chief executive officer of Draco Multimedia Entertainment.

Talk about a triple whammy. Fuck my life.

Worse, for the first time in my life, *ever*, I had no desire to do anything but lie in bed, sleep, or stare at the ceiling. Even reaching for a glass of water and pushing myself upright enough to sip it was too much. Emilia solved that issue by buying me multiple insulated cups with big, flexible plastic straws so I could drink while still lying down. I was a pathetic mess.

Emilia hovered over me too much, to the point where I had to chase her out of the room, ordering her to go study where she was meant to study—in her office.

That first week was me hanging on to the edge of a precipice by my fingernails. But it got better. *Slowly.*

Into the second week, Jordan showed up with random paperwork. He passed through on his way to or from the office.

His gaze never quite met mine—and I preferred it that way. There was definitely a lot of frost between us.

Emilia let that small amount of work slide, but she watched me like a Rottweiler. If I so much as opened my laptop—which, coincidentally, never seemed to be where I left it—she'd appear, ready to shut it again.

God help me, but she was driving me insane.

The only peace I got was when she was at school—which was a lot of the time. And I missed her after she was gone an hour or two, despite my irritation when she was here. It was a lose-lose scenario. My own private *Kobayashi Maru*.

Nothing made me happy. Or everything made me miserable. I hadn't decided which.

By the end of the second week, when I was beginning to feel slightly better, I was surprised to get a visit from Heath, of all people. I assumed he was here to talk about his role as dude of honor to the bride. Strangely, he arrived at a time when he knew damn well that Emilia was in class.

By this time, I was able to sit up. So we sat out on the deck outside my office and sipped lemonade—I'd been forbidden alcohol by the doc. This lady was number one on my shit list these days. Okay, number two after Jordan. Or maybe further down if I counted the rest of the bastards on the BOD.

I tried not to think of that while I made awkward small talk with a sullen Heath. Emilia hadn't been kidding about how depressed he was over Connor staying in Ireland. Ten minutes in the guy's presence and I needed to return to bed—badly.

We talked about random shit, the game, whatever. In truth, I hardly ever spent time alone with Heath, and that was sad because he was my friend—for the same length of time that I'd been friends with Emilia. I was *this* close to suggesting we bust out the laptops and game instead of sit here and stretch a conversation between us.

"Mia says you had no idea who implemented Lord Sisyphus's Wedding Quest or even what it does," Heath said as he squinted out over the balcony, looking down onto the boats puttering in the back bay.

"Yeah...I'm surprised you found that," I replied. "A few people have talked about it on social media. They are calling it the new hidden quest, but the hype hasn't quite picked up yet."

"Word on the street is that the quest chain is broken. People can't get past the initial dialogue with the quest giver."

I scratched my jaw. "Huh. That's weird. My guy in play testing says it's working perfectly. He tested it himself."

Heath shrugged and took another sip of lemonade. His shoulders sagged more with each passing minute. "Maybe you should delve into it, since you appear to have more time than you know what to do with."

I rubbed at my swollen neck, still sore as hell. But since I wasn't shaving, my neck was itchy. It was a conundrum that was bugging the hell out of me—like everything else.

"Yeah, maybe I will."

A few more minutes passed, and Heath got squirmy, so I gave him an out by telling him I was feeling tired again—not a lie. I was *always* tired these days. He stood up and fumbled in his pocket for his keys. But instead of following me off the balcony so I could at least walk him to the top of the stairs, he fiddled with his key ring. Then he set two keys down on the outdoor table before turning to follow me.

I recognized the keys immediately. They had a distinctive shape to them—a lopsided oval head with big letters spelling *Porsche* engraved across them. I paused, not moving to let him by when he asked me to.

"What's that?" I nodded toward the table. "Why are you leaving your car keys here?"

"They're *your* car keys. I'm giving back the Porsche. She's parked in a safe spot right on this end of Edgewater Street. You won't be able to miss her. I'm sure Mia can move her into the parking structure later."

I blinked. "That car is yours. I signed the pink slip over to you. You've been driving it around for over a year."

His head drooped when he realized I wasn't going to let him by until he explained himself. "I'm giving her back. Thanks, man, but...I can't take care of her like she deserves to be taken care of. And I get twitchy whenever I park her. I'm always afraid some asshole is going to scratch her or some bird is going to shit all over her. I can't enjoy myself when I take her out anywhere. She's made me a nervous wreck. Isn't that like a woman?" He shrugged. "No wonder I'm into guys."

I was puzzled as I tried to follow what he was saying. He loved that car about as much as I did. He'd nearly peed himself when I'd given it to him. *And* he called it *her*. He was attached. *Definitely* attached.

"I'm not taking it back." I folded my arms across my chest. "It's yours. Once I've given something away, that's it—it's final. You should know that by now."

"Please take her, Adam. I can't. I just... I can't right now." His voice shook when he said it. I averted my eyes to afford him some dignity, recognizing that he was in a vulnerable state these days. I shifted my weight from one leg to the other.

"I'll take it under one condition." I met his gaze again. "That we agree that it's still yours and I'm only holding on to it for a while. I'll drive it around and get it serviced like I did before. But it's yours. And you'll come get it when you're ready."

He hesitated. "I'm only saying yes because I don't have the energy to argue with you right now."

"Good. I don't have the energy to argue, either. Now...how are you getting home?"

He held up his phone. "I just requested an Uber." He stopped me when I went to follow him. "I'm good. I can see myself out. You need to go to bed. You look like shit."

I grimaced. "Thanks. I'm afraid that, in my weakened condition, I could take a nasty spill down the stairs and subject myself to further school absences," I quoted.

He grinned, half his mouth drooping, as if, in his depression, he couldn't allow himself to show full amusement. "Save Ferris," he replied quietly.

He followed me until we reached the top of the stairs. When I turned and stopped, I put my hand on his shoulder. "If you ever need me for anything, man, I'm here. And, of course, Emilia is never too busy for you. You know that." It was awkward and stilted, but I thought he understood the sentiment.

He nodded and avoided my eyes. "Thanks, man. Appreciate it."

And he was gone. I watched him go and puzzled at it. I'd have a talk with Emilia later when she got home to keep her apprised of the situation. I had a feeling that Heath had a long road ahead, and I knew enough of depression, having seen it in family members while still at a young age, to know that he was about to drown in his own.

He needed a support network, and that was what we had to be for him. If we could only figure out how.

I crashed for a long nap, astonished that the thirty-minute conversation with Heath had taken so much out of me. I woke up around dinnertime. A text message from my chef advised she'd left dinner on the warmer. Another message from Emilia awaited, informing me of her late night tonight. She'd rushed home to check on me between obligations, but hadn't wanted to wake me up because I was fast asleep.

After dinner, I took Heath's advice and grabbed my laptop—since Emilia wasn't around to pry it from my hands—and started the quest by opening up a dialogue with the new Town Crier, who stood beside General SylvenWood.

FallenOne says, "Hail, Town Crier."

Town Crier says, "The high lord of all the land is about to be wed. His lucky bride? The princess Emma."

Town Crier has offered FallenOne: Lord Sisyphus's Wedding Quest.

You have accepted the quest – Lord Sisyphus's Wedding Quest.

Your first task: Go to the place his lordship first met his princess and lay a bouquet of roses on that spot.

I scowled at the screen, puzzling over that. How the hell was I, or any other player, supposed to know where this fictional persona—that I sometimes played for official in-game events—had met a completely nonexistent—except for the purposes of this quest—princess? What the hell kind of quest *was* this? Quality assurance, my ass.

It seemed…personal, though. Like, applicable to things only I knew. And she knew. Could Emilia have been the one to have it implemented?

I shook my head, dismissing that possibility almost immediately. There was no way in hell that she was that good an actress.

"*Hey.*" Emilia entered the darkened bedroom. I hadn't even heard her come in or seen her flip the light switch in the hallway. In here, sprawled on my side of the bed, only the glow of the computer screen served as a light source.

"Are you working?" she asked without preamble, her voice tinged with unspoken accusation.

"*No*, your majesty. I'm playing DE."

Her mouth opened. "Hah. I didn't realize you played anymore…I thought you'd quit when we stopped getting together as a group."

"I haven't played in months, since our group last ran around together. But I wanted to get to the bottom of this Lord Sisyphus mystery."

She flipped on the light, and I squinted. She entered the room, apologizing as she pulled off her hoodie. "It's a mystery? You still don't know why it's there or who put it there?"

"Nope."

"You're the CEO of the company. They can't hide that from you, can they? You should demand answers. You're the boss of them."

I avoided looking up at her—shame, anger, and embarrassment burned in my chest. *If she only knew…*

The news of the BOD's ultimatum was still like an anchor weighing me down. Not an hour went by where I didn't think about it or how to rail against it.

Sighing, I closed the laptop, mid-game, knowing it would log me off automatically.

"You feeling okay?" she asked. "Do you need me to refill your water bottle?"

"I need you to come over here and talk to me for a little while."

She smiled. "Okay."

She plopped down on the bed and took my hand. I told her about the weird visit from Heath, and she asked me questions. She resolved to check in with him and also speak to Kat. But she said that he'd gone into a similar depression when he broke up with his previous boyfriend, years ago.

We were quiet for a long stretch, each lost in our own thoughts. She stared up at the ceiling, her fingers fiddling with mine. But she seemed to be very careful about not touching me in any other way.

I didn't feel much like it these days.

I didn't feel much like anything. It was too exhausting to even feel.

"You okay?" Her soft question broke the silence.

I gave a slight shrug.

"You seem down. I know that getting sick and incapacitated can be extremely hard on a person like you, so...just checking."

"A person like me?"

She smiled. "Yeah, the ones that are always going constantly and never resting. The ones with too much purpose and not enough time."

"'Too much purpose'? Is that my problem?"

"I'm starting to come to the conclusion that your addiction isn't to work. It's to achievement—you're addicted to accomplishing the next big thing."

I didn't like that word—addiction. It had too many painful associations for me. But she wasn't wrong, either. Problem was, I had no idea what that next big accomplishment would be, and with all these struggles with the company, I was beginning to question my direction there, as well.

"Sometimes I feel like...I'm standing at a crossroads. Like something big is about to change what I need to focus on."

She turned and looked at me for a long time. My eyelids began to feel weighted down. "I've been wondering when you'd get the itch to start finding the next big thing to work on."

My eyebrow twitched. She wasn't even surprised by this news. Why did I get the feeling that, in so many ways, Emilia knew me better than I knew myself? I gently brought her hand to my lips and kissed it.

She got ready for bed soon after that and fell asleep in minutes. And even though I was practically smothered in a layer of exhaustion myself, I couldn't sleep. I lay in the darkness staring up at the ceiling, feeling more helplessly enraged over the powerlessness of my health, my company, my future. I was hanging on a precipice, all right. In more ways than one. And that only brought on another headache.

Fuck. My. Life.

Chapter 12
Mia

IN A STROKE OF THE WORST LUCK EVER, ADAM'S WALTZ with the Epstein-Barr virus led to me showing up alone at a neighborhood dinner party. The good news? I only had to walk a few hundred yards to the other side of Bay Island in my heels in order to attend. The bad news? The company. They were nice people, our neighbors, but...*so not my crowd.*

There's fish out of water and then there's...human visiting an alien planet. I was Spock, the only Vulcan in Starfleet. *Beam me up, Scotty. There's no intelligent life down here.*

I would have loved to cancel—citing Adam's illness as the excuse, of course. But Adam and I had already backed out of previous dinners three times. I feared that our chance of offending the neighbors was reasonably high—even with the very legitimate excuse of his health. So here I was, taking one for the team. Hopefully, my teammate would be duly appreciative.

These things were bad enough when I had Adam at my side. Then I had a captive audience to rain down all of my snark on— usually in the form of muttered comments only he could hear. He at least pretended to find them amusing.

Here I was, in Newport Beach's most exclusive neighborhood, where I now lived. And I was their neighbor, the future wife and future co-owner of a neighborhood home, of that "tech genius kid," as I sometimes heard them refer to Adam. Indeed, Adam was, at the very least, a decade younger than any of them. And while some, like him, were self-made, most were from second- and third-generation wealth.

"Mia, so good to see you," Sonya, my hostess, greeted me at the door. She was one half of a power political couple. She touched her cheek to mine and kissed the air. "How is the sick fiancé? Probably playing it up, like men always do."

"Sonya, so glad to see you," I said, handing her the bottle of wine along with some of Chef's fresh gourmet butter, packaged in a fancy stoneware crock. Sonya remarked on it, saying she couldn't wait to try some. I was relieved, almost letting out the breath I was holding. Hostess gifts were a source of half a week of stress for me. It was almost by accident—or the good fortune of having fantastic advisors like Adam's chef or his assistant— that I made any of the right moves.

I moved on to shake the hand of Sonya's husband, Congressional Representative Alan Thurston, an attractive man at least a decade and a half older than her. "Thanks for the invitation, and Adam is so sorry he has to miss out."

In truth, Adam was at home playing DE in his pajamas, the fucker. He had cried exactly zero bitter tears that I was going without him. For the sake of his health, he'd refrained from teasing me about having to go alone. But I could tell that he'd been tempted to skirt dangerously close to that edge.

There were six couples in all—correction, five couples and me and my phantom date who was cruel enough to update me every so often via text message about his progress on the wedding quest. He was probably snickering each time he hit send, goddamn it.

If he wasn't so sick, Adam Drake's ass would be Alderaan and I'd be the Death Star. He'd be feeling a *great disturbance in the Force*, all right...

Nevertheless, dinner was pleasant. The house, of course, was gorgeous, with a complete glass-encased dining room displaying an impressive view. I made small talk, and people asked about wedding plans and made the usual jokes about "entering into holy matrimony." And I pretended to be amused, laughing my fake laugh.

After dinner, however, shit got real. The men all sat at the table talking business and current events while the wives moved to the couch to sip coffee and gossip. Oh, the willpower I had to summon to keep from rolling my eyes at how little things had changed since the days of *Downton Abbey*.

All the men needed were their cigars and smoking jackets to complete the image. *Ladies, have we not come further in the past century?* We'd gained the right to vote, to own land, and have our own bank accounts. Yet here we were, separating by gender and talking shop.

"Mia, you are looking wonderful. You've got that pre-wedding, blushing-bride thing going on with your skin." Sonya, our hostess, smiled as she raised her coffee cup—with more Baileys than coffee in it—to her lips.

I raised a self-conscious hand to my warm cheek. "Oh, thank you."

"Maybe it's her joy over not having to go to school anymore," Susanna, the neighbor who lived in the house to our right, added cheerfully.

I frowned at her. *Not go to school?* What on earth was she talking about? My obvious confusion brought her up short, and she did an almost comical double take.

"Aren't you quitting medical school? I'm sorry. I assumed you wouldn't need to attend anymore."

Wouldn't *need* to? What the hell? Why would she assume that? Was I only attending school and dedicating all that time, energy, and brainpower to pass the time until I snagged a wealthy husband? Perhaps her whole "career plan" was designed around catching a rich man. But *mine* wasn't.

Adam would be my ideal mate if he only had twenty dollars in his bank account. I was certain of it.

When I replied, it was through lightly clenched teeth. "I've got almost a year and a half down...no reason to quit now."

Her smile stilled in her flawless face, her skin glowing bronze from a fake tan. "But it's not only the four years of schooling, though. After all the school, there's an internship and residency. And beyond that, a fellowship."

I kept forgetting that Susanna's dad was a retired doctor—a renowned cosmetic surgeon. But she rarely let anyone forget it for long. She was *still* talking. "I can't imagine doing all that while trying to set up household, maintain a marriage, and, of course, having babies." She patted her own recently announced baby bump.

I fought to keep my face from showing what I was thinking. Naturally, the subject of babies would come up when any woman was about to get married, but it was still a sore subject with me. And because of that, of course, I was reminded that Adam and I hadn't even discussed it yet. I groaned inwardly. Yet another tense conversation to have on top of the issues with his working *and* the problems he was having with Jordan.

So many conversations to have. And yet we hadn't had them. We danced around them like pros instead.

I took a deep breath and let it go. "Yes, I'm aware it's a big life commitment, but I'm still really excited to be a doctor someday."

"And Adam is on board with that plan?" asked Trish, a flawless blonde who, for most of the night, had been quiet. Trish was the closest to me in age, and yet she'd grown up a socialite and was now on her second husband, wealthy media magnate James Sinclair.

"Of course," I replied, sipping at my coffee and looking around for something—*anything*—to catch my eye so that I could change the subject. "Oh, that painting above the mantel is gorgeous. Is that Corona del Mar?"

I knew it wasn't. I didn't give a shit. Sonya quickly corrected me. Subject changed.

Things diverted to a safe subject for a few minutes then circled back around to me. And this time, it was marital advice. *Just great.*

I was *so* going to make the fiancé pay for this.

"Don't ever refuse him," advised Audra, the oldest of the group, in her early fifties. She'd been married the longest amongst us—though she was her husband's second wife. It was heavily rumored that she'd been the home wrecker responsible for the demise of his first marriage.

I frowned. "Uh, you mean don't disagree?" Because I'd fail that one instantly. No wonder she was still married to her hubby. Why get rid of the perfect "yes" woman?

"No, I'm talking about sex." I almost spat out my coffee. "He'll come home late from work or a long trip and want some. You might be tired or you might not be in the mood, whatever. But don't *ever* reject him. If he doesn't get it at home—and if it isn't spicy and exciting—he'll find it elsewhere. And easily. *Too* easily."

I almost swallowed my tongue. There was a lot I could say to *that*. Like what about when *I* wanted it and *he* was too tired or not in the mood or jet-lagged or whatever? Equal opportunity sexual demands.

"That's the key," Trish inserted. "Finding the way to make him happy, *keep* him happy, and minimize conflict. It's a balancing act."

Not even fifteen minutes into this post-dinner girls' chat and my cell phone was burning a hole in my pocket as I willed it to ring. *Please, goddamn it. Please.* If I could send a Jedi-like mind message to Kat the way Luke did to Leia at the end of *Empire*, her head would be ringing off her shoulders right now. With no small despair, I realized that the prearranged time wasn't for another hour yet. *Shit.* One more hour of this.

"How old are you again? Twenty-four?" Sonya asked, refilling her coffee cup. "You have a few years yet. But definitely before you hit thirty, you should start. Don't you think, Julia?"

"Botox?" The redhead, whom I'd just met, perked up. "Oh God, yes. I started at twenty-five. Best decision *ever*." She smoothed a finger from the corner of her eye down across her cheek, as if to show off how much her muscles could not function of their own accord. She turned to me, stone-faced. "If you want a referral to my dermatologist, I'd be glad to pass along her number."

Botox? WTF? They couldn't possibly be serious…and I was sure my disbelief was all over my face, because Audra, who sat right beside me, patted my knee. "You don't have to start that young. You have perfect skin, but there's a lot to be said for preventative measures. You have to plan ahead, because otherwise, you'll be thirty-something and his eye will stray." Nods all around, except Julia, who sipped demurely from her cup. "Because it's *everywhere.* All the time. In their faces. It's really hard for them, you know. They constantly have to say no to what is openly offered to them, you know what I mean?"

Just nod, Mia. Nod. But no…I frowned, completely baffled as to what she was talking about. "No."

"Sex, Mia. Women," Trish supplied. "Women are all around, circling like vultures who can smell the death of a marriage from miles away. And sometimes—many times—they don't wait till the demise of the marriage to close in." Everyone avoided glancing at Audra during this speech.

"He'll get attention, that's for sure." Sonya nodded with a smile hovering on her lips.

"He already *does*," Trish cut in before cheerfully turning to me. "Your future hubby is *very* easy on the eyes." I gulped, suddenly feeling nauseated. "You know it's already happening, don't you? When he's gone on trips or whatever, he's getting sex offered to him on a silver platter every day."

At my stricken expression, she smiled. "You have nothing to worry about now. He's desperately in love. Make sure to keep it that way. Average guys cheat all the time. It happens even when they *aren't* constantly offered the golden opportunities that ours are."

Julia chimed in. "But sometimes giving a pass to a brief indiscretion is the easiest way to handle it when it *does* happen. Instead of blowing it all out of proportion."

Now I could barely swallow. Adam and I weren't even married yet, and already they had him cheating on me and me forgiving him for it. I was *this close* to barfing up my dinner.

"Unless you've got a cheating clause in the prenup, of course," added Audra, laughing. "Then you can take him to the cleaners." The women erupted into laughter, and that caught the attention of the men, who wandered over to join us. Naturally, the conversation shifted to a safer subject. *Thank the Maker.*

But I was left to stew on their words…on things I hadn't really thought of before. Like Adam being offered sex at every turn by dozens, *scores* of beautiful women with model-shaped bodies and perfectly maintained hair and skin. None of *them* would come home to him in baggy hospital greens and fall asleep exhausted before he could even strike up a conversation.

Adam had already had a semi-crazy stalker from work. Cari, an intern, had gone from crushing on him to harboring a whacko obsession. It had grown to a point where Adam had had to fire her for doing some horrible, cruel things. Things that had been motivated by her jealousy of *me*.

But to think that there were dozens or more where Cari had come from…and some not so crazy. And probably a lot smarter. Most of them wouldn't give a shit about his workaholic tendencies. They would like what they saw beyond even his monstrous net worth. It didn't help that Adam had movie-star good looks.

He really was the perfect package, and up until this moment, I'd had no problems gloating to myself that he was *all mine*.

Doubts, insidious with their quiet whispers, began to raise their voices. He was determined to get us married *now*. Why? I was completely on board with that plan. But what if, someday, I wasn't enough for him? What if, in a moment of weakness, he gave in to just one of those many, many temptations? No man was perfect, after all...

Thankfully, not long after that, Katya's phone call interrupted my mental stewing and allowed me to make quick excuses to my hostess. I told them I had to go home to check on Adam. One of the husbands joked that I should wear a naughty nurse's costume to cheer him up as I tended to him. None of them knew that Adam was at risk of a spleen rupture, so I laughed it off instead of sharing that personal tidbit about our imposed sex blackout.

I trudged back to our house, lost in thought. Pressing my thumb to the biometric lock, I entered, quietly shut the door behind me, and climbed the stairs. In our room, Adam was lying in bed, still playing on his laptop.

I was so agitated that I stalked straight into the bathroom to collect myself. As I removed my earrings and other jewelry, I stopped before wiping off my makeup. Frozen, I stared at the troubled brown eyes in the mirror.

Should I let him see me with the makeup on before I took it off? It still looked good. He mostly saw me barefaced around the house. What if he thought I was plain and shabby because of how I dressed?

A lump formed in my throat, hard to swallow, difficult to breathe through. My mouth went dry. I'd been unwanted before...knew what it felt like. My own father hadn't wanted me, and all that emotion had been dragged up fresh via my correspondence with Glen.

My stomach twisted, roiling with nausea.

Would Adam eventually reject me? I remembered the feeling again, from a time when he *had* rejected me. Weeks after I'd recovered from cancer, he'd sent me away to my mom's. We'd lived apart for months without communicating. It *had* helped us heal, but I'd been despondent. If he left me after we were married, it would feel like that multiplied times a thousand. *Oh God.*

And what would happen when he wanted a child? What if I couldn't give him one? Would he find a woman who could? I hadn't had a real period since the chemo had ended. Sometimes, I had a light flow or spotting, but nothing that indicated my fertility might return. There was a good chance it was gone forever.

In ten years, when he was pushing forty, he'd want a baby. And he could find some beautiful young thing who'd give him one.

And I'd be on the sidelines, standing by, watching him with his new family. Would I be the mature ex-wife, refusing to write a tell-all book about him or do interviews with the press? Would I be stoic while the world was watching, speculating on my humiliation as I suffered in silence?

Oh, God. I doubled over the sink, yanking on the faucet, feeling every single failure acutely, real and imagined, historical or present. In spite of earlier fears, I splashed cold water on my face. But it did nothing but make my mascara run. How could I face—

"Did you have a good time?" Adam interrupted when he poked his head into the bathroom. I stood there gaping at myself like a fool in the mirror, the water still running. Blinking, I switched off the faucet.

"Yeah, sure," I mumbled, avoiding his gaze in the mirror. "How are you feeling?"

He frowned. "What's wrong?"

I sighed. I didn't want him to see my turmoil until I got a better handle on what exactly I was feeling. But hiding things from Adam was ridiculously difficult. He was too observant, and I was too poor an actress. "I'm tired."

He stepped into the bathroom, moving up behind me, not taking his eyes off my face. "You seem…upset."

I opened my mouth to make an excuse. But inexplicably, this whole mess of emotion rose up, and suddenly, I was spewing out those feelings everywhere.

"You don't think I should do Botox, do you?"

He looked at me like I'd grown a unicorn horn out of my forehead.

My eyes flicked back to my reflection. "Or maybe I should wear makeup more often?" I smoothed fingers over my cheek. "Do you think I dress too much like a student still?"

His face scrunched up like he'd tasted a lemon. "Have you been watching *Real Housewives of Orange County?*"

I clenched my teeth and my fists, almost stamping a foot in frustration, demanding he take me seriously despite the nonsense coming out of my mouth. "I mean it. Do women offer you sex all the time?"

Now his eyes goggled. "Well, even if they did, I have a semi-explosive spleen, remember?"

"It's not funny, Adam," I whined. Then, inexplicably and much to my enduring embarrassment, I burst into tears.

"*Whoa*," he said, true concern written all over his face as he moved forward to pull me into his arms. "What the hell's going on?"

Without a word, I turned and sobbed into his shoulder, already mourning the demise of our marriage due to his infidelity with at least a half-dozen phantom women decades younger than me.

"Come here. Come on." He gently coaxed me out of the bathroom and guided me to sit on the bed beside him. "Did the Real Housewives get to you tonight?"

I shook my head, sobbing into my hands. "I don't know if I'm ready for this. I'm not ready for your world."

"Emilia!" His voice was firm as he pulled my hair back from my face. "Slow down."

"I don't want to quit medical school." I sniffed.

"What the hell? You don't have to quit school. You're not making any sense." He ran his fingers through my hair. "Who told you that you did?"

"But there are charities to run." My chest heaved as I gulped more air. "And—and benefits to organize, and your foundation—" I was sobbing so hard that it was difficult to breathe.

"*Emilia*," he practically commanded. "Slow down. Now."

I put my hands to my face, unable to control the agitation. "I don't want to be the starter wife, Adam."

"That's good. I only plan on having *one*."

He reached over to the nightstand, grabbed a few tissues from the box, and pressed them into my shaking hands. "Take a breath and calm down."

I easily detected the worry in his voice as he watched me slowly gain control of my emotions. I wiped my face and sniffled. The entire time, Adam stroked my back and my hair.

"Now," he said when I'd been quiet—aside from my hiccups— for several minutes. "Let's talk about it calmly. Obviously, they told you a bunch of bullshit that's got you scared."

"They weren't being mean." I shook my head. "They were trying to be helpful in their own way, from their own experience. And it...opened my eyes to what it must be like for you. When you're traveling or out in the world—being a billionaire and everything."

"I'm still *me*." He frowned. "I'm still the same person whether I'm here or 'out in the world.' Still the same person you met three years ago. And yes, my bank account got bigger, but that doesn't mean anything."

I turned to him, my fist tightening in my lap, squeezing the tissues into a tight ball. "No, it's naïve and simplistic of you to say that. Your world *has* changed. Maybe you don't see it yet, but it *has*." He stiffened beside me, and when he would have interrupted me, I rode over him. "You're in the one percent of the one percent and—and women are going to chase you even more now than they did before. And believe me, I didn't like what I saw before."

"So should I be worried because men are going to chase you? You're beautiful, young, brilliant. I've seen the way men stare at you when we go out, even when I'm standing right next to you and sending them death glares. Should I be worried, too?"

I shook my head. "It's not the same thing."

"No? Why not?" He put his hand under my chin, guiding me to look at him. "We're getting married. I have to trust you as much as you trust me."

I shrugged, conceding the point without admitting I was .

He picked up on that, pulling me closer to him. I relaxed against his chest. "Now, so you know, no one can chase me if I'm already caught."

I swallowed. "It's not that easy. A lot of women—probably most of them—won't give a shit that you're already married. Your wedding band might even encourage them."

"What does it matter whether *they* give a shit or not? *I'll* care about being married, about my vows to you. That's all that matters. A woman could walk up to me and drop her dress, and it wouldn't matter."

I scowled at him. "You're such a liar. You'd look."

He shrugged. "Yeah, probably. It's a guy thing."

"So is cheating."

He shook his head. "Not for *me*. I have some amazing self-control skills, if you'll recall. It wasn't easy keeping my hands off you all that time. But I did. And now...you and I together are more than that. More than the sum of our sexual attraction."

I *thought* he meant that as a compliment, but I was perplexed. And apparently, that puzzlement was on my face, because he elaborated.

"I mean, we're like an epic quest—this complex algorithm of experiences, memories, feelings, and promises to each other. Of shared parts of our lives that we've been through together. It's a bond that's way stronger than sex."

I pulled away to gaze up at him. "And the new and illicit thing is never going to tempt you the least little bit?"

Something about that apparently bothered him, because his forehead creased. "I'm not saying I'm never going to look. That would be stupid and unrealistic. And I'm not going to blow sunshine, because then you won't believe me on the stuff I'm serious about." He ran a hand through his hair. "I'm *always* going to weigh what I'd lose against the worth of any heat-of-the-moment encounter. And *every single time*, that heat of the moment will never live up to what I have with you. *Never.*"

How could he be so romantic and yet so calmly rational at the same time? I didn't know, but my smile had now grown along with my confidence. And my trust in him.

It appeared that he was going to say something, but thought the better of it. So I leaned forward and put my hand on his arm, urging him to say what was on his mind.

"*And*...maybe you should recognize that part of this fear is based on your personal experiences, too. And the things the Real Housewives said tonight played into fears that are already there."

He was talking about my father—the biological sperm donor. The original cheater in my life. Except my mom had been the poor, unsuspecting young woman that he had cheated on his family with. And then he'd deserted us and gone back to them.

"Okay." I nodded. "I acknowledge that some of the stuff they were saying triggered my own deepest, darkest fears."

He frowned. "Deep down, you still think I'm going to leave?"

I bit my lip and thought for a moment. "Not *logically*, no."

He smiled and smoothed a strong thumb over my damp cheek. "I've watched you puke and pee yourself—sometimes at the same time. If that didn't scare me away, what would?"

I shrugged, looking away. "Gray hairs? Wrinkles? Saggy boobs?"

"You'll be more beautiful." He shook his head, sighing. "Most men that stray…they're doing it because of their own fragile self-image. They're flattered by the attention that feeds their ego. They're cheating to fulfill a bottomless pit of need."

"They're not cheating because they had a fight with their wife or she's too tired to get dressed up and be glamorous or hang all over him?"

He shrugged. "Some, probably, are unhappy at home. There might be times when it's hard for us. *But* we've proven we can get through the hard times, haven't we? You should believe in us more."

I straightened, suddenly worried that he thought I didn't believe in us. "I'm sorry. I do. I honestly do. This is completely born of my own insecurity."

He scowled. "Then stop it, because like men, women have those needs, too—to have their self-image reinforced. Maybe I should be worried you'll cheat on me."

I glanced up at him to note the smile tugging at the corner of his mouth.

"Well, there *is* my sixty-five-year-old research mentor…"

The cocky smile vanished from his face, and I started laughing. His mouth dropped, and I fell back on the bed. As he had days of stubble growth on his jaw, I suspected he was going to close in for another whisker burn, but I held out my arm, barring his access as he rolled onto me.

"Wait—I do have another thing I need to ask you."

"Before I execute your punishment?"

I bit my lip and nodded, giving him my best puppy-dog eyes.

His gaze narrowed as he scanned my face, from eyes to lips, likely suspecting that I was working him over—which I was. "I don't trust that look."

"What look? I do have something else I need to ask you."

He kissed my neck instead of delivering the threatened whisker burn. I smiled, warmed by the familiar zing his lips evoked anywhere on my body. He was getting frisky now that he was feeling better. Unfortunately, despite the length of time since we'd last had sex, I'd have to shut this down. But I enjoyed it for the moment. He kissed a trail up the column of my throat.

"Well, the Real Housewives were talking about prenups..."

He froze. There was a distinct hesitation before he resumed kissing me without comment. "Are you absolutely positive my spleen is still too swollen? Because I can assure you other parts are swelling right now." He nibbled on my ear, and lust flared as my eyes rolled back into my head. Damn, this moratorium on our sex life had been murder.

Strange that he hadn't answered my question...but that was my last thought on the subject as he slowly turned me into goo with his hot mouth.

"We can't. Not until you see the doctor on Monday and she says it's okay."

"Goddamn it." He rolled off me. "I can't even cheat on you with my hand."

I busted up, laughing.

"It's not funny," he whined.

"It's effing hilarious. You're not the only one feeling horny."

"I'd offer to alleviate your suffering for you, but you're a cruel woman who has mocked my misfortunes. If I suffer, then you've got to suffer along with me."

I snickered and rolled on my side to face him, holding up my palm. "I have a hand, too. And I *can* cheat on you with it."

"Yeah. Between that and my dirty underwear—"

"T-shirt! It was your t-shirt. Jesus."

We went back and forth like that for a few more minutes before he sobered and looked at me for a long moment. "You feeling better?"

"Yeah. I am." I sighed. "I'm glad we had this talk despite how distraught I was when we started."

"And here I was feeling sentimental about us when you got home. It all went out the window when I you started crying."

I kissed his cheek. "What got you sentimental?"

He pointed to his laptop, sitting at an awkward angle on his nightstand. "The quest. It's all about *us*. Are you sure no one questioned you to get the details about our relationship?"

I blinked, stunned. "No. Like...how is it about us? Show me."

He opened up the laptop and logged into the game, explaining where he'd gone so far, running errands to help Lord Sisyphus find and propose to his bride.

"First, it said go to where he first met her, and I was stumped for a while. Then I thought about *us* and how we first met at that hotel conference room. And I took a chance and went to the best inn in town. Upstairs on a long table, there was a glowing vase. I clicked on it to put the flowers in the vase."

I smiled, hearing him talk in such animated tones. It had been a long time since he'd had this much fun playing a video game. I suspected that, for far too long, the game had been work for him.

"*Awesome.* Then what?"

"I had to find a map to a faraway kingdom called Amah Dastam and help get the princess there to meet Sisyphus."

"Amah Dastam? Amah Dastam."

He watched me carefully. "Say it fast."

"Amah Dastam." I nodded, the light bulb suddenly going off. "Amsterdam. Holy crap. That's, um, kinda creepy. What's next? Will Princess Emma start a virginity auction after penning a controversial virginity manifesto?"

He faux-scowled at me. "She'd *better* not." He slammed closed the laptop with a yawn.

"You could use a nap," I said, fully aware that it was bedtime anyway.

He grinned at me crookedly—sporting that scruffy look, he was devilishly handsome, and I silently cursed the fact that I couldn't attack him. This would have been the perfect moment. *Damn sex ban.*

"I think I do, too." Exhaustion, as palpable as his, gnawed at me.

Minutes later, we were in bed, but by the time I moved over to his side to cuddle, he was already fast asleep.

***

The next morning, he was already awake beside me, lying in bed and tapping away on his laptop when I rolled over and cracked my eyelids open.

Through my blurry morning vision, I caught a glimpse of the weirdest thing ever on his laptop screen. An animation displayed what appeared to be the trajectory of a rocket that launched from somewhere off a map of Florida (complete with estimated time stamps, launch angle, altitude estimations, and other numbers scrolling across the screen).

Clearing my throat, I frowned. "What's that?" I asked.

Shockingly, he jumped and slapped his laptop closed, a guilty expression on his face, as if I'd caught him watching hardcore granny porn. After taking a moment to collect himself, he grimaced, seeming upset that I'd seen it—whatever it was.

I sat up and stared at him. "What was that?" I repeated.

He jerked his shoulder in a sharp shrug. "Nothing. That wasn't for your eyes."

"Was it aerospace fetish porn or something? It looked like a rocket launching from Florida." I smoothed a hand through my bed hair. "The trajectories? The explosions over the Caribbean. That seemed...elaborate." Then I smirked. "And *orgasmic*."

His lips thinned as he reopened the device, the screen pointed away from me this time. "It's nothing." Clicking a few buttons on his keyboard, he adjusted the angle. All I could see was his blank desktop.

My eyes narrowed. "It seemed like something to me."

Scowling, he didn't say anything.

I turned toward him, a new—and worrisome—suspicion arising. "It has something to do with the wedding, doesn't it?"

He folded his arms across his chest. "Don't ruin a surprise."

My jaw dropped. "That didn't appear to be a mere *surprise* to me. That looked like full-blown simulated nuclear war."

His gaze went up to the ceiling. "It's not a missile."

"Then what the hell is it?"

He shifted on the bed. "It's a rocket."

"Like...fireworks? Because even I know that launching fireworks from Florida is not going to do us any good in St. Lucia."

His mouth quirked. "It's not *exactly* fireworks."

"It's *actually* a rocket?"

"It's a *surprise.*"

I leaned toward him. "Adam Drake, if you don't tell me what that was, I will pitch a fit. I promise you I will go Bridezilla on your ass. Are you launching a rocket?"

He shot me a dark look. "Yes."

"For what purpose?" Oh, God...*Overblown* wasn't even beginning to describe this shit now. "Is it launching us to the moon? Are we going to have a *literal* honeymoon? Should I pack my spacesuit?"

He rolled his eyes. "It's a...special project I've been working on."

"This entire wedding has been a special project—a special *over-the-top* project. *Please* tell me what the rocket is really about."

His handsome features revealed nothing. "It's...supposed to launch a payload into the upper atmosphere. Some harmless, inert debris that will burn up upon reentry while producing the effect of shooting stars. Our vows will be said at sunset, and the payload discharges in conjunction with that."

Silence. I blinked at him, trying to absorb it.

He threw me a glance. "Are you okay?"

I squinted at him. "I don't know. I'm not sure how I'm supposed to react upon discovering that my fiancé has lost his ever-loving mind."

His jaw worked. "What? You don't think it's cool?"

"Adam, major *nations* don't pull stunts like that for the opening of the Olympics. It's out of control—" Cutting myself off at the hurt look on his face, I sighed and began more quietly. "I'm sorry, but—"

172 | BRENNA AUBREY

He gave me a stiff shrug. "You aren't that into it. I'm getting that message loud and clear. It's tiring to be the only one excited about this wedding." He slapped the laptop shut again, jaw tensing. "Hopefully, you're more excited about the marriage than you are about the wedding."

Now it was my turn to get defensive. I could feel my blood pressure increasing, my fists tightening. "That's ridiculous. Just because I don't care about an excessive party does not mean in any way that I don't want to marry you or that I'm not thrilled about the fact that we are going to spend the rest of our lives together."

His cheeks flushing with anger and his glare darted out the window. So odd, this behavior.

Now he was up and pacing. My eyes caught on how his pajama pants and t-shirt were slightly loose on his body, which was thinner than before his illness. I made a mental note to say something to Chef about it. Now that he was eating again, he'd need to up his caloric intake.

"What's this all about? What's going on? Come on. If you can't talk to me about it, who the hell else are you going to talk about it with?"

"I haven't lost my mind." He raked a hand through his hair. "I wanted *you* to have a day that's all your own, where your every wish is granted and you feel special—like a princess."

I bit my lip. Having never entertained a girly princess fetish, nor worshipped the Disney princesses, I'd been a different type of girl. My aspirations had tended toward Dr. Quinn, Medicine Woman instead or, if a princess at all, Princess Leia, rebel leader. Maybe Xena, Warrior Princess. But his words were so damn sweet that I caught my breath.

I swallowed the big lump in my throat. Getting up, I came around the bed and held my hands up to cradle his face. "That's so sweet—" He jerked his head up and away, turning his back on me. I studied his hunched shoulders, his stiff posture.

"Adam, you're going Napster on this wedding." I referred to the infamous Silicon Valley billionaire who had been publicly ridiculed for spending approximately twenty million dollars on his over-the-top "old forest" Tolkien-esque wedding among the redwoods in Northern California.

Adam scowled. "Give me a break."

"You're launching particles into the atmosphere, you're...having God knows what else done. I *have* been reading the emails, despite what you think. Chefs and bakers flown in on private planes. *You* don't even fly on a private plane when you can avoid it. Have you calculated the carbon footprint alone from all this?" I threw my hands open wide, a pleading gesture, shaking my head. "This isn't you. This isn't *us*. Shouldn't the wedding be about who *we* are as people? As a couple? As the new family we are about to form?"

He continued to stare out the window, hands on his hips. At times like these, I knew that provoking him was akin to poking as sharp stick at a grouchy bear. It was usually best to leave him alone and let him contemplate. Adam was, after all, a ruminator. And he was getting pissed off about my constructive criticism. Okay, maybe it wasn't *as* constructive as it could have been.

But damn it, I couldn't let this stand. It was my wedding, too.

"You and I and this new entity of *us* is more important than a party. And I get that you are bored out of your skull right now without work—"

"Bored?" he snapped, jerking his head around toward me. "You think I'm doing this because I'm bored?"

I bit my lip. Yeah, the bear wasn't liking that sharp stick much. "Well, you work so damn much all the time, I'd guess you have no idea what to do with your time now that you can't. So you're channeling all your energy into this."

He turned to me, shoulders tightening. Now he looked downright pissed. "Don't do that."

"What? Blame your compulsive work habit? Why not? I've only been refraining from saying anything because I figured your body did it for me this time." I gestured to him in his pajamas, as if to signal his illness, the onset of his mono and the part his tendency to overwork and undersleep played in that.

"Okay, now you're pissing me off."

"If the truth pisses you off, then so be it. I'm not going to skirt around the issue. This time, your body shut it down. But what happens when you start feeling better? You're going to return to your frenetic pace again. We both work hard, and up until recently, we were able to make it work. But it *was* getting fucking ridiculous toward the end." I paused only to suck in enough air to continue the tirade. "You weren't even sleeping in bed with me. I mean, I'm willing to take second fiddle to work *sometimes,* but—"

Before I could finish, he turned away from me and stalked out of the room, fists closed at his sides.

I trotted after him. "Adam, where are you going? I was talking—"

"Leaving before I say something I'm going to regret."

"Like what?"

He ground between clenched teeth, "If I say it, then I'll regret it, which was why I was leaving the room."

"*Stop right there.*" And he did—so abruptly that I almost collided into his solid back. He stood still as a statue without turning to face me.

I talked to his wide shoulder blades, his stiff spine. "I'm trying *really* hard not to be a nag but...damn. Shit gets old when my soon-to-be husband is consistently choosing work over me. I'd like to come first—even if only sometimes."

His head dropped forward, and he palmed his forehead. "You have no fucking idea how I've chosen. What I've had to fend off for *us.* If you did, you wouldn't say that."

I drew away. "Sorry, but I'm gonna have to call bullshit on that."

His open hand darted out and smacked the wall. It wasn't a violent outburst, but it was loud, and I jumped. He turned to me, and that vein in his forehead was protruding in such a way as to create a whole new mountain range across his features. Yeah, he was *pissed.* I'd poked too hard.

I blinked, and he froze when he noted my startled reaction. We stood like that for one minute, two, staring at each other in wonderment and shock at what had just happened. We hadn't argued like this in a long, long time.

Suddenly, I shook my head, as if waking myself up from a bad dream. "What is this? Why are we fighting like this? What is this *really* about?"

Seemingly exhausted, he hung his head, shoulders slumped. That same hand with which he'd hit the wall now braced him against it.

Taking a deep breath and releasing it, he looked up with guarded eyes. Like he had shields up, phasers set to kill.

I swallowed hard and steeled myself for his answer.

Chapter 13
Adam

I HAD NO IDEA HOW TO ANSWER HER. NOT IN ANY WAY THAT wasn't going to dig me in deeper than I already was.

"This conversation is over," I muttered, turning on my heel into my office and hoping she wouldn't follow. Of course, I knew better, but I'd expended every ounce of energy I had for the day—and it wasn't even nine a.m. yet. Sinking into my chair with a long sigh, I glanced at her through the doorway.

I'd left a stunned fiancée standing out in the hall, staring at me in wonder. After a long moment, I finally spoke, "You can leave and we can cool this down and talk later. Or we can talk now, but I'm warning you that I'm still pretty pissed off." I wasn't about to admit that I had to sit down or I would have fallen over, but likely, my exhaustion showed anyway.

She slowly entered, giving me a once-over with an aspiring doctor's eye.

"I agree that we probably shouldn't continue that argument. But I have to know, and it really can't wait. What did you mean by that?"

My eyes avoided hers, and I rubbed my forehead, trying to think my way around the subject. This was the last thing I wanted to discuss with her—especially now. Especially after all the vulnerability and insecurity she'd revealed to me last night.

And her words. *I'm not ready for your world.*

She had no idea what "my world" was demanding of me—and of her. What I'd been trying to protect her from. And the mere thought of holding that back any longer was making me want to fold up in my chair.

"What did I mean by *what?*" I asked stalling.

She sank into the seat on the other side of the desk, opposite me, a frown creasing her forehead. Even when I was irritated with her and she was obviously annoyed with me, she was the most beautiful woman I'd ever laid eyes on.

My throat tightened so that I could barely swallow the emotion that rose up. And suddenly, a flash of memory—that moment last night when she'd told me she couldn't do this. That cold fear chilled my veins. I dreaded that she'd say it again, or worse—act on it. My chest tightened as I remembered those warm tears I'd wiped from her big brown eyes when she'd cried into my t-shirt.

Her voice was quiet when she spoke. "You said that I had no idea about your choices and something about having to fend things off for us. What does that mean? There's obviously something going on that you aren't telling me."

I rubbed my forehead, staring out the window. The bright sunshine glinted off the water of the back bay, and even in the chilly late fall weather, boats bustled toward the harbor and the ocean.

"Adam...please tell me."

Unsure how long I'd sat staring out that window while she waited for my answer, I was yanked back into the present by her plea. She was leaning forward, both palms pressed flat to the desk, eyes wide with concern.

I took in a deep breath and then let it go. Tell her? Or blow it off and risk another confrontation? Let her have her way with the wedding and keep the prenup issue hush-hush?

A new headache threatened, blossoming behind my eyes, my temples. I didn't want to think about it. With my eyes closed, I muttered, "It's not a big deal. A small conflict I ran into with the board of directors. It will resolve itself."

Her brows came down in a frown, her eyes still glued to me and a very plain *I smell bullshit* expression all over her face. "A...conflict? With the whole board or only with Jordan?"

I stiffened at the mention of the name, and her eyes flashed as if she'd hit on something she'd been searching for. "It *is* something to do with Jordan, isn't it? I've been trying to find out what. I should have asked you weeks ago."

I blinked.

"Or maybe I should ask him?"

My jaw clenched so tight that it ached. I spoke to her through clenched teeth. "Don't you dare talk to that bastard."

Her jaw dropped. "Uh. *What?*" Was she shocked that I'd forbidden her from speaking to my *former* best friend? Or was she shocked at the general animosity in my voice? My fist clenched at my side as I realized that in my weakness I'd let loose more than I'd planned.

"What the hell is going on? He's your best friend."

"Nope. Best friends are supposed to have your back."

"And he doesn't?" She let out a breath and slumped in her chair, staring at me like I was an alien species brought to Area 51 for examination. "Enough of this. Tell me what the hell is going on, or I'll pick up the phone and call him and air our dirty laundry. You should know better than to keep important secrets from me."

I laid my head against my chair, eyes darting up at the ceiling. She was right. It was way past the time for keeping any more secrets.

"Jordan wouldn't stand behind me versus the BOD when they were pressuring me to do something I didn't want to do. So yeah, I'm pissed at him."

Silence from her end then the drumming of fingernails against the desktop. I tilted my head at an angle to get a glimpse of her, hoping the answer would satisfy her, while knowing it probably wouldn't. She was watching me like a hawk.

"And what was the issue? Does the board want you to sell more shares in the company or something?"

"No."

She hesitated longer. More drumming. I knew the determined expression on her face. She was on the scent of something and wasn't about to give up. Exhaustion gripped me, and all I could think of was how much I wanted to go to bed and lie down and sleep for a week rather than discuss all this with her. My body might force me to give in before I could think about any other options. *Shit.*

"You might as well tell me what it is. I'm not going to let you go to bed till you do."

My eyes closed. "Cruel woman."

She bit her lip. "Adam…"

"All right, all right. The BOD is pressuring me to sign a prenuptial agreement."

"Okay, and…?"

My eyes popped open again, and my gaze found hers. She was staring at me with that expectant look on her face, resting on her elbows against the desk, her fingers laced in front of her. Her reaction was completely bewildering—as if I'd told her I needed to zip down to the grocery store to get a carton of milk.

"*And*...that's it. Jordan sided with the board instead of helping me fight it. And they were getting ugly about it."

"Like—how ugly?"

"Like threatening to remove me as CEO..."

She blinked. "But—why wouldn't you want a prenup?"

I rubbed the tense muscles in my neck. This was a puzzling reaction that I hadn't anticipated.

She waited while I wondered and tried to think my way through the brain fog. My body may have been wanting to shut down and go to sleep, but my brain was now skipping along as fast as it possibly could. Which right now, admittedly, was suboptimal brain speed.

"Because I don't want to be forced to sign something about my personal life. And I don't want to force you to sign to prove to the world that you aren't a gold digger."

Her brow scrunched. "You mean...to prove to *you* that I'm not a gold digger, right?"

I shifted in my seat. "I don't think—"

She held up her hand. "Calm down. I know you don't think that. But you assumed I'd think this was an excuse in order to get me to sign. Hence all the cloak and dagger, the hiding it from me."

"Emilia—"

"I'm hard-pressed to understand your need to jeopardize your career because you don't want to hurt my feelings."

I blinked, now completely confused. "Shouldn't I be worried about your feelings?"

Half of her mouth quirked up in an ironic smile. "Yes, of course, but this is business. I understand that. I'm a big girl."

I gave my head a weak shake. "I know you are."

"And do you know that you have a *ferocious* instinct to overprotect?" She raised her eyebrows, as if daring me to disagree. Which, in truth, I couldn't. "And while it can be endearing—and so much of what I love about you—sometimes it goes too far. *You* go too far."

I leaned forward, resting my elbows on the desk, and opened my mouth to protest.

She stopped me with a curt chopping motion. "The BOD wants to protect the company in case something happens. You should be happy about that. They see the prenup as a way to protect your assets, and it's true that you would profit from it."

"I don't want to benefit from something if it comes at your expense."

The corner of her mouth twitched, as if she wanted to smile, but couldn't. Then she nodded slowly. "I could profit from it as well, don't you see?"

I licked my bottom lip, considering, waiting for her to continue before I'd concede or reject her point.

"A prenup can protect me, too. In lots of ways." She began counting on her fingers. "First, it eliminates any doubts you might have about my intentions."

"I have none."

She shrugged. "But if you—or anyone else—did, they'd be eliminated. Second, suppose there *were* ever a problem with us...like my Botox backfiring and you wanting trade me in for wife 2.0 or something." I rolled my eyes, and she laughed. "But seriously, when a marriage breaks up, it's usually very ugly. There are hurt feelings, threats, and broken promises. And there can be a lot of hate. A prenup saves us making any spur-of-the-moment decisions motivated by anger or revenge or whatever. It's a contract that a bride and groom hammered out when they were calm, rational, excited about the future and in love."

I frowned. "In a perfect world, it works like that, but ours isn't a perfect world."

"We can be fair to ourselves now. Talk it through and make the agreements we both can live with. It will likely never need to be applied. But...it's kind of like insurance."

Jordan's argument, brought up to me again. By the person I loved most in the world. I blinked.

"You're holding three fingers up in front of you—was there a third point?"

She smiled. "Yup. A prenup would remind both of us why we are really together."

I mirrored her smile. "Oh? And why is that?"

"*Love*, baby."

I swallowed, suddenly aching to pull her into my arms.

"You okay?"

I nodded, still staring. "I'm a bit in awe."

"Of what?"

"Of *you*. You are..." I couldn't even get it out. The word sank in my throat as I choked up. My throat clogged with sudden emotion.

She seemed to pick up on it immediately, getting up from her chair and moving to sit on the desk, facing me. She leaned forward so that her long hair brushed against my chest. "I am...what?"

I reached out, pulling her against me, into my lap. "You're amazing, incredible..." My voice died out, and I fought to suck in more air. "You literally take my breath away."

Her mouth curved into a grin, and she bumped my shoulder with hers. "All those compliments without sex? Wow, I really must be all that."

I nibbled at her collarbone. She sighed, the warm air splaying across my cheeks. "You *are* all that. I shouldn't have coddled you. Stupid me, for forgetting how strong you are and not trusting you more."

She chuckled. "You'll learn, young padawan. I have faith in you." She slipped her head onto my shoulder. "So are we going to do this, then? This prenup?"

I hesitated, feeling that wall inside me come up again. The resistance came so naturally, without conscious thought. That same resentment burned. "I have a big problem with the board of directors telling me what I can do with *my* life—and forcing me to sign a paper that has nothing to do with them."

She reached up and traced my earlobe with her finger. In spite of my preoccupation, the touch sizzled down every nerve ending in my body, right down to my gut, where that fire for her always smoldered.

"With regards to your share in the company, it *does* have to do with them. They want to protect the company. *And* they are watching out for everyone who relies on you. All your employees, the stockholders. If anyone ever sabotaged the company, it would be all of their livelihoods, too. A lot of people depend on that genius brain of yours to keep them employed."

I clenched my jaw. "I'd never suspect you of wanting to sabotage the company whether or not you signed a paper. Or no matter how awful a situation we ended up in."

She kissed my cheek. "But that's because you *know* me and you love me. The board doesn't. It's business. Marriage is for love. It's for building families. Divorce is business. Since we are never going to get a divorce, this is all for show."

I said nothing as she combed her fingers through the scruff on my jaw.

"So this was your big issue with Jordan? Because he sided with the Board?"

I nodded.

"He was doing his job, Adam. He was being a damn good CFO."

I blew out a breath I didn't even know I'd been holding. "He didn't stand by me."

"But can't you see what a shitty situation this must have been for him? Put in the middle between you and the board. And if I know him, he was trying to find out any angle he could to prevent you having to go through this. Am I right?"

I thought about it. He'd been doing the research—as he'd told me—asking his people to determine the case I might have for fighting the board. He'd been the lone guy out in the middle of two war fronts, waving a white flag and hoping nobody lobbed a grenade in his face.

"He's your friend—the friend who covered for you when you went on leave from your job when we first got together. Jordan held down the fort when I was sick and you weren't working, so you could take care of me. And now, doing the same thing while *you* get better. Asking me regularly about your health, worried as hell. He *does* have your back."

I shrugged. His behavior was *still* irritating. And it still hurt.

"You've been stressing out for months over this...and overworking to compensate. And you damaged your health. Totally not worth it. Let's resolve this, okay? Let's do the paperwork."

I mulled that over, but apparently not fast enough. She shifted to face me. "Tell your lawyers to send me something to look at, okay? A draft or something? We'll hash it out."

I shrugged.

She got in my face, putting the tip of her nose to mine. "*Listen. I'm going to insist on this. It's about time I get what's due to me.*"

I raised a brow at her. "And what is that?"

"You still haven't paid me my 750K from my scandalous virginity auction. I refused to be stiffed." Then she bit her lip to keep from laughing, an action which failed miserably after only a few seconds.

Her laughter was infectious. I finally cracked a smile of my own. "Maybe I'm simply making sure I get the most out of that money."

"Oh, I'd say that you *have*."

Despite my exhaustion, a heated tongue of lust licked its way up my spine. If I had the energy—and a non-explosive spleen—I'd try something right this minute. My hands inched up her thigh, aching to touch her everywhere. Instead of acting on this, I simply took a deep breath and relished the feeling, like a thousand-pound weight had been lifted from my shoulders.

"Come on, Adam. I know your stubbornness has gotten you far in life, but this is not the hill you want to die on."

I closed my eyes and opened them again, leaning forward to kiss her on her neck. "Fine. We'll do it. But I intend to be extremely fair. As fair as possible."

She nodded in response.

I held her gaze. "You need your own lawyer, someone not associated with my lawyer. It needs to be totally independent, okay? Peter could probably give you a name. Obviously, he can't do it for you because he's family, but I'm sure he'll know of someone."

Her eyes widened. "Oh, I bet Lindsay would be a better person to ask for a referral." It made sense. Lindsay was an excellent lawyer herself and had been through her own divorce a few years previously. Emilia had good instincts. I had no doubt she'd pick a competent lawyer for this.

"Whoever you hire, have them send me the bill. I'll pay it, no questions asked."

She shifted on my lap. "Sounds extremely fair, Mr. Drake. Now, about that 750K…"

I leaned forward and caught her earlobe between my teeth. "I do recall that you said 'no deal' to that."

She rewarded me with a delighted sigh. "Maybe I figured out that getting the man was worth a whole lot more."

My hand was on her ass in less than a second flat. "Like…how much more?"

"Like…worth all the bugs you kill for me—for life. And all the tight hugs. And the stimulation."

Now we were talking. I ran my other hand up her thigh. "Stimulation?"

"*Mental* stimulation."

I pressed my mouth to her succulent neck.

"I'm exhausted. Let's cuddle."

"You're still under doctor's orders to rest. *No* work. *No* hanky-panky."

I fought laughter at the archaic term. "Hanky-panky? For real?"

"Nope." She shook her head, kissing my nose. "*None.*"

I got my hand up her t-shirt. "What about a little...panky?"

She snorted, pushing herself off my lap. "You need to go back to bed. You're about to fall over. And *I* need to go get a lawyer." She leaned forward, grabbed me by the wrist, and tugged to pull me out of my chair. "There will be neither hanky nor panky."

I sighed. But, admittedly, all my body wanted to do was collapse and doze for a few more hours. I'd fantasize about seducing her later.

After a nap.

***

Between long bouts of sleep and occasional phone calls to my lawyer, I spent hours over the next week working on my Dragon Epoch mystery.

For the quest, I helped Lord Sisyphus gather his friends. When Princess Emma fell ill, I went on the hunt for a magic elixir to cure her. Once she was well, I escorted Princess Emma to a beautifully secluded beach at sunset, where he proposed to her and she accepted.

I even helped his cousin win a duel so that the wedding date could be established.

All uncomfortably familiar. But not in a creepy way.

Whoever had set this up—and it was elaborate enough to have required some time to develop—knew a lot about Emilia and me. And they knew something of the trials we'd endured to get where we were today.

Once I'd collected bottles of different types of tasty spirits from the different parts of Yondareth, I was on the verge of quest completion. It was almost time for Lord Sisyphus's Wild and Crazy Bachelor Party.

And with the drop of one simple line, I discovered the person responsible for the wedding quest.

My gratitude to you, FallenOne, for all of your help. But you must be careful when arranging my honeymoon travels to the exotic city of Pah-Arees. My boss, the King, just might end up stealing my long-awaited vacation.

Pah-Arees. That obscure reference could only mean one thing...because his boss *had* taken his long-awaited vacation from him—at his behest. To Paris. And though he'd been glad to offer it to us, he'd never ever let me hear the end of it when I'd taken Emilia to the City of Lights on the trip of *his* dreams—that he had spent months planning for himself.

Jordan.

Well. I'll be damned.

Chapter 14
Mia

A PPARENTLY, I WAS REQUIRED TO READ THROUGH A full disclosure of Adam's assets as part of the prenuptial contract agreement. Who knew? I certainly hadn't.

And though I'd never tell Adam this in a million years, the disclosure packet was, um, *overwhelming*.

By California law, both future spouses had to fully disclose their assets to their partner before anything could be signed. As part of my due diligence, I read through the list of Adam's assets and their estimated current value. The document, bound as a booklet, was easily the size of a sturdy medical school workbook.

His collection of assets was as varied and interesting as the man himself. As I turned page after page, I'd tried to squelch feelings of inadequacy with the knowledge that my disclosure could fit on an average-sized Post-it note. And most of that was gifts from him, like my car, my computer, and various other things.

And, of course, there was my debt, too. Adam had the normal type of commercial debt associated with running a big company. He had no personal debt whatsoever, aside from the obnoxious mortgage on the house.

Me? I had medical school debt accruing. In fact, Adam was footing that bill, too, without a word—and likely would be upset to hear me refer to it as a *debt* to him. But I'd always fully intended to repay it. I'd be adding that to the prenuptial documents as soon as I met with the lawyer I'd retained.

But for now, per her instructions, I was supposed to read through all of this and highlight any items I wished to know more about.

The more I read, the harder I was finding it to breathe as I sat at my desk in my study and pored over the seemingly endless list of assets.

The gaming company, the virtual reality hardware company he had recently acquired, a heavy chunk of investment in a firm called XVenture—aa private space agency that intended to send astronauts on manned missions soon. He had partial ownership in hospitality industry properties, like Emerald Sky in St. Lucia, among others.

It went on and on.

Jesus. He wasn't even thirty yet, and he owned half the country, it seemed.

"How's it going?"

I jumped almost out of my skin. Adam's bearded face hovered about a foot from mine, leaning over me to see where I was in the document.

"Shit, you scared the crap out of me."

"Sorry." He frowned. "I thought you heard me come in. I wasn't trying to sneak around."

"You're getting too stealthy. Might have to consider working for MI6 on top of all this other crap you're involved in, because *clearly*, you need more projects."

"Huh," he said, still reading over my shoulder. "You're still only on page four. Everything okay?"

I flipped back a page to point to a highlighted line item. "Sure. But I want to know why my future husband owns the complete licensing rights to PuffPuff the Pink Poodle." I tapped at the item with my pen. "This might be a deal breaker for me."

"What?"

"What what? PuffPuff the Poodle? Seriously?"

"Hello Kitty got popular again, didn't it? And the Smurfs? Why not PuffPuff?" I stared at him wide-eyed, and he continued, albeit slightly self-consciously, "It was a sound investment. Those are the full rights, movies, merchandising, video games, everything."

I snickered at him. "Are you going to write a new game? Retro games are all the rage. Maybe square-shaped PuffPuffs to incorporate into Minecraft? Maybe PuffPuff Pokemons to capture with your Poke balls?"

He pointed a long finger at me. "Someday, you'll eat those words, young lady, and I'll be laughing all the way to the bank when PuffPuff makes a comeback."

I grabbed his finger and wrapped my hand around it, making a fist. "Them's fighting words."

His dark eyes got that familiar gleam. "Wanna wrestle?"

I let go of his hand and waved at the tome in front of me. "I'd love to take you up on that, but some douchebag rich guy dumped this big old encyclopedia of his immensely huge and girthy assets in my lap, and I have to handle it."

"Ohhh...handling immense and girthy assets in your lap." He laughed. "I love it when you talk dirty to me."

"Especially when everything I say to you is taken in the dirty way."

"I can't help it." He bent over, planting a kiss on my cheek. "You're too sexy."

I swatted the hand that was now groping my boob. "Go away before I start demanding half of the licensing rights to PuffPuff the Pink Poodle and foil your attempt at world domination."

He straightened, laughing. "Just you wait. You'll see."

"I'm sure I'll be eating those words." I sighed, giving a dismissive wave of my hand.

"And a whole lot more." He leered before vanishing out of the room again.

"No workouts. No working—not even phone calls," I called after him.

"Blah blah blah," he replied from down the hall.

Ahh, conjugal bliss. We were already enjoying it without the obnoxious over-the-top wedding and ridiculous paperwork.

As the night passed, I made it deeper and deeper into the document. I found no lurid surprises, no secret support payments to illegitimate children, no illicit hideaways for kept lovers, no secret bribery or blackmail payments or the like.

But reading through Adam's accomplishments made me feel like I'd been standing still during these six years of my adult life. He was on a single-handed mission to change the world— investments in leading-edge and green technologies dominated the list. And space exploration.

All this money. And all these decisions...no wonder he was so goddamn busy all the time.

Cora, our housekeeper, brought me my dinner in my study instead of calling me down to eat. She told me that Adam was sleeping and gave me our chef's instructions on how to heat his dinner when he woke up. I nodded.

I'd mentioned to Chef the needed increase in his protein and caloric intake, and she'd said she'd noticed his weight loss as well. "We can't have him not properly filling out that tux for the wedding."

Somehow, her words had caused a lump to form in my throat. Oh yeah, the wedding. I wanted to forget about it. *Just jitters.* Like the other night after the Real Housewives had triggered my freak-out.

I picked at my dinner and, though it was good, couldn't bring myself to finish it.

Feeling the need for some fresh air, I took the disclosure document with me out onto the deck that wrapped around the back of our house.

I snuck down the length of the deck and sank into the lounge outside our bedroom door. Adam had pulled the French doors ajar, like he often did, to bring in some fresh air. I kept quiet, continuing to plow through the damn paperwork, wishing the mounting uneasy feelings away.

About an hour later, the natural light of the day was dying in a golden blaze, and my attention had been drawn away to the beautiful sunset. I became aware of the sound of stirring from inside the bedroom. The door to the deck swung open, and Adam stepped out onto it, wearing only a t-shirt and his underwear.

He did a double take when he saw me there. "Hey. What are you doing out here?" His eyes flicked to the disclosure document lying open across my lap. "It's getting dark. Still reading all that? How has it not put you to sleep?"

I picked up the booklet and dog-eared the page I'd been reading, setting the thing aside. "It's very interesting. I'm discovering all your sordid secrets. Your pink poodle fetish, for instance."

He busted out one of his signature cocky grins. "Just you wait." He approached, sinking down onto the ottoman across from me.

I eyed his bare legs. "You better put some clothes on, or our neighbors will be pulling out the binoculars. Trish Sinclair did inform me that you are very easy on the eyes."

He laughed. "I'm sure I look particularly fetching right now." He ran his hand through his respectably thick beard. God, it was a disgrace to cover up that face, but it wasn't like I could demand he shave every day while he was sick.

"You hungry? Chef left you some dinner. I'll warm it up."

He rubbed the back of his neck. "In a few minutes. I'll get it."

I stretched my legs out straight, settling my feet gently in his lap. He took one in his strong hands and gently massaged the arch. Shocks of awareness zinged up my legs from that simple touch.

"You seem quiet," he said, sending me one of his careful looks under his thick, dark eyelashes.

I reclined, enjoying his touch even though it had aroused me in seconds. Of course, these days, going without, I got aroused from passing him in the hallway, from *smelling* him. It didn't help that he was so goddamn sexy all the time. And that beard held no small appeal. It was driving me half to distraction—especially when he wore his glasses. An...*interesting* look for him.

Relaxing in my chair, I sighed. "Mm. That feels good. And I'm quiet because I don't have much to say. There's a lot to take in. I didn't realize that getting married was going to remind me of studying for the MCAT all over again."

His brow twitched. It had been a joke, of course, but as always, Adam picked up on every tiny subtlety—in the tone of voice, body language...

Should I tell him about my concerns or give it a pass? He'd fought like a dragon from his game to prevent me from having to do this. He'd put everything on the line. I didn't want to confirm that his fears had been right. That I wasn't ready to face this after all.

"You need to eat," I declared, changing the subject. "You've lost weight."

"I've still got these to tempt you with." He grinned, flexing his biceps.

"I'm already a puddle of lust due to the outfit you're wearing. Boxer briefs and t-shirt. Man lingerie. *Mangerie?*"

He chuckled, but his eyes returned to the booklet. "I'll go eat in a minute. Come with? We can talk about all that if you want."

I worried my lip, but nodded, getting up. Adam disappeared into his closet and came out in a clean shirt and pair of sweat pants. I gave him a smooch on his hairy cheek.

"I'm proud of how you're handling this no-work challenge," I told him.

He shrugged. "I still don't really feel well enough, to be honest. And...I've been philosophical about it. Thinking about why it happened and what you said when I was diagnosed. That it was my body's way of telling me to slow down. I mean...it could have been a lot worse than mono. It's been a challenge to remember that work-life balance thing."

"Of course. You're a natural-born overachiever." I smirked, holding up the thick disclosure document as we made our way down the stairs to the kitchen.

I pulled the tray that Chef had prepared for him out of the fridge and followed her directions for reheating. He flipped through the document that I'd left on the counter near where he sat.

"You took a lot of notes," he murmured as I set his plate down in front of him and went to pour him some ice water to drink with dinner.

"Well, I figure you can't be the only overachiever in the family. I'm going to have to run to keep up with you. That's the realization I came to today as I was poring over that."

"Well, it takes one to know one."

I shook my head, laughing. "You're no average overachiever, Adam Drake. You're in, like, the one percent of overachievers. I mean...I don't even understand half the stuff in that portfolio. Those notes you saw are stuff I had to Google on my phone to figure out what was being listed—the mutual funds, the venture capital shares, the vested funds, the charitable institutions, the licenses, the NPOs. It's endless. No wonder I hardly ever see you."

He shook his head. "Most of that stuff takes care of itself. I don't deal with it on a daily or even a monthly basis. That's all stuff for the financial managers and whatnot. Did you...did you get a chance to go over the contract?"

I nodded grimly. "Yeah, I have objections there."

His brows knitted, and he appeared disappointed. "Really? Well, we can rework it however you need."

I leaned forward, my elbows resting on the counter in front of him. "Good, because there's no mention whatsoever of a free lifetime subscription to DE in the event of a divorce. I might someday have to learn to live without you, but I'm not going to live without DE."

His jaw dropped before he started laughing. "Ahhh, I think I can work that out."

I nodded. "And sex?"

He raised his eyebrow, but didn't speak as he slowly took in a forkful of herbed mashed potatoes.

"Guaranteed number of orgasms per week?"

He choked on his food. I pushed the glass of water forward so he could reach it easier. Once he was through coughing, he sucked down a gulp and replaced the glass, watching me with narrowed eyes.

"I didn't think you could put that kind of stuff in there."

I waggled my eyebrows at him. "You can put anything in those. Another factoid I learned from Professor Google today."

He took another bite and then—taking care to swallow first before continuing—he continued, "I'm going to make sure I ask this with a clear windpipe but...anything else you'd like to add?"

I rested my chin in my hands and stared off into space, thinking. "Workweek hours limitation. Definitely."

His expression turned skeptical.

"No more than forty-five hours a week, I think? Sixty under special circumstances."

"Jesus. I hope you're kidding. And how would I even prove special circumstances?"

"A signed note from your CFO."

That made him belly-laugh—and realize that I'd been pulling his leg, hopefully. I'd never be *serious* about him getting a signed note from Jordan.

I busied myself about the kitchen, and we chatted about other stuff while he finished eating. I insisted, like an overprotective nanny, that he clean his plate.

Then we moved into the living room, where I checked his throat and ears with my otoscope. I also touched his neck glands to monitor tenderness and swelling.

"Noticeable improvement. You're being a good boy and getting your rest."

"I may be getting my rest, but I'm not a good boy," he said. To reinforce his point, he reached out, hooked an arm around my waist, and pulled me into his lap where he sat on the couch. "I'm having dirty, not-nice thoughts about my sexy doctor."

"Now, now...better not go there. We don't know what that spleen looks like."

He heaved a deep sigh. Likely, he'd been hoping that smaller neck glands meant he could return to certain activities he very much enjoyed before getting sick.

"You've gone for longer without sex before, and you weren't even sick."

"Well, it doesn't help that I have to see you and all your sexiness walking around the house, every damn minute of the day."

I quirked my mouth at him. "I wasn't trying to be sexy in my shabby yoga pants and big t-shirts and my hospital greens. I'm sorry, but how can you find hospital greens sexy?"

"You're wearing them." His hand slipped down to the small of my back, holding me against him. "That makes them sexy."

I kissed his cheek then gave his beard a good-natured tug. "Enjoying this? Because you're losing it before the wedding, you know."

"I am? What if I want to be the beardgroom?"

I groaned. The pun didn't merit acknowledgment of its awfulness. As I tried to get up out of his lap, however, he held me fast to him. I turned, and he was watching me with serious, even concerned, eyes.

"So are you *really* okay about the prenup stuff?"

I hesitated. How much should I tell him, really?

The truth. Put it all out there and trust that he'll know enough about himself and me that he won't have to go nuclear...

"Okay, so if I tell you the truth, I don't want you to freak out and go into overprotective mode. We've had problems with that."

He blinked. "Okay, *now* I'm concerned."

I shook my head. "If you want me to spill all, then you have to promise not to go into beast mode."

He sighed, glancing away.

"Promise!" I repeated.

He rolled his eyes. "Okay, I promise. Now tell me the truth."

"Well, it's freaked me out a little, but not why you think."

"How do you know what I think?" His forehead wrinkled—frown almost concealed by the thick beard.

"We've known each other a while." I idly combed my fingertips through the coarse hair on his jaw. This thing on his face *was* oddly fascinating. "I'm suspecting you think I'm getting all emotional about the business details and the implications that you don't trust me."

"And that's not what has you upset?"

I traced the line of his cheek. "Upset is too strong a word. I'm not upset. Just...uncomfortable?"

"About?"

"About the coldness of a contract."

Despite his mouth being mostly shrouded in darkness, I could tell that was a cocky smirk hovering on his lips. "You can say that without even a little a sense of irony?"

I shook my head smiling. "Oh, I get the irony. Our whole relationship started with a contract...or did it? Our relationship started long before all the paperwork came along."

His gaze flicked off to the side and then back to me. "True."

"It's...hard to imagine, I guess." I tilted my head slightly, our temples touching. "I know how I feel now. I know how I hope I'll feel in ten years, and looking at that agreement..." I shook my head to mask the hesitation. "It's hard to imagine a time when you and I will part ways and become strangers again—or distant acquaintances at best."

"That's because it's not going to happen." His arms around me tightened almost imperceptibly.

"But it *could*."

"Any marriage could, Emilia. That's the risk you take. But ours isn't any more likely than anyone else's. In fact, less so. Studies show that couples who were friends before they became lovers have a better chance of making marriage work. And we were friends—good friends. For over a year."

I grinned at him.

He narrowed his eyes, and I grinned wider.

"What's the smile for?"

"You've been reading studies. About marriage. You're such a nerd."

"If you're only realizing that now, I don't hold out much hope for you."

"You're a nerd's nerd, Adam Drake. A goddamn sexy nerd." I shifted in his lap to hug him around his ribcage. He rested his head on my shoulder.

"So that means I can keep the beard for the wedding?"

"Hell no."

"How about some...panky?"

I shook my head. "Consider this good practice. Abstinence can help us for when we're old."

His hands were on my butt again. "You think old age is going to stop me?" he asked, his thick brows rising as I smoothed my fingers over his pale forehead, noting the dark circles still under his eyes. He might be *feeling* a lot better, but he wasn't looking it. Not yet, anyway.

"Oh really?" I kissed his nose. "So you're already planning on being a dirty old man?"

That cocky grin that usually made my panties start to smoke... It really should be illegal for a man to be this sexy. "With you, my thoughts never really leave the gutter. I won't lie."

I smiled. "So in my retirement, I'll need to take up knitting so I can fight you off with my knitting needles."

"Even that won't stop me. Come here." He pulled me flush against him. "When we are old, I will take every opportunity to jump you. I won't need Viagra."

I hummed, scouring his face. "Not all that different than the present, except when a virus is stopping you."

"All right, I get it. No panky. Let's cuddle."

"Huh." My mouth quirked.

"What, huh?"

"I mean...that's probably the very first time you've ever suggested cuddling to me and *meant* that you wanted to cuddle."

I pushed against his chest in order to pull away, but he didn't budge.

"I feel bruised by your implication." His tone of voice told me the exact opposite.

"No, you don't. 'Let's cuddle' is every dude's euphemism for 'I'm going to convince her to have sex. She just doesn't know it yet.' Except newsflash, dude, she knows it."

He frowned. "Have you been reading an illegally gained copy of *The Bro Code* or something?" His arms slackened, and I pulled away, sitting back. Turning, I ran my hand over his tousled hair, attempting in vain to tame it. Not only did he need a shave, but also a haircut.

"I'm an observer of life. I know how you not-so-smooth operators work." I winked. "So you've got me all snuggled up against you, right? And then you slowly, subtly start to 'rub' me somewhere seemingly innocent, like my back or my stomach or something. Your hand moves in circles, growing wider and wider so that you eventually touch more 'interesting' spots, like the bottom of my bra or the top of my panties."

"Sounds about right." He reached out as if to demonstrate, and I knocked his hand away, laughing.

"And then *oops*, your hand slips under the elastic, all while *cuddling*." I made air quotes with my fingers. "You wonder why suddenly she's in the mood because you've been not-so-subtly putting the moves on her, all in the name of *cuddling*."

His features were all innocence. "I can't help it that my hands and innocent touches drive you insanely wild with desire. It's not like I can turn that off."

I snorted. "You're *way* too full of yourself."

He licked his lips. "I can't wait till *you* are way too full of myself."

My head leaned forward, touching my nose to his "Well, you've got the *dirty* and *man* parts down perfectly. It's a matter of time before you get the *old* down." Reaching out to smooth his cheek, I could tell he was exhausted. Despite his frisky talk, he was leaning his head on the couch again, eyes drooping. "Now, I think you have sleep in your future, and I have to get back to that girthy tome. C'mon, old guy. Time for bed, gramps."

And by the way he hardly protested, I could tell I was right.

Chapter 15
Adam

THREE AND A HALF WEEKS AFTER MONO BODY-slammed me and demanded I slow down, I completed a half-day at work. It was the longest half a day of my life. Or it felt like it, anyway.

Nevertheless, I managed to keep a brave face for the duration before going home to collapse. And wisely, on Emilia's advice, I'd scheduled hat day a Friday so I wouldn't need to show up the following day, even if I wanted to.

One of the first things I did was something I'd studiously avoided before falling ill—met privately with Jordan.

Just as two years before, when I'd taken a leave of absence, he'd had to do the heavy lifting for me while I was sick. All this in spite of the tension that had boiled up between us.

Emilia was right. I owed him a lot. I owed him an apology.

Yeah, I was still sore from the things that were said. But since my conversation with Emilia, I'd had a week to think things through.

Jordan sat across from my desk, methodically running down the checklist of the most important items to be handled now that I was here. I listened carefully, jotted notes to myself, and asked few questions. When he finished, he gave a pointed glance at his watch and pushed himself out of his chair.

I capped my pen and leaned forward. "Can you stay for a few more minutes?"

Jordan's brows twitched together briefly as he sank again into the seat. "Sure, man. What do you need?"

"I need to apologize. To you."

He blinked then jerked his head to gaze out the window, ducking to examine the sky. "Huh."

"What?"

"Just checkin' to see if pigs are flying. No flying pigs yet."

I leaned the chair back, watching him. "I deserved that."

He didn't say anything, instead clenching his jaw so that his cheek bulged. Then, getting up, he turned away from me and he went to the window to peer out of it.

The silence grew, and I cleared my throat, suddenly uneasy. I stood from my chair, and for lack of anything better to do with my hands, I stuffed them into the pockets of my jeans. "I said some shitty things—"

"Shitty things were said all around," he interrupted. "And I get it. Tensions are high. Emotions are high. You're facing a huge life change. *But* I can't help but wonder, after this, if being the best damn company officer I can be *and* being your friend are mutually exclusive."

I straightened, studying his posture—the rigidity of his shoulders, the hands clenched into fists. "Of course not," I said quietly.

"Really?" He turned to me. "Because that's sure as hell not what it feels like from here."

I paused, realizing that I should have expected this. I should have prepared for the pushback. I had no idea, in truth, what I *had* been expecting. A few jokes. Jordan blowing the whole thing off with his usual brand of salty humor. Maybe some well-deserved putdowns aimed in my direction. His usual BS. I braced myself to take my lumps.

He put a hand out toward me. "We've been friends for a long time, Adam, and business partners for almost as long. I've messed up in the past. I fucked up *huge* last year, and you had my back then. I'll always be grateful for that. And if you know me, you know that loyalty means a lot to me. And you've earned my loyalty many times over."

I blinked, at once touched and troubled by his speech. It was true. He was loyal—sometimes to a fault. In so many other ways throughout our history, he'd been there for me. Jordan had even been an asshole to Emilia when we'd had our relationship troubles—out of protectiveness toward me.

"But I like to think that *I've* earned *your* loyalty repeatedly as well. And your trust. And I felt neither."

My jaw dropped—it wasn't hard to hear the hurt in his voice, and I was a first-class dick for having caused it. "I do trust you, Jordan."

"*Really?* You have a strange way of showing it. You treated me like I was only out for myself. And you wouldn't meet with me so we could find a solution everyone could live with."

"Well, like you said, we all screw up sometimes. I'm trying to tell you I'm sorry."

He took a step toward me. "And I'm not trying to be a hard-ass here. As far as I'm concerned, this is already the past and water under the bridge." He mirrored my stance, putting his hands into his pockets. "*However,* that doesn't mean that I'm convinced this isn't going to keep happening over and over again."

"This was a...special case. I saw this as an attempt by the board to control my personal life."

"Yeah, *control*. That's a big issue for you, man. We've talked about it before. Your need for control is based on the fact that you don't trust anyone else to do as good a job as you can." He sighed.

I opened my mouth to contradict that statement, but shut it again. He was right. And I'd been a colossal asshole, because Jordan had done a good job. He'd always done a good job. He'd been doing his job when he broached the prenup issue, and I'd blown him off, insulting him in the process. My face flushed hot with shame. I looked away to cover the uncomfortable moment, and he continued to talk.

"The outcome of this company is in the board's best interest, too. And yeah, sometimes you have an employee who can't get his shit together—like Alan—and you have to can them. But the rest of us are right there with you on the front lines, trying to make this the most awesome company it can possibly be." He shook his head, his own face flushing—I assumed with anger or frustration. Probably both. "You've gotta loosen up on the reins and let us do our job."

For lack of anything to say, I nodded. I felt like a fool standing here speechless like a chastened schoolboy, but what the hell else was I going to do? I knew this was a problem. Emilia pointed it out to me often, and I'd fooled myself into thinking I'd been listening to her all this time. Did she feel this same level of frustration with me, too? Did *everyone*?

"I'm saying this as your friend, not your CFO," he continued. "There are only so many hours in the day for Adam, the control freak; Adam, the visionary who's going to change the world; and

Adam, the loving husband. You can't be all of these people *all* of the time, so you're going to have to make some choices—hopefully good ones. Or continue to drive yourself to an early grave, not giving a shit and letting everyone who loves you pay the consequences."

I sucked in a breath, folding my arms over my chest. My lumps indeed. Jordan was dishing them without hesitation today—*and* without buffer. And as hard as it was to hear, I resolved to take his words to heart. Because they echoed that voice that had been talking inside my head since I got sick. They echoed what Emilia had been saying for some time now. Everyone I cared about had been singing the same tune, and now their voices were unified into a great chorus in my imagination.

And it was my choice to listen or blow them off, yet again.

I swallowed. "We all have learning curves. This one has been mine."

"Wow," he said, shaking his head with a grin. "Did Adam Drake just admit that he's still got shit to learn? If there's no flying pigs today, then I'm thinking that maybe hell froze over instead. I won't be able to check on that until I die, though."

"Smartass motherfucker," I muttered, shaking my head. "You're really making me pay for this shit, aren't you?"

"That's what friends are for." His gaze met mine and held for a few moments of awkward silence. A light bulb went off in my head. Emilia had once called me on my work addiction shit, but Jordan's words made me realize that I had no addiction to work.

I had an addiction to control. And all this time I'd been treating the by-product—long work hours and preoccupation with everything to do with the company and my business—and not the root of the problem.

212 | BRENNA AUBREY

If I didn't get a handle on this, it could ruin everything good I had going in my life. It would erode my professional relationships, my personal friendships. Possibly, eventually, my marriage.

I rubbed my jaw to cover for my shock at this conclusion. Jordan was watching me closely. I gestured to his chair and sank back into mine. "You've been a really good friend. And I couldn't have asked for a better CFO."

My voice sounded...off. And I desperately needed some time alone to think this shit through, but Jordan moved to his seat, sinking into it. He sat in silence, swiveling nervously on his chair. Then he cleared his throat and spoke. "I couldn't have asked for a better friend, Adam. Thank you."

We both looked at each other, a bit stunned at the emotion of the moment. Then Jordan shook himself and blinked. "Fuck, what is this, a therapy session? Am I about to grow tits?"

I shrugged. "Well, that would certainly be convenient."

He ran a hand through his hair. "Goddamn. I feel the need to use power tools while simultaneously barbecuing a side of beef and guzzling whiskey."

I laughed. "Maybe we should take Liam up on his offer to fight it out with swords and armor."

"Yeah, that's old-school macho. Why not?" We chuckled, the weird moment finally broken. Jordan leaned back, scratching the edge of his jaw, and flicked a glance at me. "So I have to ask—"

"It's handled," I interrupted. "We're hammering out the document now. She'll sign it when we're satisfied."

His brow twitched. "Glad to hear it. Hope it wasn't too stressful for her."

"It wasn't stressful at all. She completely understood."

If we had not had the previous uncomfortable conversation, I would have expected the next words out of his mouth to be *I told you so.* Mercifully, they weren't.

Jordan nodded. "She's a smart one. I'm glad it wasn't a problem."

"It forced us to open up to each other about a lot of important things. It's been good."

He hesitated and then nodded. "I'm not going to pretend I know everything you're going through or your circumstances."

"You will, soon enough."

He shook his head. "April and I already discussed it, and it's a non-issue for us. There will be a prenup—when the time comes."

I suppressed a smile. So my suspicion that all his anti-marriage talk was mostly for show was correct.

He shrugged. "I haven't even popped the question."

"*Yet.*"

He shot me a sly smile. "You're my guinea pig. I'm going to observe and see how the married state treats you." I laughed, and he sent me a sheepish grin. "But speaking of all this...I made mistakes, too. I assumed that everyone approached a given situation the same way I would. I don't know much about your childhood, but what I do know..." He shook his head, shrugging. "Growing up, I lived a privileged and sheltered middle-class life. I shouldn't have assumed. So *I* am sorry. There. Now snowballs are waltzing through Hades at this very minute."

I nodded. "Thanks, man. Appreciated."

He bounced his foot some more, shifted in his seat, then leaned forward to get up. "Well, I'd—"

"I've got one more thing for you."

He stopped. "Shoot."

214 | BRENNA AUBREY

I laced my fingers together on the desk in front of me. "Will you be my best man?"

He blinked. "Define 'best.'"

I laughed. "What about best asshole, then?"

He nodded. "I can do that."

"Good. I'd say you've more than earned the slot over my cousin."

"I'm sure he's glad he's off the hook for the toast." He grinned.

"Also, I want to thank you for the quest. That was legitimately impressive."

He laughed and rocked in his chair again. "Ah, the highest form of compliment from the master of quests himself. I am deeply honored." He put his hand over his heart. "I only wrote the storyline. I commandeered Tony in development to implement it for me."

I shook my head. "Should I sue you for stalking? How'd you know all those details about my and Emilia's relationship?"

"I was around for most of that stuff at the beginning, and also…girls talk. Mia told April everything. April helped me write it all out and put all the romantic fluff into it."

"Maybe I should demote you as CFO and put you in charge of creative, then? It's gotta be more interesting than financial reports."

He glared. "Says you. Financial reports get me hard. *Spreadsheets* make me—"

I held up a hand. "TMI."

"True story." He laughed. "Lucas told me you put him on the spot in play testing when you were digging to find out who was behind the quest. The guy almost shit his pants and was practically hyperventilating when he came to me. I paid the poor bastard a bonus out of my check to make up for it."

I laughed. "I'll make sure to apologize to him today. Thanks for taking the best man gig. No bachelor party, though."

"Overruled. But don't worry; there won't be a stripper." I rolled my eyes. "Don't think I haven't figured out what you're up to. Putting me in a tux to stand next to you at the altar? All to give April ideas."

"This will probably be the first wedding you've attended where you don't bang a bridesmaid."

He got up from his chair. "I'll be shagging the hottest chick there—aside from the bride, of course. That's my consolation."

"Better get that diamond ring picked out." I winked. "A wedding is the perfect place to pop the question."

He made it through the door, but not before flipping me the bird.

***

A couple weeks later, Emilia signed the finalized prenuptial agreement. No commentary. No resentment. No pomp and circumstance. We had witnesses document the occasion for us and certify that there was no coercion on either party's part. We were signing of our own free will and accord.

When we returned home, she found the document that I'd left for her. It sat in the middle of her desk in an antique-looking envelope, sealed with a red wax seal and ribbon, all official and old-fashioned like.

Once she noticed it and sank slowly into her desk chair, I made myself scarce. I'd written her name in blue fountain pen on

216 | BRENNA AUBREY

the outside. She'd know immediately it was from me. If not from my writing, then definitely from the fact that no one else called her by her full name.

A week before, I'd typed out the rough draft.

I, Adam Drake, hereby give my prenuptial promise to Emilia Kimberly Strong, the woman who will soon be my wife. And that's forever... So the promises I make here are the promises I make for that forever.

There is no "if" or "when." There is only us.

Together, we've created a new, unique program. A code that only you and I could write, giving our lives to each other. The test will be when we compile—and set that code to run. And yes, every day will be a trial run. But we can make those a triumph. Every day.

I went for a walk—since I wasn't cleared to go running yet. The doc had declared my spleen still swollen, though much improved. She wanted to give it another week or so, to err on the side of caution. And Emilia was watching me closely to prevent me cheating. I had privately nicknamed her the Enforcer.

But the doctor said I'd be fine in time for the wedding. Thank God.

Any more hurdles getting this woman to the altar and I'd lose my mind. *Not long now.*

After hitting the end of the beach this side of the jetty, I turned back toward the house a half-hour later. I caught sight of her running toward me down the paved walkway and bike path that lined Newport Beach. She must have used her phone app to locate me.

Once she caught up to me, cheeks flushed and out of breath—and more beautiful than ever—she might have tackled me were she not overly concerned for my delicate spleen. I stopped, facing her, and she gazed up at me, all round-eyed. Reaching out, she wrapped her arms around me, snuggling close. I returned the hug and kissed the top of her head, overcome with feelings as strong as if I'd been toppled by one of the waves currently pummeling the shore. *Love. Pride. Peace. Satisfaction.*

"Wow. I should have waited to give you that next week when I'm cleared for sex," I murmured said into her hair, breaking the sappy sentimentality of the moment. "I think I wasted a great way to get you in the sack."

She gazed up at me, grinning. "Oh, don't you worry. Nowadays, merely glancing my way would get me in the sack."

"Good to know. One more week and you aren't going to be able to keep me off you."

She smoothed her cheek against the fabric of my shirt, her arms gripping me tighter. "I'm counting on it."

"So I take it you liked the note?"

She laughed. "You are the reigning king of understatements."

"I'm an arrogant prick most of the time. I don't know how you put up with me."

She leaned up and kissed me, but didn't dignify my statement with a reply.

I hesitated then smoothed a hand down her back. "I want you to know that I'm serious about all of it. About our forever."

She touched my shaved cheek with her palm. I closed my eyes, relishing the feeling. "Of course, I knew that already. You're always serious about everything, Adam Drake. In fact, some would say you're *too* serious."

"But *you'd* never say that?" I raised a brow.

She smiled. "I keep you down to earth when you're getting too uppity." She tilted her head, her smile fading only by a small fraction. "It's so weird, but the entire time I was reading that, I kept thinking of the first day I met you."

The regular weekend crowd had made it to the walking path and were filing around us. I took her hand, and we slowly headed toward the house. "In the game?"

She shook her head. "No. In person. That day in the hotel conference room."

I laughed. "That day was an epic miscalculation on my part. I walked in there determined as hell to scare the shit out of you, my one objective." I took a deep breath. "Instead, I entered that room and saw you, and it felt like I'd stepped off a cliff and was free-falling."

"And *I* thought I'd been snapped up into a raging storm." A breeze picked up the ends of her hair, and they danced around her shoulders as if they'd been imbued with magic. "Hurricane Adam. That's what I mentally nicknamed you."

"That storm was the future, smacking us the face. And we weren't aware."

"I keep wondering when I first knew it. Like...knew it without admitting it to myself."

I could answer to that for myself, but said nothing. Instead, I pulled her hand up to my mouth and kissed it.

"Maybe it was our first date," she mused.

I laughed. "What exactly are you calling our first date?"

"That night in Amsterdam." She winked up at me.

"Oh, huh. *That* night. The night I realized I was in a lot of trouble where you were concerned."

"Really? Tell me more."

I hesitated, wondering how she'd receive any new information regarding that entire trip, *especially* that night. The night that started it all. But after these past few weeks and the way she'd taken everything else in stride, could I ever be anything less than completely honest with her?

Time to find out. "Well…you remember that phone call?"

She took a few steps in silence. I picked up scraps of other conversations around us and the ever-present call of gulls on the beach. "Of course. That phone call is the whole reason that things went on and on between us. If it hadn't been for that call, we would never have— Well, I mean, I know now that you had no intention of…" Her voice faded out when she saw the expression on my face. "Now you've got me wondering if that was more than a mere random occurrence."

I crooked a smile. "You know me. I never leave anything to chance. We weren't going to do anything that night. I'd had some safeguards installed."

"*Safeguards?*" Her pace slowed as she chewed on that. "Like what?"

"In the limo on the ride back from the dinner and dancing, I texted Jordan and told him to call me in an hour." I gauged her expression. "And then ordered him to keep calling if I didn't pick up the phone. Just in case."

"Just in case you went too far?"

"Yeah."

She frowned. "So…there was never an ill-timed emergency?"

"No." A few more steps. "I invented the emergency. Then I logged into the server to run a routine backup."

We walked on in silence as she continued the pace, continued to hold my hand, but stared down at the pavement in front of us in deep thought.

"Does that make you mad?" I asked.

"No. A little confused. You're not really the type of person who needs to invent an excuse to get out of something he doesn't want to do."

"The phone call wasn't for *you*. It was for *me*. And it wasn't about *not* wanting to do something. It was about wanting it too much." I twitched the hand I was holding, lacing my fingers tightly through hers. "All through dinner, dancing, I realized this might get a little—or a lot—out of my control. I decided to enact a failsafe plan ahead of time."

She laughed, and I relaxed, not even realizing that I'd been mentally holding my breath. "It's hilarious that you enlisted Jordan to purposely cock-block yourself ahead of time, from thousands of miles away."

"Glad you find it funny."

"I didn't at the time." She sent me a glance from the corner of her eye. "I found it incredibly frustrating."

A skateboarder, heading straight at us, swerved at the last minute. I cast a scowl in his direction as he passed.

"That makes two of us. And the beginning of long weeks of frustration."

She smiled wryly. "Not unlike recent events. I wonder why this keeps happening to us?"

My hand tightened around hers. "Let's hope we've seen the last of it."

The breeze kicked up a notch, raising the ends of her hair to form a halo around her head. She released my hand and reached up to grab at her hair, slipping an elastic from around her wrist to form a makeshift ponytail. "It's a small price to pay for the love of a lifetime, right?"

"We'll make up for it, I'm sure."

Two more minutes and we were at the gate to the small bridge that led to Bay Island. I opened it for her, and we crossed in silence.

She stopped at the halfway point over the bridge, gazing down over the water.

I halted beside her. "What's up?"

She didn't say anything for another stretch of minutes before letting out a breath I didn't even notice she'd been holding. "Something that wasn't mentioned in your letter. Something I think we need to talk about."

I turned around to face her, mildly alarmed by her serious tone. She took up both my hands in each of hers. With our arms, we formed a bridge of our own, parallel to the one upon which we now stood.

Her head came up, and I suddenly perceived that she was on the edge of tears. Resisting a frown, I swallowed, bracing myself for whatever it was.

"What about—babies?"

And there it went, the bottom of my stomach. Stupidly, I hadn't expected that question. And I had no answer for it.

Those brown eyes bored into the back of my soul. "Will there be babies, Adam?"

Somewhere in the deepest reaches inside of me, someone flipped the switch on a deep freeze. I swallowed again. *No.* I wanted to say it in the most final of voices. I wanted to put that foot down now. *Nothing that threatens your health. Ever. Ever again.*

But I said nothing.

She blinked, continuing to stare. And those eyes—those beautiful eyes—welled up with the largest, clearest tears I'd ever seen. "Please, Adam," she whispered hoarsely. "I need an answer."

I shook my head. "I don't know."

Was it my voice that trembled like that?

The tears breached the rims of her eyes, spilling in thin streams down her sculpted cheeks. How could happiness turn to sorrow in the literal blink of an eye?

This fabric we'd woven together, this mesh of *us*, was made of joy, of pure love, of humor, of shared experiences, pain, sex, arguments, discussions, and practical jokes. But there was that one sharp pinprick of sadness that we always seemed to avoid acknowledging.

That one razor-edged sting that could draw blood with its sharpness.

That loss.

"So it will only ever be the one?" Her voice trembled, and she bit her lip then took a breath to continue. "The one lost baby we can never hold? Never watch grow up?"

Her face, so filled with emotion, highlighted the void inside myself. Like there was a barrier containing my feelings where this issue was concerned. This part of my heart was tucked somewhere far back in a deep, dark corner.

Resolution filled me. I wanted to answer her in definitive terms. But how could I? Given the tears, given how difficult it even was for her to bring it up, I knew this was important to her.

This loss still haunted her. In truth, if I could stand to admit it, it haunted us both, even if for different reasons.

The least I could do was give her hope.

But I wouldn't give her empty promises, no matter how much she needed that hope.

So I needed to decide here and now what I would give her. What I *could* give her.

"I'm not going to say no," I murmured. *No matter how much I want to.* The fear, it was rising up again, choking me. Memories of the tears we'd shed during that dark, troubling time. Memories of carrying her, passed out in my arms. Memories of coming that close to losing her. Could I bring myself to face that fear again? *I want to say no—but I won't.*

She nodded, lifting one hand to swipe across her cheeks. "For now, I only need that. A promise that you'll keep an open mind when the time comes."

An open mind. Something I definitely wasn't known for.

I remembered Jordan's words now, that decision I'd come to the day in my office when we'd talked. I loved that control. I'd mainline it like a drug if I could. Twenty-four-seven. Without hesitation.

I was addicted to control, and I wanted *this* control over our future. No kids. No pregnancies that might damage her health. Just us. Her and me.

But every addict had to face the challenge of resisting his drug of choice, right? Had to fight against that pull to indulge? *An open mind.* Despite everything in me crying out against it, I pushed against that barrier. It would be a struggle when the time came. And I knew it. But it wasn't a battle I needed to fight *now*.

I took a deep breath, mentally fortifying myself. "I can do that."

"You can?"

I nodded. "I promise you an open mind, Emilia."

That smile...the one that pulled at the corners of her mouth and crowned her flushed, tear-stained cheeks. That was worth the promise alone.

Just please, God. How I hoped that promise wouldn't come back to bite me in the ass someday.

Chapter 16
Mia

ONSIDER THIS 'PERSONAL PRENUP" MY HUSBAND'S *Manifesto, to use your terminology. Should I start out with a list of all the marital injustices enacted against wives throughout time immemorial, or should I just start with us?*

I vote for us. Because that's the only thing within my power, and though I can't see the future, I know that—with you by my side—every joy will seem brighter, sharper, more colorful and every disappointment will be duller, more distant.

I've made mistakes in the past, and they were painful for both of us, but I'm being philosophical and calling them learning moments instead of mistakes. Because I have learned from them, Emilia. And I promise you...

I promise you I will never take my vows to you lightly.
I promise to be open with you when I feel we might have the slightest hint of trouble
I promise to listen when you come to me with a problem.
I promise to compromise.
I promise to cherish the moments we are together.

Downstairs, the front door opened and closed. I tucked the document back into its envelope after having reread it so many times I couldn't even count. Soon, the print would start fading along the creases from unfolding and refolding it so often.

Hopefully, he had no idea. He'd never let me hear the end of it.

Grabbing my purse, I bounded down the stairs to kiss him goodbye. It was midafternoon, and he'd done another almost-full day at work. Unfortunately, I had to go. Bride business and all that.

"I bought the new Marvel movie and downloaded it to the TV. Don't you watch it without me," I ordered as I pulled him into my arms.

He bent down and kissed me. "Nope. But you better not be out all night, or I will."

"I'll be back after dinner. It's just Heath and Kat."

His brow furrowed. "How's Heath doing? Better?"

I nodded. "Yeah. I've been touching base with him every day and giving Kat pep talks for how to deal with him. Together, we'll hopefully keep him on track."

Adam nodded.

"Go take a nap. You look tired."

"Maybe."

My brows came up. "What's this *maybe*? You want me to rat you out to your doctor?"

His mouth quirked. "You're tedious."

I smiled. "It's Wife Prep 101. Be prepared for me to bring the nag. Go. Nap. When you wake up, I'll be back to watch the movie with you."

My meeting with the bride's dude and his assistant went well. Kat was all kinds of excited to get to St. Lucia. In three short weeks, we'd *all* be there. December had just started. The days were shorter and chillier—even for California. Though there still wasn't enough of the much-needed rain.

The Caribbean would be a nice change.

I got home to find Adam sitting downstairs in the audiovisual room with a book in his lap, patiently waiting for me to return. He'd napped. I could tell by his messy hair.

And he looked yummy—even in board shorts and a long-sleeve t-shirt.

Hunger is the best spice, my mom often liked to say. And when it came to Adam, I was ravenous.

We didn't make it that far into the movie before realizing that we couldn't keep our hands off each other. It all started out so innocently, too. Snuggling together in a big recliner made it difficult. His chest was hard, drawing my hands to it as if that was their sole purpose. Soon he was reciprocating, lightly touching my breasts. These advances were not unwelcome.

Adam paused the movie right in the middle of Captain America's rousing speech so he could pull me into his lap and kiss me soundly. Our lips locked, and I scooted up his lap, settling right against his prominent erection. *God*, he felt so damned good.

He rewarded me with a deep groan as I rocked against him. This sex blackout had been torture. *Only a few more days.*

But some make-out time wouldn't hurt, would it?

Adam's hands were up my shirt, slipping inside my bra to tease my nipples. But he didn't seem satisfied with that level of access. His tongue pushed deeper into my mouth as his hands grew more frantic. With a growl, he tugged on my bra, and the garment creaked in protest.

"You're going to break it," I muttered against his mouth.

"I don't fucking care. I will buy you dozens of bras. I need to suck on your nipples." He tugged again, and the plastic piece holding the strap on snapped. "*Now.*"

"Yes, *sir.*" I laughed, leaning back to pull off my shirt and bra in one fell swoop.

"Ohhh, yes…that's what I'm talkin' about." He reached up and cupped me with his big hands, fingers closing firmly over my breasts. "Shit…I missed this."

I leaned into his touch, replying, "Me, too. I was trying to be good and not change in front of you or anything."

Without another second's hesitation, he leaned forward and fixed his mouth firmly on one lucky nipple as I arched my back, closing my eyes and seeing stars. Hot arousal bloomed between my legs as my nipple tightened happily in his hot mouth. *Jesus.*

"We, uh,"—*Gulp.*—"We should probably—"

He rubbed the edge of his teeth against my nipple, looking up at me with those burning, dark eyes.

"Oh, fuck." I groaned. *It felt so damn good.*

"I'm gonna make you come."

"You shouldn't…" I breathed though *damn,* I wanted that more than breathing right now.

"Why the hell not?"

"Because *you* can't."

He sighed, pulling away. "In two days, the doctor is going to tell me that I'm cleared."

"I saw the sonogram of your spleen. It was bad, Adam. I want to make sure you aren't permanently impaired."

"Sex is not going to impair me. Sex is natural. Sex is good. Sex is best—"

I burst out laughing and ran a hand through his messy hair. "If our roles were reversed, you wouldn't be touching me with a ten-foot pole. Don't deny it. I'm not the only overprotective one in this family." He opened his mouth to protest, but I prevented it. "Who's the one who insists on doing breast exams on me every few weeks, even though I do them myself at the prescribed times?"

He ran his thumbs over my nipples again. "That's because I love your boobs. It's no chore doing an exam."

"Adam…" I bent to put the tip of my nose to his, but he wasn't returning my gaze. He was transfixed by what he was doing to my nipples. And I had to admit it felt damn fantastic.

He glanced up, those dark eyes meeting mine. "If you're going to make me wait for an all-clear, I'm not going to be happy."

"What would *you* do? Be honest."

He gritted his teeth, jaw bulging. I had him, and he knew it.

His hands dropped from working their magic on my chest. I almost cried. "Fine. But if I don't get any, neither do you."

I stuck my lip out. "Meanie."

"Oh, I'm going to be *extremely* cranky these next few days. Better be prepared for it."

I stooped to scoop up my shirt from the floor and slip it over my head. "You've been legit ornery for the past few weeks already. I'm prepared."

"And yet you still want to marry me."

I waggled my eyebrows at him. "Yup. You're stuck with me, Drake."

He took a deep breath and let it out in a long-suffering sigh. Reaching around, he grabbed my butt with both hands and pulled me against him. "Best news I've heard all week."

Then he scowled and pushed me off his lap. He wouldn't turn the movie on again until I moved to my own recliner, declaring me—and my boobs—too much of a distraction.

After I stopped laughing, I complied, warning him that once he got the all-clear, we'd be all over each other.

A storm was coming, and it would be raining orgasms. Hurricane Adam, indeed.

***

The next day, Adam was still moping as we got ready to go to a lunch meeting. I would have offered him an out to stay home, but he was the one who had set up the meeting in the first place.

And I wasn't going to this meeting without him. Even if Mom and Peter were going to be there, too.

After a few months of exchanging emails with Glen Dempsey, I'd finally agreed to meet him in person. We'd reserved a room at a local Italian restaurant, La Cucina, which had a window overlooking the cliffs of Corona Del Mar, a golden sand beach.

We stepped into the restaurant, expecting to be the first ones, being that we lived less than ten minutes away. But Glen sat at the table, chatting with my mom and Peter, who had all preceded us. We entered, and Glen shot out of his chair. Peter and Mom followed suit.

I paused, waiting stiffly as Mom introduced us, studying my older half-brother. He did not resemble me in the least. After seeing photos of his other family members, it was easy to see they all resembled their mother.

He was of medium height and stocky build, fair coloring, with the palest blue eyes I'd ever seen. And he had the best smile. Wide, honest, open.

He appeared to be everything his father was not. At least from what I could judge. I knew next to nothing about his father aside from the crumbs I'd suffered to hear from my mother.

Glen's eyes widened. "Hi, Mia. It's an honor to finally meet you."

He was as affable in person as he'd been in his emails. I smiled, reaching out my hand to shake his. "Glen."

He shook my hand. "You're as beautiful as your mom."

Mom and I thanked him in unison.

I introduced him to Adam. Glen shook his hand, congratulating us on our impending wedding. Then we all sat. I buried the awkwardness of the moment and wondering what to say as I studied the menu.

Thank goodness for appetizers—and wine—to loosen the mood.

Glen wasn't the awkward one. It was all me.

"Thank you again for sending me that folder of medical information," I said after the small talk lulled.

He smiled. "It was the least I could do. And I mean that completely. The least anyone in our family could do for you."

I blinked and avoided peering at my mother. "It—it must have been difficult for you to get your father to sign the release for his records."

Glen hesitated then returned his eyes to his plate as he cut his meat. With a shrug, he replied, "He's a man of sense. When sense is pounded into him, he responds appropriately."

I nodded, but didn't reply. It still stung, the knowledge that Gerard been reluctant to give his medical records to me, even while I was undergoing treatment for cancer. That he hadn't cared enough to respond to my mother's request.

Glen cleared his throat and met my gaze. "I'm not going to defend him, by the way. He hasn't done right by you, and that's on him. But I will say that you haven't missed much, Mia. Honestly, he hardly knows the three kids that grew up in his house. He's a crappy father."

In spite of that downer pronouncement, it was still a little gratifying to hear. That his neglect and disdain hadn't been personal to only me. Those feelings came with more than a small pinprick of guilt, however.

"I'm sorry," I murmured for lack of anything else to say.

"Don't be. One by one, our relationships with him have deteriorated or become damaged beyond repair. One of my sisters cut him off completely. The other barely speaks to him. I'm the only one who tolerates him, and that's more for my mom's sake."

I nodded, chewing my chicken breast thoughtfully, wondering about his mother. What kind of woman must she be? Was she like the Real Housewives from my dinner out—the ones who spoke of tolerating their husbands' indiscretions out of necessity?

"She's aware of you, by the way. She's known for quite some time."

Silence. I peeked at my mother, whose features appeared perfectly smooth and unaffected. This wasn't news to her, then. But did she appear paler, or was I imagining it?

"Well, I'd say I'm sorry if my existence has caused her pain—"

My mother nudged me under the table. Not lightly, either.

"More like my father's existence has caused her pain," he scoffed.

Whether Glen was exaggerating the idiosyncrasies of his father in order to put me at ease, I didn't know. But I was grateful to him for the effort, nevertheless.

Our lunch was pleasant, and when it was time to go, Glen asked for a moment alone with me. After a nervous glance at Adam, who nodded his reassurance to me, the rest of the party left to wait for me at the entrance of the restaurant. I stood in front of Glen, shifting from one leg to the other.

He pulled an envelope from his jacket and held it in front of him without offering it to me. "I need to explain this first before I give it to you. I didn't know about you until recently, but as I said, my mom has known for a long time now. She didn't actively monitor what was going on with you, but was aware of your circumstances and your age. All of us received a trust fund dispensation at age eighteen to cover our college with our full payout of the trust fund at age twenty-three, or whenever we graduated college. She insisted my father set one up for you, which he did. But he refused to make you aware of it."

I swallowed, blinking, suddenly aware of an invisible weight slamming against my chest.

He held the envelope out to me. "This is the information on how to access the trust fund."

My hand trembled as I took it from him. "I don't want his money."

He put his hand over mine, a firm grasp holding tightly. "Take it, Mia. It's yours. And don't do it for him. Do it for my mom. It would make her happy."

Inexplicable tears prickled my eyes. "She sounds like a wonderful lady."

"She is. The best. He never deserved her."

"I hope she divorces him."

He laughed. "She did. Very recently."

"Maybe I could meet her someday."

He nodded. "I think she'd like that. But one thing at a time. I don't want this to be weird between us. I have no idea how you establish a sibling relationship with an adult you've never met before, but...I'd like to try. I'd like to tell people that I have another sister. I went from being the baby of the family all this time to having a younger sister."

He released his grip on my hand, and I pulled it away. "Thank you, Glen. For being such a decent human being. For restoring my faith in that half of my family tree."

He smiled. "I can't vouch for the old man, but thanks for not judging me based on him."

I laughed. "I may once have. But never again."

"Can I give you a hug?"

In response, I stepped forward and hugged him. "Thanks for doing all of these things you didn't have to do."

He patted my back. "I *did* have to do them."

We walked out, but not before I invited him to attend our wedding. He was delighted to receive the invitation.

Adam only asked me a few questions on the way home. He left me alone once we got there, after I told him I had a lot I needed to think about. It was bizarre, really. Suddenly, I had money. How did one deal with becoming instantly wealthy?

I'd been struggling with that question since I'd become engaged to Adam. Now, that issue was hitting me from a completely different angle. After taking a long walk by myself, we had dinner, and I told him about the trust fund.

"You were young when you got this kind of money dropped into your lap." I was speaking of Adam's first big break—when he'd sold a program to a huge gaming company for millions of dollars at the ripe age of seventeen.

He laughed. "Yeah, it was weird. I had no clue what to do with it. I paid off my uncle's mortgage. I paid Liam's college tuition— before he dropped out. And I did a few other nice things with it. I went to Europe on my own. Kids' stuff. It's a lot of money to dump on a kid's plate."

I shrugged. "I was thinking of using it to pay for my medical school."

He frowned. "Well, I guess you could. But you know you don't need to. I'd like to see you find a way to do some real good with it. Maybe when you are a doctor. *But,* you don't have to make that decision tomorrow."

We continued to eat for another minute before he stopped chewing. He was looking off into space, as if thinking…then he let out a groan.

"What's wrong?" I asked when he grimaced.

"This means we have to redo the prenup document."

I made a face, and he laughed. "Don't worry. I'll call the lawyer. Hopefully, this won't be too much of a pain."

***

And, fortunately, it wasn't.

But I couldn't help but wonder…if I'd received that money at the time I'd started college, I would have been in vastly different circumstances. And so many things would have been done differently.

I would most likely have never done the auction.

And the auction had brought me Adam.

And I'd take Adam over a thousand trust funds. So, for that, I owed the biological sperm donor—or, rather, his ex-wife—my thanks.

The next day, Monday, when I got home from labs, Adam was sitting on the bed with the TV on. He'd had an enforced— by me—day off. But I quickly noticed the laptop on one knee, which he promptly slammed shut when I came in. His phone sat right beside him, and a remote to the TV was on the nightstand next to him.

I raised my brows. "Working?"

He sighed. Damn, he looked pale. "Checking emails. I really need to hire a new IT director."

"But not today. And probably not until the new year."

He shook his head, his eyes gravitating to the TV screen, which was blaring the news—a special report. There were shots of the International Space Station and mentions of NASA and astronauts.

"I've mostly been following this. Did you hear?"

"I've been in class all day—heard nothing." I turned to the TV. "Did something happen?"

"There was an accident. Two astronauts were doing an EVA—a spacewalk. There was an accident. One astronaut's suit was breached, and he was killed."

"Oh, *shit.*" I sank down on the bed, staring at the screen. "That's horrible."

"Yeah, the other astronaut on the spacewalk, Ryan Tyler—I know him. He was on the station the same time I was and even helped me with my training. Real kickass astronaut. A heroic sort of guy."

Sadness tightened like a cold fist in my chest. "This is awful. I don't think anyone's ever died *in* space before."

Adam shook his head. "Nope. Only on the way up or the way down...or in training."

I listened as the newscaster repeated the known facts of the accident while saying a lot was still unknown, and they were waiting for a spokesman at NASA to start a press conference within the hour.

"It sucks," Adam muttered. "I wish I could do something to help Ian. I can't even imagine what he's going through right now. Of course, the news outlets are going to spread hearsay and repeat rumors that will be harmful to the space program. It always suffers after accidents. Programs get canceled, and people will forget that going into space is important for everyone's future."

"Maybe the future of going into space shouldn't even be in government hands, then." I turned back to him. "Maybe it should be for visionaries with the means and the motivation. Someone said it's going to take a bunch of smart billionaires banding together to accomplish major changes in practically every field. I happen to know a *very* smart billionaire."

He glanced at me out of the corner of his eye. "Are you referring to my little investment in XVenture?" he asked. XVenture was the private space exploration company I'd seen on the disclosure document.

"It didn't look like a *little* investment, but yeah, that's what I mean. Like...maybe it will take a visionary billionaire with motivation to do something more than the government is willing to do."

"Maybe." He rubbed his jaw and continued to stare at the screen, but I was convinced that he was listening closely to me.

"You remember what Spider-Man said: 'With great power comes great responsibility.'"

"Spider-Man didn't say that. Uncle Ben did."

I shrugged. "I simply mean that you have the power to change things."

He nodded, still watching the television with a troubled expression. Without asking him if he needed a hug, I leaned over and gave him one anyway. After the press conference, I finally convinced him to turn off the distressing news, and we had a quiet dinner alone and tried not to talk about it.

But the wheels were turning inside that brilliant mind of his, and I wondered what the result would be.

Adam had his doctor's appointment and ultrasound for his all-clear tomorrow, and I hoped he'd feel better with some good news. The countdown to our wedding had begun. Only two weeks now.

In the bathroom, before bed, I noticed the telltale dark spot on my panties. After months and months of being AWOL, it looked like I might have a normal period.

Best not to count my chickens before they hatched. It could vanish as quickly as it had come. I cleaned up and took care of it, but didn't mention it to Adam.

He'd find out soon enough.

Chapter 17
Adam

INSIDE MY CLOSET THAT NIGHT, AS I DRESSED FOR BED, I reached into the back and pulled out my dark blue flight suit from the Soyuz mission I'd flown from the Baikonur Cosmodrome in Kazakhstan over four years ago. Running my fingers around the mission patch and my name, *A. Drake,* stitched over the right breast pocket, I remembered that euphoric feeling of weightlessness, of the importance of the things being accomplished on the International Space Station.

In the news, talk of scrapping the station had started based on the dangers inherent with an aging facility that circled the earth every ninety minutes. A real possibility existed of pulling all astronauts and cosmonauts from their missions and bringing them home.

People forget so soon that what they were doing affected all of humanity and was *important* for its future.

I couldn't get the news out of my mind, nor that urgent call inside myself to do something to help. Maybe *this* was the next step for me. The next move beyond where I was. Something important for humanity's future. A new purpose.

Already in my head, a list formed. A lengthy to-do list that didn't involve wedding stuff for once. The first thing would be to send Ryan Tyler my condolences.

Then I'd get on the phone with my friends at XVenture and start proposing some ideas. If it weren't on the back of such sad news, I'd feel elated to have a new project to work on.

Instead, there was muted hope. A hope that I could have a hand in helping change the world.

Maggie, my assistant, promptly set up the appointment for me to meet with the CEO of XVenture in the New Year.

***

The next day brought the best, albeit expected, news. I delivered it to Emilia with a wide grin when she got home—late—from her last study session before her winter break.

"Clean bill of health," I murmured into her ear after I'd grabbed her around the waist in the kitchen and kissed her soundly.

She turned in my arms, pressing her front to mine and throwing her arms around my neck. "Oh, *man.* I'm so happy. Just in time, too."

"Yep, just in time for my suave advances." I winked.

"You and I have a different definition of *suave,* I think."

I shrugged. "Hey. It's been six weeks. I'm off my game. Cut me a break, would ya?"

She went up on tiptoes and kissed me. "I would absolutely *love* to cut you a break except I, uh, have an issue."

"Uh oh." I braced myself to hear it. What could it be? Had she failed a test? Forgotten some important wedding detail? *Oh God,* had she found a lump? My heart began to race. "What?"

She shot me a tentative glance. "Uh...wrong time of the month?"

Relief and frustration mingled together, making me at once glad and annoyed. I relaxed my arms, dropping them from around her. One hand went to rake through my hair. "Well...fuck."

She reached over and smoothed my cheek. "I'm sorry. *But* I think I could make *you* happy tonight, regardless."

I stared at her. "Like how bad are we talking here?" Since her chemo treatment, her periods had been light, and except for a day here or there, they'd hardly hampered our sex life before this.

"It just started, but isn't pretty." She quirked her mouth. "Let's say this one is restoring my faith that my fertility might return. It's like a murder scene. You don't want to go there."

I grimaced. "Murder scene? Ugh. Don't make me nauseated again."

"*Nauseated?*" Her jaw dropped, and she faux-punched my arm. "Oh my God. You are green around the gills. Stop being such a boy."

I held up an arm to fend off her attack. "I *am* a boy. We don't come with that equipment."

She folded her arms across her chest—tightening her shirt over her magnificent chest. I couldn't tear my eyes away. Leaning a hip against the counter, she huffed, "*Well,* you live with a girl. You're about to *marry* a girl. And girls get periods. It's a natural part of our lives. So get used to it."

I looked away with a resigned sigh.

"Wait..." She pushed off the counter and walked slowly toward me, arms still folded. "You're not...*afraid* of my vagina, are you?"

I laughed, shaking my head. "No, I'm not."

"You are! You're afraid of my vagina."

I held out my hand like a traffic cop trying to halt her advance. "It's the murder scene thing. I am not CSI Newport Beach. I don't need to know about the murder scene." She made a scoffing noise, halting mere inches from me. "I am *not* afraid of your vagina."

She swung on me again, and I blocked it easily as she tried gamely to keep from laughing. "What do you have to say for yourself?"

"I like your vagina. I give it five-plus stars on Yelp. *One of my very favorite places to hang out.*"

That got me a few more hits on the chest before I wrestled her into submission, pinning her arms to her sides. Then I kissed her deeply. By now, I was feeling exhausted and not caring much that I wasn't getting laid that night.

Also, I realized how relieved she must be. She'd expressed anxiety before that her periods were not "normal—which, being a guy, I was clueless as to what, exactly that meant nor did I want to know. But given the recent conversation we'd had about babies, I knew that the possible loss of fertility was upsetting to her, and that this was a good sign. She seemed happy about it, too.

And so, instead of pouting that it was hampering my sex life, I was happy for her instead.

"Look at the bright side," she began.

"There's a bright side?"

She smiled. "Yeah. At least I won't be on my period while we're on our honeymoon."

I nodded, agreeing wholeheartedly that was a good bright side.

The timing would work out perfectly.

Unless, of course, our crappy luck interfered again, which was definitely a possibility.

***

Days later, I was back to work after my rest break—the last one I'd take before the wedding—when the news hit.

On the eve of the release of our newest expansion of Dragon Epoch, to coincide with the Christmas rush, our data center suffered a distributed denial of service attack from an unknown source. For hours—which threatened to stretch out into days—our servers were completely crippled and unable to run the game. Our website and forums were also down. We were very limited in how we could communicate with our players.

How do you spell disaster for a gaming company? DDoS.

Jordan wanted to call an emergency BOD meeting, but I was too busy for that. We lost millions of dollars for every hour the servers were down. And if we did manage to get them up again, it did not prevent another DDoS hitting quickly thereafter.

Attacks like this usually came in waves, and our IT security firm was inadequately equipped to handle them. And with Alan gone and no IT director to replace him, I had to do the heavy lifting.

Jordan paced my office. "Someone needs to go to the data center."

I massaged my forehead at my desk. "Yeah, I know. I'll get Emilia to pack me a case."

He blew out a long breath. "She's going to eviscerate you. You're supposed to be on a plane the day after Christmas. We will get someone else."

I blinked at him. "Who?"

Jordan looked stumped. "I can try to supervise it."

"Do you know how to implement protection on the last hop IP?" I asked.

He stared at me like I was speaking Martian. I might as well have been.

"Uh. No. You probably should go."

I ran my hand through my hair. "I swear to God, if I had a decent IT guy, I would not be going. But we have five days until Christmas."

He whistled. "You're the one who's going to have to explain it to the soon-to-be wife. I want no part of *that*."

"Goddamn it." I rubbed my eyeballs through closed lids.

Jordan gestured dramatically to the phone. "I'll handle the board here. Call her and get your ass on a plane."

I called Emilia and hedged *a lot*. To be honest, I had no idea when I'd be home. It could be tomorrow or it could be the wee hours of Christmas morning. Things like these were hard to tell. I'd know more once I got up north to deal with our data center.

"What is a DDoS, and why are they attacking Draco?" she asked over the phone.

"DDoS means distributed denial of service. Someone is using a bunch of zombie computers to flood the servers with data so they can't function." I paced a circle around my office, stopping at my desk every so often to jot a note down for my assistant.

"Why would someone do that?"

"No idea. Bored hacker kids or an organized effort from outside the country. It could be anyone. They might not even be purposely targeting us, but someone who uses the same data center or network. Hopefully, we'll be able to tell more after we get it up and going again."

She sighed. "Okay. When do you leave?"

"As soon as possible. Can you send me a bag of stuff?"

"I'll bring it myself. I can meet you at the airport in twenty minutes."

Maggie found me a charter flight that was ready go to within the hour. As I'd only be flying a short distance to Northern California, I'd be there quickly. As promised, Emilia met me at the airport with a packed bag. "Good thing I'm on winter break. Of course, you could have Cora do it for you. Does a billionaire even *need* a wife, anyway?"

I smiled. "*I* do." I kissed her and bade her goodbye, hardly wanting to let her go. But I left her with a promise: "I'll be back for Christmas."

Except I wasn't. At least not for more than a few hours. And she flew out the next day. Without me.

Chapter 18
Mia

I WAS PRACTICALLY CERTAIN THAT EVERY BRIDE'S DREAM of an exotic destination wedding did not include flying to said destination without her groom. But here it was, six short days before our wedding, and I'd seen Adam for a total of six hours—most of which were spent sleeping—before flying out without him.

After spending five days in Silicon Valley cleaning up the data center mess, he still had work to do at the office to close out "everything I had to skip by going up there."

To say I was irked was an understatement. But what could I do?

If I hadn't been joking about that workweek hours clause in the prenup, I could have invoked it, but I thought any reasonable person would acknowledge these extenuating circumstances. And reluctantly, wedding or not, I did.

But that didn't mean I wasn't going to give him hell for it anyway.

Him: *I slipped my sweaty workout t-shirt from this morning into your luggage so you have something to cuddle tonight.*

I tucked my phone away without reply, face flaming with embarrassment. I was *so* exacting my revenge for that. Besides, I'd already grabbed something of his to take with me—not that he'd ever know if I could help it. But damn, how that cockiness needed to be brought down a peg or two. Or maybe two thousand.

Men.

Me: *Not necessary. I'm finding myself a new bridegroom upon arrival in St. Lucia.*

I smiled smugly to myself when he didn't reply immediately. Let him stew on *that* as we boarded our flight—only the second time ever I'd been on a private plane. The last time had been a surprise trip that Adam had sprung on me. This time, we'd planned it well in advance and were flying the entire wedding party straight to St. Lucia.

The plane was much larger this time, carrying our thirty-ish closest friends and business associates to the Caribbean. Mom and Peter were snuggled together on a couch, reading. April, Jenna, and Alex all sat around with champagne flutes while William, beside Jenna, carefully looked around the plane, as if staking out the exits. Then he grabbed an emergency procedures card from a seat pocket and began studying it. Lindsay was sitting beside Adam's cousin, Britt, and her husband, their heads bent together in a tête-à-tête.

Yes, everything had been perfectly planned. Everything except for leaving without one of the main participants in the wedding, that was.

Even *Jordan* was on the flight with us, steadily getting hammered.

Drunk Jordan was fun, though. It took the edge off his usual abrasive cockiness. And I thought he felt sorry for me, which would have been insufferable any other time, but was a welcome distraction now.

"Hey, Mia," he greeted as he plopped down on a couch next to me. I threw a glance around the plane to locate April in case I needed her to take her man in hand. People were sitting in clumps talking giddily about the experience, or, in the case of Heath, stretched out on the back row of seats, snoozing.

It was going to be a long flight.

And no Adam. *That* thought made my blood boil. What if he missed the wedding?

"Hey, Jordan," I replied between my teeth, then downed the rest of my wine, and set the glass aside.

"I hope you aren't too bummed about your sweetie being left behind."

"Huh. Why would I be bummed? It's not like it's some ordinary vacation. Like we aren't getting *married* or anything."

He frowned. "I know. I know. I'm sorry."

I shrugged, suddenly wishing I had more wine to drink. Jordan noticed me staring wistfully at my empty glass, called one of the two flight attendants over, and asked for a refill for me. I thanked him when she left to fill the order.

"Why didn't *you* stay and handle it, then?"

"I think you know the answer to that already."

I quirked a brow at him and nodded, happily taking the next glass of wine from the flight attendant. I sipped deeply. "Control freaks gonna control."

He shrugged. "Well, in his defense, without an IT guy, Adam is the man for the job. I don't know shit about that part of things. I'd only know who to yell at to get it done."

"That's the difference, though. You'd let other people handle it. He insists on doing it himself."

Jordan opened his mouth to defend his friend—he'd die defending Adam, I was certain. He was like Zoë Washburne to Adam's Mal Reynolds. The perfect right-hand man.

"It's okay. Adam is not in the doghouse with me. I'm irked, sure. It's our wedding. He did all of the planning and managed all the details. But here I am, alone."

"Well, even superhumans can't foresee the future."

I sighed. "You're right."

"He'll be here in time. The wedding isn't for five more days. If I have to fly back and drag him here, he'll be here."

"Well, *that's* reassuring."

He grinned that infuriatingly charming grin of his. "Drink up, Mia. There's plenty more wine where that came from."

Me: *Fabulous flight. Arrived here safely. About to enjoy four relaxing, exasperating, stressful days till the wedding. Am hoping other half of wedding party shows up soon.*

Him: *I will be there. I promise you. And long before the wedding starts.*

I swallowed a lump in my throat at the realization that he was no longer joking around with me or teasing me. Things must be really hairy at home. I was worried for him.

But as each day passed—our day out on a catamaran, snorkeling; the day we all went parasailing on the bay; the day we went to visit Diamond Falls and then had a bonfire on the beach—I was the odd one out. Almost everyone was paired up, either with a boyfriend, a flavor of the month, or a BFF (as Kat stuck close to Heath's side most of the time).

Every day, I got a bigger bouquet of flowers and a sweeter, longer note from my absentee fiancé. But that didn't quell the frustration and loneliness. I wanted *him* here, not his goddamn flowers and notes.

Finally, I was notified that he was on a plane and would arrive late morning...

The day before the wedding.

Oh, I wasn't going to let him forget this anytime soon.

Payback could be a bitch, and so could I.

Chapter 19
Adam

WHEELS DOWN, HEWANORRA AIRPORT. ST. LUCIA. At last, I was in the same geographical location as my fiancée, approximately thirty-six hours before our wedding. And I was certain she was going to have my balls for this.

I'd forgotten to bring my industrial-strength cup for protection.

Me: *Just landed. About to transfer to helicopter. Will be there in 45.*

Her: *At last! We are down on the beach already. I left your swimsuit on the bed in my room. Change and then come down and meet us. I'm in Cabana #1. We have picnic and spa later, then wedding rehearsal & dinner.*

Me: *Got it. See you in an hour or less. Can't wait.*

No reply. Huh.

With the exception of the last one, her texts had become more and more terse over the past few days. But I'd attributed that mostly to increasing stress as the wedding date approached without my arrival. I was right there with her on that stress level. In the end, I'd had to cut and run with the majority of the issue solved.

Again, it came down to that control issue, and I mused over it during the quiet moments on that solitary plane ride, realizing what the hell I'd been doing. I'd almost missed my own wedding. Because of a *server problem*. Because I couldn't back away once the main problem had been solved.

Because I had control issues. I needed to wake the fuck up before I lost what I loved most. I thanked all the powers that be that she was patient enough to put up with me for this long.

Starting tomorrow, the day I became her husband, I would be making some major changes. I'd have priorities, damn it. And I'd never do anything like this to her again.

Over a half-hour later, we touched down on the helipad of the Emerald Sky Resort and Spa, which, for the current week, was catering only to our wedding guests and the wedding party. One of the perks of being a joint owner of the establishment.

The lush resort perched on the side of one of the jagged green mountains that St. Lucia was known for. It overlooked a beach, several stories below. Each room, referred to here as a "haven," had its own infinity pool, and some also came equipped with hot tubs. The rooms were open on three sides to the Caribbean air.

The hotel manager greeted me with a room key and told me the number. I let myself into our room, and true to her word, a swimsuit sat on the bed.

Someone *else's* swimsuit.

I picked up the shiny scrap of fabric. A bright blue Speedo. A *Speedo.*

Convinced it was either a mistake or—more likely, if I knew my betrothed—a practical joke, I proceeded to look through all the drawers and the closet for my stuff. Emilia had brought my suitcase along with hers on the private flight so I wouldn't have to bother with luggage. That way, I could rush to the airport at the drop of a hat and fly out the first moment I could.

So now...here I was with not a scrap of clothing in sight except for what I had on my back. And this goddamn Speedo.

I was not dressed to hit the beach, either, wearing khakis and a button-down shirt with leather loafers.

Fuck it.

I pulled off my pants and underwear and put on the Speedo, taking time to inspect the result in the mirror. The swimsuit left *nothing* to the imagination. Nylon lined my crotch, emphasizing the lines of my dick and sac. Looked like Emilia had found a way to have my balls after all, no athletic cup needed.

Oh, I was so demanding payback for this one. Everything I owned was on display for all to see.

Not being able to fathom being seen in public like this, I slipped the pants back on and tossed my underwear onto her pillow as a calling card. *Something for you to cuddle tonight, my love.*

Maybe I should let her have her laugh. *No, Emilia. Not this time.*

She probably had my proper swim trunks in her beach bag. I'd change into them once I hit the cabana.

Me: *Here. On my way down. Interesting choice of swimsuit.*

Again, no reply.

I made my way down to the beach, choosing to use the steep, winding stairs over the elevator cut into the side of the cliff.

It took me no time to find our sand-colored cabana with a big white 1 painted on it. I lifted the flap and entered. It was completely empty but for a couple of beach bags, an ice bucket with a chilled bottle of unopened champagne, a cooler full of water bottles, and a tray of snacks.

I popped a piece of cheese in my mouth—as I was *starving*—and dropped my pants, digging around in the beach bag for the swim trunks I was certain were there.

I rifled through towels, bottles of sunblock and lotion, and pairs of sunglasses—grabbing out mine, I tucked them into my shirt pocket. That was a good sign. If my sunglasses were in here, my shorts *had* to be.

Still bent over, I heard someone enter the tent. I resisted the urge to turn around. Let her get a nice, long view of my ass in a prone position. It was what she'd wanted, right? I kept digging, trying to ignore the fact that she was probably getting her laugh anyway.

She moved up behind me and grabbed my ass. And not lightly, either. She squeezed the hell out of it.

"Well, *these* are new. Nice ass, *Beast*."

I stiffened, standing. That wasn't Emilia's voice. I turned, my gaze meeting April's shocked blue eyes. My best friend's girlfriend had grabbed my Speedo-bedecked ass.

"Holy *shit!*" Her hands went to her mouth, which was O-shaped. Her eyes were like saucers in her face. All I could do was laugh at her hilarious reaction. She took a step back. "I'm so sorry. I thought you were—"

"Obviously."

She rubbed her forehead, flush with embarrassment. "Crap, I can't even believe I just fondled you."

I laughed even harder. "I'll keep it secret if you do."

"Keep what secret?" Emilia burst through the tent flap and took in April's stunned expression and my laughter. Her eyes dropped to my Speedo. "Nice ass."

I only laughed harder, and April retreated again. "Oh shit. I gotta go. I thought this cabana was ours— Oh, uh—bye, Mia." She paled. And for April, also known as Snow White, that was a feat. "Sorry, Adam." She apologized, bursting out of the tent.

"Tell *Beast* I said hello," I called after her.

Emilia stared at me expectantly, her arms crossed over her chest. She was wearing a bikini I'd never seen before—pale pink and white checks. *Delectable.*

But *not* happy.

Before I could say anything, she scoffed. "You look familiar. I think I know you from somewhere."

I grimaced at her, indicating the insufferable Speedo. "Is this my punishment? People can see everything I own in this thing." I tugged at the crotch self-consciously.

She twitched her brows suggestively. "It's a fantastic example of a banana hammock. Maybe I wanted to show off to the world all the goodies I'm about to get."

"Very funny." I raised one brow at her. "Where's your wet t-shirt, then? So I can show off all the goodies *I'm* going to get?"

She stuck her tongue out at me in reply.

"How many more mischievous jokes do you have in store for me?"

She grinned, delighted. "This was the main one. I was going to try and substitute it for your tux tomorrow, but Jordan talked me out of that."

Someone should inform Jordan of how much his girlfriend appreciated a Speedo-bedecked ass.

Emilia let her arms fall from her chest, and she took my breath away in that bikini. This Speedo was about to become a problem as my eyes slid down from the curve of her breasts, across her smooth stomach and hips, and down those long, delicious legs of hers.

"Come here," I ordered.

"Why should I?"

"Because you look good enough to eat, and I'm starved."

She laughed, stepping forward. "Still not suave, Drake." Once she was close enough, my arms were around her, my hands on the soft, soft skin of her lower back. I pulled her up against me and kissed her neck. God, she smelled so good.

She drew away to scan my face. "What was April's problem?"

I shrugged. "Maybe she got freaked out because she saw me in the Speedo and was turned on. But I had to remind her that these goodies belong to you."

Emilia laughed. "Officially. As of tomorrow at sunset."

I kissed her again "These goodies haven't been used in a while. I think we need to test them out before then."

She was already unbuttoning my shirt, kissing her way down from my collarbone across my chest. "I completely agree. Don't want to accept faulty goods."

She licked my nipple, and it zapped me like an electric shock. I moaned, putting my hands in her hair. "I need to fuck you. ASAP."

"I could get on board with that plan." She led me over to the outdoor couch in the rear of the tent. With a flick of her wrist, it unfolded into a double lounge. Slowly, she spread her towel on it and lay down, stretching herself out like a banquet, all ready for me to consume.

I laid down my towel just as she had and landed beside her, pulling her into my arms immediately. "I've only seen you in this bikini for five minutes, and it's already driving me insane." With my index finger, I stroked the velvet skin on the inside of her breasts. *Like heaven.*

Her eyes snapped shut, and she pressed the whole length of her body against mine. Our mouths found each other, fastening together. I tasted her lips, her mouth, her tongue.

Kissing her was amazing, but after all this time, I was beyond desperate to get into her bikini. My mouth traveled down the column of her neck, down her breastbone, between the two pink-checkered-covered mounds.

"You taste like suntan lotion," I groaned as her fingers glided through my hair, teasing my scalp.

"I didn't put lotion *everywhere.*" She smiled lazily. "Certain parts have nothing at all."

"Yeah...my *favorite* parts," I murmured as I untied the string to her bikini top. She lounged with a long, contented sigh, happy to let me devour her. And I was happy to do the devouring.

When I touched her nipples, they tightened immediately, firing me up more. Her husky moans were music to my ears. My cock swelled inside that ridiculous Speedo, and I pulled away, taking two minutes to tear it off while also making sure to remove her bikini bottoms.

I settled on top of her. "I'm cutting to the chase, here. I figured you don't mind." At last, she was naked and underneath me. *Finally.* And everywhere our skin touched, it burned. She leaned up and, with a delicious moan, took my mouth again, opening her legs for me.

And I was in such a trance that I almost—*almost*—entered her right there and then.

Rocking against her, I breathed heavily, suddenly snapping into reality with an urgent thought. "Please tell me there are condoms in the bag."

Moving her hips again in such a way as to demand I enter her, she let out a long breath. God, it was so tempting. But these days, we strictly observed the adage *No glove, no love.*

Her reply came in a gruff whisper. "Um, what? Why would there be condoms in the beach bag?" I let out a long sigh of frustration, resting my forehead against hers. She smoothed her hands down my back. "Use the one in your wallet."

I raised my head and looked her in the eye. "I *never* carry a condom in my wallet. That's something only frat boys—and Jordan—would do."

She leaned up and kissed me again, her tongue tempting me with every fluttery movement inside my mouth. She was so goddamn irresistible. "Why don't you pull out this time?"

Shifting my hips a fraction, I was all ready to take the plunge before actually considering *that* insanity. I shivered against her. "There's no way in hell that I'm trusting myself to pull out. Besides, that is the *least* effective method ever."

"But what about your *legendary* self-control?"

"Today, I've got none. Damn it."

"Shit." Her head flopped on the headrest, and we held each other's gaze for long minutes.

"Let's go up to our room. I have condoms in the luggage," I said.

"We're not in the same room tonight." She sighed. "It's the night before our wedding. Your luggage is in the honeymoon suite."

"Then let's go there."

"We've got the picnic and bay tour in a half-hour." She rolled her eyes. "After that, we have our spa appointments. Today's agenda is packed."

I chewed on my bottom lip. "Tonight after dinner?"

"Our rehearsal dinner?"

I hesitated. "Sure...we'll have time. We'll meet in the bathroom of the restaurant. A last sexcapade while we're still unmarried people." She laughed and shifted under me, and I had to suppress a groan at how good it felt. I kissed her nose. "We better get dressed before I consider doing something very foolish."

Her eyes closed. "I don't wanna. I want to be ravished."

"Oh, you will. You *will* be ravished...but not right now." I pushed off her. "Now I have to figure out how the hell I'm going to stuff all this back into that fucking Speedo."

She cackled with laughter before pushing herself off the lounge and moving over to the beach bag, unzipping a side pocket—*a secret compartment!*—pulling out my trusty swim trunks and flinging them at me. "No way is that banana going back in the hammock. At this point, it would be indecent to walk around like that."

"Not liking the marble bag look anymore?" I gave her a goofy grin before pulling on the trunks.

"You mean the weenie bikini?" She winked. "You've got the goods, sure. But I think you forgot how to use them."

I jutted my chin out at her. "Tonight. Wear easy-access underwear." She flung the Speedo right at my head, and I dodged. "Or better yet, go commando."

"So full of talk."

"Oh, I'm making it happen. Just you wait."

But for the moment, we had an agenda to follow, and I would have protested the goddamn agenda were I not the person who had created the shitty thing in the first place.

Chapter 20
Mia

"**M**AKING IT HAPPEN" WAS EASIER SAID THAN done. What I'd realized hours ago, after the sailboat tour of the bay—and what Adam was coming to realize only now, in the middle of the rehearsal dinner—was that the day before a destination wedding, the bride and groom are *never* left alone. It was like some secret, unwritten rule.

For all that they'd be bending over backward to give us our privacy on our wedding night and during our honeymoon, our friends and family were having none of it right now.

The girls wanted to get together for appetizers before the rehearsal. The guys had made it to the bar for beers and dude talk—which apparently included a surprise dunk of the groom in a hotel swimming pool.

Fortunately, he'd been able to change into dry clothes quickly, so that he wasn't dripping all over the wedding rehearsal. Afterward came the quiet, intimate rehearsal dinner with our tiny wedding party: Heath, Jordan, my mom, Peter, and the two of us.

The good part? Dinner was intimate and quiet and really rather nice.

The bad part? Dinner was intimate and quiet and nearly impossible to slip away from long enough to go have a quickie in the bathroom.

While we awaited dessert, Adam nudged me hard under the table and began to excuse himself for a restroom break. I folded my napkin, planning to follow suit when Peter stopped Adam, saying he was about to make a toast to us.

Well, shit. How could we miss that?

With a stony face, Adam raced off to the bathroom and returned in a few minutes. His dark eyes found mine, and I shrugged at him. Despite his grumpiness, he looked good tonight, even with the last-minute clothing change. His dark, damp hair had been slicked back, and he was freshly shaved. He wore a light blue, exquisitely tailored button-down shirt, chinos, and deck shoes.

I smoothed my cute floral cotton frock across my lap, all too aware of the barely there, "easily accessible" panties I'd worn underneath. All he had to do was stared at me, like he was doing now, and they grew damp. I squirmed in my seat as Peter cleared his throat and took up the fresh flute of champagne the server had placed before him—as he had done with all of us.

We all mirrored his action. "Tomorrow is the first day of the rest of your lives, and this step you're taking will be the most important. Adam, I've known you your whole life, and since you were a small boy, I've watched you overcome obstacles that would have stopped men three times your age. You have grown into the strongest and most determined human being I've ever met. You're at once a man I admire and, also, part of my pride and joy. I can't tell you what it means to me to see you so happy.

Mia completes you, and everyone who knows and loves you knows that."

I stole a glance at Adam, and he was already watching me. My cheeks flamed as I suddenly felt coy and a bit ashamed of plotting our escape from these wonderful people who loved us so much. I swallowed a lump and turned my eyes back at Peter, incredibly moved.

"Mia, who'd have known that when you'd enter Adam's life, you'd change so much?" he said, taking my mom's hand with his free one. "You've made this family whole in so many ways. Like your husband-to-be, you are a fighter. You're his match in every way, and I'm certain that, together, you'll be an unstoppable force. Just remember to always talk to each other. Even when what you're talking about makes you vulnerable or afraid. Keep your hearts open to each other, but shored up against anything and anyone else that stands in your way.

"These words of advice are not so eloquent as I'd like them to be. From a humble man who has recently gotten a new lease on life. And I can't wait to see what mischief the two of you get up to. I have a feeling that, in your own ways and using your own special gifts, you're both going to change the world. To the wedding couple."

"Cheers," chimed Mom.

"To Adam and Mia!" Jordan toasted as we all sipped. Then, once we had, he added, "Damn. Topping that toast tomorrow night is going to be a bitch." We all laughed. "I guess 'Down the hatch, grab some snatch' is out?"

"Unless you want your ass handed to you," replied Adam, mildly amused. The rest of us snickered.

When we stood, Mom came around the table, kissed and hugged Adam, and then turned to me. "Have a great night, baby girl. You're going to be a beautiful bride tomorrow. I can't wait." She held my face in her hands and kissed both cheeks, tears brimming her eyes.

"Thanks, Mom," I whispered.

Adam's hand was on my elbow, steering me toward the way out. He whispered in my ear, "We have time to hit the suite before—"

As we exited the restaurant, there stood the group of girls— Alex, Jenna, April, and Kat, with Heath in tow. They pounced. "This is a bride-napping. She's ours tonight."

Adam's hand tightened on my elbow, telling me he wasn't about to give up when we were so close to our goal.

I faked a big ol' yawn. "I'm, um, feeling really tired. Thought I'd go get some beauty sleep."

Kat's eyes narrowed. "You can sleep in tomorrow. The wedding isn't till sunset. C'mon. You two are going to be stuck alone together for the next three weeks. This is your last chance for girl time."

Stuck with Adam alone for the next three weeks sounded like heaven to me.

"We have to go over some important paperwork," Adam bullshitted. Was that his new euphemism for hot monkey sex now—*paperwork?*

Kat scoffed at him. "You're totally going to shag her. Don't think I don't see through that. Back off, dude."

Adam stiffened next to me, and I could feel the frustration running off him in waves. I turned to Kat. "Give us a sec?"

I pulled Adam aside and hugged him, kissing his cheek. "I think we'll have to save the consummation for our wedding night."

His gaze hardened and flicked to the side. He was trying to curb the feeling and go with the flow, but it wasn't going so well. "You know, for two people bound to 'change the world,' we sure are having an inordinately difficult time sneaking off for a few minutes to hook up. This is ridiculous."

I put my hand on his smooth cheek. "Think how amazing it will be tomorrow. And—uh oh, I see Jordan loitering at your six o'clock. I bet he's going to drag you off for some guy time." I put my arms around his neck and kissed him soundly. "Now go. Have a few drinks. Have fun with the guys."

"I want to have fun with *you*." His arms encircled my waist. "Alone time fun."

I smiled. "Unless you've packed our mystery honeymoon with an obnoxious schedule, consider that our preferred activity for the next three weeks."

Stepping away, I released his hand and followed the girls out. We climbed to the topmost deck of the resort. There, beside a shimmering azure pool and our own private bar, we had our girl time. People grouped up in clumps, and I flitted from one to the next with a drink in my hand, taking care not to have too much. While they all got smashed, I was only pleasantly tipsy. Perhaps I'd be able to slip away and find my groom tonight after all.

In fact, I was scoping out a possible escape route on the back stairway when I ran into a couple ferociously sucking face.

Stumbling, I stepped backward up the stairs, but they heard me, pulling away from each other. When the light hit them, I let out a breath. "Get a room," I told Jenna and William with maybe more snark than was necessary. Well, at least *someone* was getting some action tonight.

"We have a room," William replied happily. Jenna's cheeks were flushed, her blouse untucked—as if he'd had his hands up her shirt. His shirt was halfway unbuttoned. I cleared my throat and averted my gaze as they made themselves decent.

"Maybe you should use it, then," I grumbled.

Jenna came up the stairs with a radiant smile on her face, and William abashedly followed her. "This setting and all these wedding events are so damn romantic. And you two are such an awesome couple. Let's just say we were overcome, victims to passion," Jenna beamed.

William frowned at her overdramatic, and somewhat comical, admission. I counted at least three hickeys on his neck. *Damn, Jenna..."overcome" or 'in heat'?* If it were anyone else, I would have pointed them out for optimal mocking purposes, but I could only imagine how much that would mortify William.

"I can't wait to see you in your dress tomorrow. You are going to be the most beautiful bride. This wedding is going to be *unforgettable*." Jenna hugged me then stepped aside. She was not entirely sober and wobbled where she stood. Fortunately, William *was* entirely sober. He put a large hand on her tiny waist to steady her.

Then he turned to me, and, to my surprise, he bent and kissed my cheek. "I'd say 'Welcome to the family,' but you're already my stepsister, so that isn't necessary." I laughed—I couldn't help it. William, as impeccably logical as always. "But I'm so glad that Adam is finally getting married. If anyone needed to find the right partner, it was him. And you are definitely the perfect one for him."

"Thank you, William. Maybe *you two* are next."

William turned and gazed at Jenna, who appeared flummoxed. "Maybe we are."

I leaned forward and returned William's kiss on the cheek, and the two of them headed up to the deck to sit beside Alex at the poolside. The darkened stairway was now free and clear and led straight down to the walkway in front of my room.

I sent Adam a few texts, letting him know what I was planning. He didn't immediately reply, which led me to believe that the guys had him tied up. I was determined that if I had to make like a ninja and kidnap him from his bachelor gathering, I'd do it to get him alone for thirty measly minutes.

Those best-laid plans, however, were blown out of the water when I encountered Heath. He wasn't far from the darkened stairway, lying alone on a lounge chair and staring up at the stars with a half-empty bottle of beer in his hand.

I walked over to check on him.

Without looking at me, he said, "You should make a run for it now, so you can hook up with him before midnight."

"How did you know we were trying to hook up?" I sat beside him on the lounge.

"Because it's your wedding and you haven't seen each other in almost two weeks? Two plus two is always four, doll."

I reached out a hand and smoothed his rumpled hair. He closed his eyes and turned his head toward me. Pulling my hand away, I put it on his chest. "If I could make any wish at all right now, I'd wish for a way to mend your broken heart."

His free hand went on top of mine, and he smiled sadly. "Time will do the magic you seek. It always does."

I blinked back the sudden urge to shed tears. "Heath, you deserve to be happy."

He shrugged. "We don't always get what we deserve. If we did, Miley Cyrus would be arrested for her crimes against fashion. But...it does my heart good to see that *you* are getting what you deserve. May he always make you as happy as he does today."

I bent down on the lounge, giving him a big hug and laying my head on his chest. "Who'd have thought we'd end up on such adventures, huh? To think it all started with me roping you into helping me with that crazy virginity auction."

"It's been a wild ride," he agreed.

"Thank you for being the bestest friend a girl could have."

"Dollface, for you, I couldn't have been anything less." He stroked my hair, and we stayed like that for a long time.

But before I could make my getaway to the stairs, the girls found me, wanting more drinks, more chat, more prying of the details of tomorrow's ceremony. It took me an hour to beg off. By that time, it was simply too late in the evening to find Adam. In any case, they all walked me to the door of my room as if we were enacting some ancient bridal ritual. "We posted Heath as a lookout to make sure the groom isn't lurking around the corner. Don't want any bad luck," Kat said.

"I think she's safe to see him before midnight. We have forty-five minutes till then. But she should definitely not see him after that until the ceremony tomorrow. That's some seriously bad juju." Alex nodded.

"Not even a goodnight kiss?" I pouted. Eighteen hours. I only had eighteen hours left as a single person, and the one person I wanted to see and spend time with most was being barred from kissing me goodnight.

"*No*," insisted Kat. "Keep that man far away. You'll have plenty of time together soon. You don't want to screw it all up with bad luck. Okay, girls, line up and give the bride your advice and best wishes."

And as if they were forming a line waiting for the hopscotch court in grade school, all the women complied. I stood before the door to my room, and one by one, they approached with their kernels of wisdom.

April stumbled up on her heels and took both my hands in hers, looking into my eyes solemnly. "My advice is...always use lube if he wants to go in the back door," she slurred, punctuating with a hiccup.

My jaw dropped before I started laughing hysterically. I muttered that someone had better make sure she returned safely to her room, because she was tanked. *Lucky Jordan.* At least someone would be getting some hot monkey sex tonight, provided she didn't pass out.

Jenna came next, kissing my cheek and murmuring, "Rumi said that lovers don't finally find one another. They are in each other all along. You and Adam have been eternally circling one another and have finally drawn into each other's orbits." She placed her hands on my cheeks. "May that gravity hold you together forever."

I thanked her with a hug, vowing to aim my bouquet at her tomorrow.

Next was Katya's turn. She gave me a bear hug before whispering in my ear, "May all your pain be champagne and all your tears be tears of joy."

I frowned at her. "You stole that from a greeting card, didn't you?"

"Totally." She nodded.

Alex stepped up last and dramatically threw her arms around my neck. She spoke to me in melodically lilting Spanish. "*Que seas bendecido con la fuerza, la compasión, la fe, y sobre todo el amor profundo que dura.*" She smiled. "It's a Mexican wedding prayer."

I returned the smile and kissed her cheek. "Thanks, *guapa.*"

I waved my key card in front of the lock, and the light went green. The girls turned to leave as soon as I opened the door and stepped inside.

"Goodnight," I called down the hallway to them. Glancing down at my phone to check for any replies to my "goodnight" text to Adam, I was disappointed when I saw none. Maybe he would swing by and say goodnight in person after all? It *was* only eleven-thirty.

But there definitely would be no "one for the road" illicit hookup. My easy-access lacy panties had been for naught.

Damn. I still had a raging case of the hornies.

Sighing, I crossed the room toward the bed in order to flip on the bedside lamp. It was a temporary disappointment, really. In less than twenty-four hours, we'd hopefully be retiring to our honeymoon suite to kick off our own private sex-fest as man and wife. Could. *Not.* Wait. Hopefully the honeymoon afterward involved going somewhere with no cell phones, no computers and no—

Before I could reach the bed, movement in the dark near the bathroom almost stopped my heart. What the—fuck?

"Hello? Who's there?" I called, taking a step toward the door. The shadow moved, again—*very quickly*. I only knew a few people who moved that fast.

The figured approached, and I sucked in a breath of shock. Backing against the door, I opened my mouth to scream, but a hand smothered my cry. I saw his face and smelled him at the same time.

I reached up and slapped Adam's face.

"Ow. Shit. What was that for?" he whispered harshly.

"For scaring the crap out of me!"

"Sorry...I was trying to be sneaky. Jordan kept trying to keep me longer for 'one last night of hellraising.' I tried to find April to get her to distract him."

"She's shitfaced. It wouldn't have worked."

"I'm not interested in raising hell with Jordan. I'm going to raise it with *you*..." Suddenly, his hands were all over me in the dark. "I think you and I have some...unfinished business, don't you?" His mouth devoured my ear as his hard body smashed mine against the door. Every point, from my neck to my nipples to the place between my legs, pulsed with sexual excitement.

His mouth covered mine, his thumbs already working diligently to tease my nipples to taut points through the thin material of my dress. "You've gotta go..." I mumbled only semi-committedly when his mouth freed mine in order to speak.

"What?" he protested, refusing to remove his mouth from my skin, kissing his way down my throat.

I swallowed. *Hard.* His hands and mouth were turning me into molten goo. "It's almost midnight."

"Is your carriage about to turn into a pumpkin, Cinderella?" Now his palms were rubbing across my breasts, his touch deeper, more insistent. More convincing. Oh yeah, he knew exactly what he was doing. And *I* knew that it wouldn't be easy to convince him otherwise. I closed my eyes as his hands slid lower.

"It's almost our wedding day," I rasped as his hand cupped the inside of my bare thigh.

"I'm well aware..."

"Are you?" I questioned archly. "'Cause you almost missed it. I almost had to find a stand-in so you could marry me by proxy."

"I wouldn't have missed it if my plane were on fire."

"Well, unfortunately, you got here too late for us to catch up on fooling around before the wedding." His mouth had not stopped sliding across my skin. Now his tongue was lining the inside of my collarbone and simultaneously turning my bones to jelly. "I'm afraid all future conjugal relations will have to be within the bounds of marriage rather than illicit fornication."

His mouth found the spot below my ear—that spot he knew drove me insane. My toes curled of their own accord. "What?" he asked. "We've got eighteen hours till the wedding. We can do a *lot* in eighteen hours."

"We're getting married at sunset. We're not allowed to see each other on our wedding day until we're at the ceremony."

He huffed. "Silly superstitions."

"*Adam.*" I nudged him. "You're going to make marks on my neck. I can't have hickeys in my wedding pictures."

"That's what makeup is for," he replied without budging, continuing to nip at my throat.

"Adam—"

He pulled back a few inches to look into my face. When he spoke, it was in his stern, take-command-of-the-room CEO tone as we stood nose to nose. "I have not had sex with you in almost two months. I'm not waiting any longer. This has been ridiculous."

"The universe has conspired against us, it's true." I sighed. "But hey, we're here. We're almost married. We'll have one hell of a wedding night—*tomorrow.*"

"We sure will," he persisted as he unbuttoned the top button at the front of my dress.

"Adam, I said *tomorrow* night."

"I heard you. Tomorrow night. And...now."

I opened my mouth to protest, and he plucked another button open. "I don't just want it. I *need* it. I need to have sex with you right now. It's a serious health concern."

I started laughing. "You're not going to die from blue balls. You've survived it before."

He didn't reply as he plucked the third button open and promptly shoved his entire hand inside my dress.

"You're staring at me like I'm a steak, drooling like a starving wolf."

"I *am* a starving wolf. Watch me howl, baby."

Now both hands were inside my dress, and he was not letting up. "Adam, you're going to jinx the wedding if you don't leave. We aren't supposed to see each other on our wedding day. It's going to be twelve a.m. in a few minutes."

"You've known me for a total of three years now," he said, his voice dark with determination and desire, with a husky edge on it that made every nerve inside my body sing with pleasure and anticipation. Clearly, he could tell that my heart wasn't in this protest. "As well as you know me, do you think there's a chance in hell I'm going to give up this plan?"

"This *nefarious* plan."

"Nefarious or not, you have to admit I'm tenacious."

"Oh, yes. No one would criticize that description of you. But we should be saving all this for the wedding night. Abstinence, remember? Consummating the marriage on the wedding night and all that good, old-fashioned stuff?"

"Oh, there'll be plenty left for our wedding night, believe me." He took me by the wrist and pressed my hand to his ready erection as if to prove his point. My hand molded around his shaft, stroking him through his pants. He hissed out a breath. "And for the entire honeymoon, for that matter. I won't have done my job right if you're still able to walk normally at the end of our honeymoon."

I laughed. "You're setting the bar very high for yourself."

He was kissing me again, his hands stroking across my breasts, and I was aflame, smoldering and combusting from the inside out.

"Dammit, Adam. It's almost midnight..."

"Emilia..."

"I'm still not convinced."

He stiffened and then stepped away to regard me calmly. "Okay," he replied in a flat voice. I raised my brows, shocked—and disappointed—that he'd given up so easily. Opening my mouth to reply, I was cut off when he interrupted me again. He turned and walked toward the bathroom. "I'll be right back."

I shrugged, laughing. "When you gotta go, ya gotta go. Remember not to look at me on your way out."

I walked over to the dresser, setting my phone down, checking the time—ten minutes until midnight. I yelled, "It's ten till. Don't take too long."

"Yeah, yeah," he answered before shutting the door.

I puzzled at that, moving to a drawer to grab a sleep shirt. My fancy lingerie was all ready to go for tomorrow night, but he wasn't going to see me in it until we were official. That was being saved for my wedding night surprise. No doubt that would be eclipsed by whatever stunt he had up his sleeve for the honeymoon.

I turned toward the bed, facing away from the rest of the room and unbuttoned the rest of my dress, choosing to wait until he left to take it off. It would definitely be better not to wave my naked body at him like a red cape in front of a bull. In the state he was in, he'd charge, probably with steam coming out of his nostrils, too. I snickered at the thought of the horny bull charging. Beast mode fiancé indeed. Poor guy was so randy he was probably going to get blisters on his hand from wanking tonight.

I made a mental note to save that joke as a parting taunt on his way out the door. Suddenly, the toilet flushed, the faucet turned on then off, and the door opened. I kept my back to him as he re-entered the room.

"It's five minutes to midnight," he muttered when he stopped.

I remained facing away from him. "Yeah...so goodnight. Love you. Sleep well."

"The rule is that we're not supposed to see each other, right?"

I hesitated. His voice sounded weird, like he was trying to suppress amusement. *Like he was planning something.* I shifted from one leg to the other. "Uh...yeah."

He started walking again slowly, and I let out a breath of relief—until I realized that he wasn't moving toward the door.

He stopped when he was right behind me. I could feel his breath on the back of my neck. Trembling, I tilted my head to the side, listening. He whispered, "I have five minutes."

I swallowed. "But you can't do anything in five minutes. So scram."

He wrapped his strong fingers tightly around my right wrist. When he spoke, his mouth was at my ear, breath creating tingles that cascaded like a waterfall down my spine. This power over me was real, and he knew exactly how to wield it. "*I'll* be the judge of how much I can get accomplished in five minutes." He looped something around the wrist he held. *What the—*

"Adam, what the hell are you doing?"

He didn't answer as he grabbed my other wrist, pulling both of my hands over my head.

"Will you please stop fucking around?" I snapped in irritation. He was making it hard enough to say no already. Adam was a patient man, most of the time, having proved that in the past. Twenty-four hours more was nothing compared to the wait he'd already endured

"Oh, there *will* be lots of fucking around in here shortly."

"It's got to be midnight right now," I said, but let him continue his charade of tying me up. But when he cinched my wrists together, he pulled tight enough to pinch the skin, like he meant business. He was taking this joke a wee bit too far.

"Adam—"

"I told you I wasn't giving up." He leaned down and sucked my lobe into his hot mouth until I shuddered with delight. Then he pulled away again. "Have you *ever* known me to be a person to give up? Even when asked nicely? *Especially* when asked nicely." Suddenly, he hooked an arm around my waist, nudging me toward the closet door.

"No." My heartbeat accelerated in anticipation.

He pressed my back to the closet door and ran his eyes down the length of me. "Oh. You unbuttoned the rest of your dress. That was nice of you. I won't have to rip it now. It's a hot dress. Not as hot as what's inside it, of course."

He looped the strap, which he'd apparently pulled off one of the cotton dressing robes that hung in the bathroom, up over the door of the closet, wedging it in the doorjamb. My hands were thus suspended above my head.

"Okay, you've had your laugh. Ha ha. Now let's—" I moved against the door to try to yank my hands out from where they were tied. They didn't budge. Shit…how did he do that so easily? "I unbuttoned the dress because I was getting ready for bed—not to do you any favors."

"A happy coincidence, then." He scooted the dress so that it was now wide open, and all I had on underneath was a lacy bra and the aforementioned easy-access panties. With one quick flick of his wrist, the bra snapped open from the front. He unhooked the removable straps, and it fell to the floor.

"You need to go now." I tried hard to make my voice sound as stern as I could.

He nodded, looking at his watch. "It's eleven fifty-eight. I have two minutes."

I heaved an impatient sigh. "*What* are you doing?"

He reached up and stroked my nipple again, smiling with satisfaction as it beaded instantly under his touch. "We are in the Caribbean, aren't we? I'm a pirate, and you are my captive wench." I couldn't help it. Despite my irritation at this moment,

I found him too adorable with that gleam in his dark eyes. He was quite pleased with himself. And when he punctuated his declaration with a hearty "*Arrrrrr!*" I burst out laughing.

"Okay, you've had your fun. Now get out of here. It's, like, thirty seconds to midnight."

"Tsk, tsk." He shook his head. "I cannot do that, Miss Cinderella. *Shiver me timbers.*" He walked over to the dressing table where the hotel had left me a first-class basket of supplies and started to rifle through it, grabbing things and putting them in his pocket while muttering about "plunder."

"According to you and some supposed wedding rules committee, we aren't supposed to see each other on our wedding day before the ceremony."

I leaned my head back against the closet door with a weary sigh. "Yes."

"And our wedding day starts at midnight, correct?"

I sighed again, heavily. "Now you're being a pest."

"A pest, you say?" He moved to the lamp I'd switched on and flicked it off, throwing the room into darkness once again.

"A pirate pest, yes."

"I was going to tell you that I have devised an ingenious solution."

I rolled my eyes. "Because—of course you have."

He spun, approaching until he stood right in front of me, bending to kiss me on the lips before slipping a sleep mask over my head. He pulled it down to cover my eyes so I couldn't see anything.

"Is that comfortable?"

"Adam, what—"

"Can you see?"

"No. But that only solves half the problem, because *you* can."

"I have another one here." He tugged my mask up so I could see. He slipped an identical sleep mask over his head and pulled it over his eyes. Then he reached over and drew mine back down.

"Great, now we're both blind. This is going to be a comedy of errors."

"No way. It will help us appreciate our other senses...like our sense of touch." He reached up and trailed a light, tantalizing caress of two fingers from my collarbone, down across my breast with the slight edge of his nail. I jumped. "And smell." He buried his mouth and nose into my neck, opening his mouth to kiss it. I shivered, and he groaned in response.

"Hearing." He tilted his mouth to my ear. "I'm going to fuck you, Emilia. And tonight, all night, it's all you're going to feel, and you'll be begging for more."

His hot breath on my ear and the promise in his words made me waver against him.

"And..." His hand closed around my panties, and he gave them a healthy yank right at the seam, shredding them in a classic Adam Drake move. I gasped as he pulled my panties away. Aside from the open dress hanging on my shoulders, I was naked.

"Of course, there's *taste...*" I listened as he lowered to his knees. One hand separated my knees in order to open my legs. There, he pressed his face to the apex of my thighs. "Mmmm," he said. "Delicious. Best midnight snack ever."

His tongue snaked out and slid along the seam of my sex, pressing against my clit. I jumped as if jolted by an electric shock.

"Oh God." I gasped. This only seemed to encourage him, as he continued, pressing my legs farther apart.

"You don't want me to untie you?"

"I never said that."

"So you do?"

"I never said that, either."

He laughed and leaned forward again, continuing to tantalize me with his tongue.

"Tell me to untie you and let you go, and I will. But don't worry about us seeing each other before the wedding, because I sure as hell can't see a goddamn thing."

"I'm, uh"—*gasp*—"quite sure, oh." *God.* "Um, that...that...ah. That's not what they meant."

"Whoever they were hadn't been sexually deprived for over two months, I'm sure."

"Jeez, Adam. This isn't fair."

"You said you wanted to be ravished, didn't you? So are you going to stand there and whine about me using your own body against you, or are you going to relax and enjoy it?"

I stayed silent, concentrating on the sensations of his fingers, which he had gently slipped into me when he'd pulled away to talk. He hadn't replaced his mouth on the magic spot, though, and my entire body was throbbing and thrumming and demanding it.

"Well?" he asked when I didn't answer him.

"I'm thinking. I'm thinking!"

"Okay. Well, while you're thinking about it, I'm gonna go back to what I was doing." Then he paused. "Oh, I almost forgot...I had these in my pocket."

"What?"

"Complimentary breath mints." Then there was loud crunching and chewing and the sudden, strong smell of mint. "A whole bunch of them." I stiffened, remembering hearing that

Altoids mints were used to enhance the sensations of oral sex—as if I needed any enhancement at this point.

When his tongue reconnected with my clit, I jumped like I'd been shocked by sensations of hot and cold at the same time. Frosty heat. I shivered and instinctively moved away. With his hands on my hips, he pinned me to the door, continuing the contact. Then deepening it.

With my eyes blindfolded and my senses overwhelmed, like he'd predicted, I wasn't aware of *anything* but his mouth and his hands.

Adam licked and sucked ferociously, almost as if he were demanding my climax. And my body was more than happy to comply. In minutes, I came violently against his mouth. My head thrown back against the door, I screamed his name, my body convulsing with pure pleasure coursing through my veins.

He didn't stop.

"Please, it's too much," I slurred, barely able to form the words, as if the orgasm had fried my brain. It certainly *felt* like it had.

Slowly—too slowly—he stopped and pulled away, running his palms down my thighs repeatedly. I shuddered, overly sensitive to any touch. I almost lost my footing.

I slumped against the door, completely absorbed in my afterglow. Even as every muscle in my body relaxed and basked, a thin thread of unfulfilled desire shot through everything.

I wanted to feel Adam's weight on top of me, his body moving against mine, our sweat mingling. I wanted to feel him inside of me, filling me up, hear his groans of pleasure as he used my body for his own enjoyment. I wanted that even more than another orgasm.

I was greedy like that.

And apparently, Adam read my mind. Before another moment had passed, he opened the door, freeing the belt from the doorjamb and releasing me. My arms came down, and I stretched my shoulders, though my wrists were still tied together in front of me. Warmth flooded my arms as circulation returned.

Gently, Adam took me by the shoulder and guided me to the bed—or, at least, the direction where he suspected the bed was. His steps were halting, like he was trying to find his way in the dark.

And without too much difficulty, he found it, nudging me to lie down. "So if I said *no* right now..." I teased.

"Of course I'd leave," he replied. "But I wouldn't be happy about it."

"It's not my job to make you happy...yet."

"A happy groom makes a happy wedding." He adjusted a pillow to slip under my head as he grabbed the rope around my wrists and pulled it above my head to fasten it against the headboard.

"Afraid I'm going to run away?"

"Nope, but a good pirate always hedges his bets. I'm going to have my way with you."

"And what if I said I needed my beauty sleep?"

He ran a hand over my breasts as if to reassure himself that they were still there. "You can sleep in. We're not getting married till six."

"You've got an answer for everything." I listened while he took off his clothes—quickly—letting them drop to the ground wherever. "I don't think, in all the time that I've known you, I've ever known you take off your clothes so fast."

"I'm highly motivated," he replied. "I have a gorgeous, naked woman tied up in my bed. What better incentive is that?"

I laughed until he sank down on the bed beside me before gently rolling onto me. Then my laughter was swallowed in a gasp of renewed desire.

When he spoke again, his mouth was a fraction of an inch from mine, every inch of his naked flesh branding and fusing against mine. "Do you know what bed this is?"

I smiled, knowing full well what bed this was, but I played along. "What bed is this?"

"This is the bed where I first made you mine." His mouth sealed over my lips, and my entire body—until that moment content to bask and glow and wallow—ignited once again. Smoldering arousal burst into flame, Adam the consummate fire starter.

"Is that what you were doing?" I answered when my mouth was free again. "I thought you were proving a point. Yet again."

"I was doing that, too." He shifted against me. "But most importantly, I was making you mine. Forever."

"Funny, isn't that what you are going to do tomorrow—I mean, later today?"

He kissed along my jaw. "That's the official version. But think it's fitting that our last night as unmarried people we spend fucking like bunnies in the same bed where I first had you."

"Fucking like bunnies, huh?"

"Don't plan on sleeping much tonight." He pushed my legs open.

The next sound was the crinkle of a foil packet—that packet which we had so felt the lack of this afternoon in the cabana— and I sucked in a breath as he entered me with a satisfied sigh.

288 | BRENNA AUBREY

My heart raced in my throat as I felt the familiar stretch of my muscles around his welcome invasion of my body. He placed a long, gentle kiss against my throat.

"Fucking *finally*. The *Eagle* has landed."

"Is that what we are calling it now? The *Eagle?*"

"I promise you that after tonight you will be calling it Robocock—and enthusiastically so."

"I hope you're prepared to put your money where your mouth is."

He shifted, slipping deeper inside of me. "I'm putting my mouth everywhere tonight. Just you wait."

And then he started to move. And my world shifted with him. For it being the first time in months, it wasn't frenzied and hurried, as I'd suspected it might be. Though I knew Adam was anxious to resume our sex life and enjoy himself again, he didn't floor it all the way to the finish, though I would have completely understood if he had.

Instead, he moved carefully, slowly, as if knowing anything faster would make it too short this first time. He was savoring the journey rather than pushing straight to the end.

When he stopped, dipping his head to suck on my nipple, I arched to meet him, wrapping my legs tightly around his hips. "God, you feel so good," I muttered.

He pulled himself free of my hold, his breath ragged. And suddenly his rhythm was wobbly, as if he'd expended the last ounce of his control.

That was when he pushed hard, driving himself directly to the end.

His body stiffened. He held his breath. I again wrapped my legs around his hips, tightening the hold, and he shuddered against me then came. A moment later, he pressed a clammy forehead to mine.

"Goddamn," he finally mumbled. "That was..." He gasped. "If my spleen exploded, that was definitely worth it."

I couldn't help laughing. "No, that was *other* parts of your body exploding."

"The good parts." He slid off me to roll back to his side of the bed. But not before kissing me all over my face. "I think those parts of my body want to explode a few more times."

"*Tonight?*"

"Tonight's the night."

"You're going to have to convince me of that."

"Happily," he said, running his hands over my chest and belly as if reading every inch of them by touch. I was a map, and his hands were awestruck, reverential explorers. His boundless energy would have him exploring every inch of my terrain tonight.

Chapter 21
Adam

THE SECOND TIME WAS ROUGHER—AND LONGER. AND oh-my-God amazing.

I'd heard that a man's most reliable sense for sexual arousal was sight. Yet I couldn't see her. But I could not have been more aroused, having to work my way around that soft, supple feminine body with my hands, my mouth, my body pressed to hers.

She was still tied up—though this time to the high post at the foot of the bed, standing up. God, I vowed to tie her up more often, because this was fun. And damned straight if I was going to have my way with her now that I had her right where I wanted her.

"These last two months have been torture." I breathed into her hair at the back of her head as I stood behind her, drunk on her scent. "Sadistic doctor's orders."

"And I'm sure that's exactly why she did it, too, to torture you." There was laughter in her voice.

I nuzzled her neck. "I was talking about *you*. Walking around my house in those lace panties, those tight leggings, driving me insane."

"Because depriving myself of sex was a whole lot of fun for me," she refuted.

"Maybe I need payback. A little torture to get even."

She paused. "*Torture?*"

I pressed myself against her back, sandwiching her between my body and the bedpost, pushing my erection against her firm, perfect ass. I sank my teeth lightly into the shell of her ear. She sucked in a breath. "Maybe *more* than a little."

Pushing away from her, I turned away to guarantee I wouldn't see her. I had to honor that promise to her, after all— silly superstition or not.

I made my way over to the ice bucket, where a bottle of champagne rested in a pile of fresh ice, replaced with the evening bed turn-down service. *Perfect.*

Grabbing the ice bucket and removing the bottle, I backed toward the bed until I was almost there, replacing the blindfold over my eyes before I turned and made my way to her.

"Right where I left you," I said and landed a kiss between her delectable shoulder blades. "Good girl."

"How was I going to go anywhere?"

I bent and placed the ice bucket on the ground near her feet. "Good point." Grabbing a piece of ice, I straightened. "Now that I got that first one out of my system, at least I can wait a little while till next time."

She cleared her throat. "And when are we supposed to sleep?"

"Sleep is overrated." I took the ice cube and placed it on that spot between her shoulder blades where I'd kissed her.

She jumped and then gasped. "What the—"

But I grabbed her chin, turning her face toward me, muffling her protest, plunging my tongue into her mouth. I dragged that ice cube along her collarbone, over her breastbone, down to her navel as she stiffened in my arms, her body rigid against mine.

It felt goddamn fucking fantastic.

Her arms were tied to the bedpost at the foot of the bed. When I brought that ice cube up to her right nipple, she struggled, but couldn't evade me.

When I finally figured she'd be quiet enough, I freed her mouth from that kiss. "You okay?"

"I will be after I put ice all over *you*," she replied breathily.

I flipped her around to face me, settling her against the bedpost. "We'll see about that. In the meantime, I think the other one needs some love." I moved the ice cube to her other nipple while bending to take the cold one in my mouth. She wiggled and struggled, and I held her against the bedpost to keep her stable.

I was so hard again that it was painful. Her ice-cold nipple warmed in my mouth. *So* refreshing—my own Emilia-flavored popsicle. I laughed at the thought, and once I determined that her other nipple was ready for my mouth, I switched what I was doing, replacing the ice cube on the previous nipple. It was freezing my finger soundly with that painful numbness of cold. These incredibly sensitive parts of *her* body surely felt the numbness and pain acutely.

She was breathing hard, giving me these haunting moans that were almost muted, her voice slightly deeper than normal.

I dropped the ice cube into the bucket and slid my cold fingers into the warmest place I could find—right between her legs.

She inhaled sharply and stiffened again as I worked my fingers against her wet, hot flesh. I could barely restrain myself from pushing her legs apart right that second and getting inside her. Instead, I plunged my fingers deeper, listening carefully,

294 | BRENNA AUBREY

trying to determine how close she was by the sound of her moans and her breath. So close. *Close,* but not all the way.

"Adam," she said in that low growl that made my cock twitch in response. And seconds later, I pulled my hand away. She blew out a breath, shifting from one tiptoe to the other. "So *that's* how it's going to be?"

"Yup," I replied, smiling though she couldn't see me. "You owe me some torture."

"Just you wait. I'll be turning your own tools against you, Dread Pirate Drake."

"Arrrrrr. Will you, now? That's not happening tonight, my little wench. Tonight, *I'm* in charge." I grabbed her hips and yanked her toward me so that she was off balance—and even more under my control.

I reached up and raked my fingernails down her back with both hands, all the way down past her waist and over the curve of her ass. She hissed like a cat.

"Tomorrow, you'll be my blushing bride, and I will worship you, body, and soul. But tonight, you are my plaything."

"You are a bad man," she whispered hoarsely.

"*Pirate.*" I laughed. "You haven't seen a damn thing yet, Miss Strong." And to punctuate my statement, I firmly pinched her nipples before working them between my thumb and forefingers until they were large, hard points and she was groaning low in her throat. That sound vibrated right through me and made me throb, head to toe. The tension in my cock bordered on painful.

I bent forward, catching her mouth with mine, smothering her moans. Her teeth came down, sinking firmly into my lip.

I retreated, my lip still between her teeth. "Not the face!" I rasped. "We can't do anything that affects wedding pictures tomorrow."

Haltingly, she released my lip. It throbbed, mingling pain and pleasure. This was supposed to be a torture for her, but instead, I was the one doubting I could take any more before I took *her* again.

Jesus, she was too goddamn sexy. Without warning, I picked her up, slipping her tied wrists off the bedpost. Pulling her against me so she wouldn't fall off balance, I held her as her body went slack. Her hard nipples and supple breasts pressed against my chest. My heart thumped in double time.

"Your plaything, huh?" she asked.

I closed in, my lips hovering over hers. "Yeah."

Then I did the next thing very carefully, knowing there was a possibility, because of her past, that she might have problems with it. I pressed down on her shoulders until her legs bent and she was kneeling in front of me.

There was no hesitation, much to my surprise. The minute she hit her knees, she leaned forward and caught my cock in her mouth, sucking in only the tip before pulling away again.

Then she was moving around, reaching for something with her bound hands. I heard her nudge the metal ice bucket. *Uh oh...*

"Clearly, I should have tied your hands behind your back instead of your front."

"You need to brush up on your pirate training." She started crunching ice cubes in her mouth. When I tried to retreat, she hooked a hand around my leg to stop me.

After swallowing, she then grabbed more ice and crunched that as well. When her mouth took me in again, ice cold enveloped my heat. *And* she had ice chips still inside of her mouth. And—*shit*—it felt...incredible. Pain and pleasure mingled on the most sensitive part of my anatomy. I reached out to brace myself against the same bedpost in order to keep my knees from buckling. Her mouth slid farther down my shaft, taking me deeper. I growled, allowing the feeling to overpower me as she sucked me—*hard.*

Christ. She was getting *really* good at this. You'd never know that it was far from her favorite thing to do.

It didn't matter. Because with each movement of her head, she was seizing control of this situation, and she damn well knew it.

And I was letting her.

Because the thought of coming in her mouth right now held more than a little appeal. More than a *lot* of appeal. I slid a hand down to gently touch the back of her head, and she froze.

I didn't push it. But damn if I didn't want to. I wanted to cram it down her throat.

I restrained myself.

Barely.

It took a fuckton of willpower. She didn't move her head, though her sinful tongue continued to swirl around me, twining heat up every nerve ending from where her scorching mouth sucked me, all through my tight gut, the blood scalding my veins.

She seemed to be enjoying this power—her low moans responded directly to my rushed breathing. And that was when I decided that I couldn't take it a second longer.

I gently applied pressure to her head, pushing her toward me. Her head only gave an inch before she stopped again, holding fast to her position. I thrust my hips forward, suddenly losing control.

And that was my mistake.

Her body buckled when she gagged. I pulled out immediately, ready to untie her, ready to kneel down and comfort her, apologize.

She was doubled over, coughing.

Oh shit. I'd gone too far.

I was shocked to hear her laughing. *Laughing.*

"*What* is so fucking funny?"

"I can't stop thinking about that ridiculous name—robot cock. It distracted me and I gagged."

"*Robo*cock," I corrected. "And that was feeling good, goddamn it. You're naughty"

She let loose a long, melodramatic sigh. "I guess I am a naughty girl." The dare in her voice was unmistakable.

I reached down, grabbed her knotted wrists, and jerked her off her knees to stand in front of me. Then I bent so that we were nose to nose—or, at least, I perceived that we were. I still couldn't see a goddamn thing.

"Would you like to know what I do to naughty girls?" I turned and, pulling her behind me, peeked from under the blindfold to prevent myself from bumping into furniture on the way to the dining table. I replaced the blindfold once there.

"What are you going to do?" I couldn't help but grin. She was loving this game as much as I was. *Hell yes.* "Is this where you make me walk the plank, Cap'n Drake?" She laughed.

"No walking the plank. But you'll be riding my plank soon."

"Suave," she said.

I pushed her shoulders down, pressing the upper half of her body flush against the dining table. She sucked in air, but I couldn't tell whether it was from excitement or surprise—possibly both. Grabbing the belt around her wrists, I tied it to the chair opposite where she bent.

Then I came up behind her, fondling her round ass before opening my palm and smacking it soundly. The sound alone made me throb with need.

"*Ow*," she exclaimed. "What the fuck?"

"Bad girls need spankings," I explained then punctuated it with another smack on her other cheek. I wasn't screwing around—I knew those hits had hurt. She strained against the tie, as if she wanted to stand up, and I pressed my left hand to the small of her back to hold her down.

She hissed out a breath, and every muscle in her body tensed up.

"Are you okay?" I asked.

"Do your worst," she replied between clenched teeth.

"Challenge accepted." Two more whacks . "For the shitty Speedo." She actually laughed, though it was a tight, tense one.

I rubbed her ass. The heat on her skin from my not-so-light smacks only turned me on more. She let out a long breath and then shakily took another one. I waited another minute before I spanked her twice again, making sure she was unaware it was coming and had relaxed.

"What were those for?"

"For doubting I'd get here on time. As if there was any reality where I'd miss this wedding."

A pause. "I never doubted. However, I did like to taunt you about it."

"Should I taunt you with more spanking, then?"

She took a long breath and let it go. "I'm not afraid of you."

I said nothing, but slapped her two more times. My cock throbbed with the sound of every hit.

"What were those for?" she asked, her voice quieter, more husky. But I couldn't tell if it was because she was aroused or about to cry. Maybe both.

"Those were because this is turning me on."

"You already seem to be horny to begin with."

"You can never be too aroused." I bent and kissed the back of her neck, moving my mouth all the way down her spine, aware of every minute reaction from her.

Each involuntary intake of breath, each squirm, each shiver of creamy skin under my fingertips, each reluctant but vitally necessary sigh from her mouth went straight into my blood like a glorious drug. And the feel of goosebumps across the flesh of her soft arms, her silky thighs—it made *me* shiver in anticipation. I was high from touching her, hearing the sounds of my hands smacking her ass.

Two more smacks totaled ten, and I stopped. I could tell she was trying to hide tears from me. I touched her moist cheek. "Want me to stop?"

"I want you to stop screwing around and fuck me."

I bent and kissed her tears away. They were cold and salty. "Challenge enthusiastically accepted." Stepping away from her, I turned to find my pants where I'd discarded them on the ground. There were four more condoms in the pocket—I'd been over-the-top optimistic about this evening. I bent and retrieved them, grabbed one, and put the other three on the nightstand.

Then I returned to the table where I'd left her, eyes averted until I replaced my blindfold. I tore the foil packet and put on the condom.

"Ladies and gentlemen, for the second time tonight, he has perfectly managed a condom while blindfolded. *And the crowd goes wild.*"

"Pfft. You do it in the dark all the time. No big feat."

"I've got your big feat right here," I murmured as I positioned myself behind her. She tensed with anticipation. I bent, pressing my chest to her back, kissing her cheek, her neck, her shoulders. Then, straightening, I thrust into her.

Her gasp alone almost made me come. And if I didn't slow down, this was going to be a lot of buildup for an underwhelming result. I didn't want that.

I paused, listening to her rushed breathing. "Do you know what it feels like for me to be inside you?" I asked and kissed between her shoulder blades. She tightened around me. "It feels like stepping into a warm pool when it's cold outside. It feels like a hot shower after a long day. It feels like home."

She replied with a long, low moan, and I began to move. Taking her by the hips and holding her still, I sank in as deep as I could go, listening carefully to her. After nearly two months of no sex, she was tight. She felt incredible, her muscles clenching me like a fist. My heartbeat thrummed in my throat, my mouth dry. I imagined how she must look, spread out across that table for me.

I slowed, reaching one hand underneath her where I could rub her clit and the other to tangle in her hair. Even as I pulled at her hair, jerking her head up, I was thankful that since she'd lost her hair and it had grown back, she no longer had anxiety associated with fingers—*my* fingers, at least—in her hair.

Thank God, because I loved running my hands through it.

She moaned as I brought her closer to climax. I sank my teeth into the pliant flesh under her shoulder blade.

"Don't leave a mark," she gasped.

I released her. "Way down here?"

She didn't answer, but I concluded that her wedding dress must be backless. The thoughts of seeing her in it almost did me in.

Later today... *Finally.* She'd be mine in every way.

And she was mine right now. I deepened the pressure where I rubbed her, and she rewarded me with the familiar sounds of her climax. At the end, when she said my name as a desperate plea, that was what did me in.

Only a few more thrusts and I was coming, too, in mind-blowing waves of brain-frying rapture. A full minute of my life passed where I had no awareness of anything but the pure pleasure of emptying myself into Emilia's supple, waiting body. I couldn't move. I couldn't breathe. All I could do was experience her. The feel of her beneath me, of her chest rising and falling under mine. Of her satisfied, contented moans.

I kissed her back, her shoulder blades, everywhere my mouth could reach. Then I lifted myself off her and reached to untie her wrists. She was pliant in my arms as I helped her up from the table and guided her to the bed. It took longer than normal, but when she finally lay down, she let out a hiss of a breath when her bottom hit the sheets, immediately rolling onto her side.

"Well, *that's* going to be fun...no sitting down tomorrow."

"Roll onto your stomach." I undid the tie at her wrist with a simple pull of the slipknot. Turning from the bed, I lifted the blindfold, went into the bathroom, and grabbed a towel and a bottle of pain reliever. When I returned, I dunked the towel into the melting ice bucket and wrung it out before fumbling my way toward the bed.

I put the ice-cold towel across her ass, murmuring a brief warning first. She tensed when I did it, but offered no protest. Then, after more fumbling, I gave her two pills and a bottle of water, which she leaned up to take into her mouth straight from my fingers.

Down, boy, I had to order myself when arousal flickered again from that simple action. I moved to my side of bed, and she ordered me to cover myself with a sheet so she could pull off her blindfold and use the bathroom.

I complied. When she approached the bed, she replaced her blindfold and crawled in beside me, wrapping herself around me. "You have to be gone by sunrise."

I pulled her against me. "Why?"

"So no one sees you leaving my room in the morning."

"I hate to break this to you, but all the wedding guests already know we've been sleeping together for the past two years."

"Smartass. The night before the wedding and all the bad luck and everything."

"That did *not* feel like bad luck. That felt very, *very* good."

"Adam..."

"Okay, okay, I'll be out before five. Which means I have over four more hours." I was talking big, though. I knew perfectly well I was too exhausted to go again without some rest.

She yawned, as if reading my mind. "I'm sleepy," she whispered, putting her head on my shoulder. In minutes, she was asleep, and I relished the sound of her breathing, burying my nose in her hair and drifting off into a pure, contented doze myself.

I wasn't quite sure when it started, because I was definitely asleep at first, slowly becoming aware of a warm body pressed to mine, a weight on my chest, a mouth on my mouth. I was on that twilight edge between dream and reality, not quite sure what was real and what was manufactured by my subconscious mind. But slowly, slowly, reality took hold in an almost seamless way, and everything appeared as if in a fugue.

Emilia was kissing me, straddling me.

Without even opening my eyes, I reached up, cupping her breasts, and she shivered, sliding against me. I was rock hard again and ready and had, apparently, slept through any foreplay that had taken place.

This time was slow, and it took longer—a fact that didn't bother me one bit. Emilia reached over to the nightstand and then handed me the condom, which I quickly took care of. Seconds later, I was inside her again as she rocked on top of me, her melodious moans in my ear.

I tried to take her hips and drive her movements, but Emilia shoved my hands away, bracing herself on my shoulders as she moved at a maddeningly slow pace. I hooked my hands around the back of her thighs, running my fingers along the soft skin there. We climbed slowly, together, every movement of her hips over mine taking us one step closer.

Soon, it was too much, and my hands were on her hips again, driving us toward that finish line together. This time, she didn't shove me away, her movements becoming as urgent as mine. I was close, so close when I felt her still and tighten around me with her orgasm, nudging me over the top toward mine. And we came together—pulsing, ecstatic delight washing over both of us.

She slumped immediately, sliding to her side of the bed, slick with sweat. "Whatever that was, it was fun, and you should definitely do it more often," I said.

She sighed. "I thought you were awake. You were grabbing me and muttering dirty stuff. You must have been dreaming."

"I don't remember, but I'm sure it was the best kind of dream." I kissed her temple.

We slept again, locked in each other's arms, peaceful and secure. It should feel like this every night. And yet, after all we had done together, the last thought that zinged through my mind made me feel like a kid on Christmas Eve.

When we came back to bed this evening, we'd be married.

Chapter 22
Mia

WHEN I WOKE UP, THE SKY WAS ALREADY lightening. My first awareness was of soreness, *everywhere.* Mostly in between my legs from all the sex and the use of muscles that had lain dormant for far too long. But also on my ass, where he had spanked me. And around my wrists, which had been tied together. And, of course, the raw and tender skin from where his abrasive growth of whiskers had rubbed my skin wherever he had kissed me—which was everywhere. My stomach, my breasts, the insides of my thighs. My neck. My ears. Even the small of my back had been scraped raw by his delicious, sandpapery kisses.

In short, I hurt all over, but with an exquisite sort of discomfort.

Hot desire rushed through me at the memories of last night. Or, rather, this morning. Or... I looked up and out over the bay from the open-walled suite and noted the gray sky. Hesitating as I lay on my side, I suddenly realized that my blindfold had slipped off.

Adam was still in my bed. *Shit.*

I dove under the covers, making sure my head and every part of my body was covered by sheets. Then I turned and nudged him with my leg.

"Adam."

He didn't move.

"Adam, you have to get up. It's almost dawn."

I nudged him again, harder.

"*Adam.*" I shoved him with my leg, and suddenly, he left the bed with a big thump.

"What the hell?" he said from the floor.

I winced. "Sorry, but you weren't waking up. I didn't mean to push you out. You need to go back to your room."

"Damn, a simple shake of the shoulder would have sufficed."

"I tried. I promise. You were out."

"Some hot chick wore me down to a nub last night."

"Lucky you. Now go."

"All right, all right. Jeez." I could hear him get off the floor and gather his clothes. The sound of his footsteps then faded in the direction of the bathroom.

I stayed under the covers until he returned, presumably dressed. "I'm still exhausted."

"*Well,*" I said, "all that last night was *your* idea."

"Yes. An amazing idea at that. I'm gonna go back to bed. See you at six."

"Bye. Love you."

"Love you, too," he muttered before shutting the door, and he was gone.

I lowered the sheet, glancing at the clock, aware that I'd slept a grand total of maybe three hours the night before. Wondering if I could grab a few more, I rolled over, found one of the blindfolds, and pulled it over my head.

I slept two more hours before the excitement of the day caught up to me and I just couldn't anymore. Dark circles or no, I had to get up.

Thank God for coffee. And concealer makeup.

***

The rest of the day passed in a blur of my mom and closest friends coming up to the suite. The makeup artist and hair stylist arrived and rotated among us. We shared them—along with the nervous excitement and the jokes.

I had to conceal that I was still sore from being used in the best way possible practically the entire night the night before. *Damn,* it had been hot. But hopefully, not enough to wreck my look and make me appear half dead in the wedding pictures.

Nevertheless, the stylists worked absolute magic.

My makeup had been done to flawless perfection, every blemish concealed in a natural glow. The stylist had left my dark hair flowing around my shoulders in loose curls, as I'd wanted.

And shortly before the ceremony, my mom helped me into the dress. The gorgeous garment had been altered to fit me perfectly. Mom stood behind me in the full mirror.

The gown was floor length, figure hugging, with a backless dip that draped in folds above my waist. It was adorned with tiny Swarovski crystals and trimmed with silver thread and accents.

"I've been dreaming of this day since that morning I first held you in the hospital. You were minutes old and I wanted the world for you, my beautiful Mia," she said in a trembling voice, her eyes watering.

I turned to face her, my eyes and throat stinging with emotion. "Mom, I need to ask you to stop talking like this, or I'm going to start crying and ruin this makeup."

She nodded silently, smoothing my hair and checking her watch.

A short time later, we were on the highest patio, facing west and overlooking the pointed green mountains and the aquamarine waters of the beach far below. The west patio seemed to hang off the mountain, providing a view that looked out over an infinite horizon against a champagne-colored sky. The guests sat in white linen-covered chairs on either side of an aisle, covered by gauzy awnings.

My mom and I stood at the back, hidden by a screen, awaiting our cue. When the string trio began to play Pachelbel's Canon, Mom turned and hugged me for a long time. Then we stepped out from behind the screen, and she walked with me down the aisle to my future.

One of the defining moments of a wedding is when the groom turns and turns his eyes upon his bride in her gown for the first time. There are clips and montages all over the Internet showing that moment at different weddings. Some grooms show no emotion at all, sometimes a slight change in their eyes. Others are overcome with emotion, crying to the point of doubling over.

Adam was somewhere right in the middle of those two extremes. He definitely showed emotion, but he didn't cry. He appeared more like someone had hit him violently in the stomach with a medium-sized metal club. Like he was holding his breath, though his body was screaming out for him to breathe.

Me? I totally cried. Smear-proof makeup was my friend.

And…if I'd concede any type of princess fetish, it would be that I did feel like fairytale royalty in this moment, standing here in front of all these people in my gorgeous gown in this stunning setting.

And the prince I had caught… He was beyond handsome in his black tux—with only a vest, no jacket, and a long necktie. In spite of the beard joking, he was clean-shaven, his perfect jaw and dimple revealed once more for all to see. His hair, freshly cut and styled, was combed to perfection. And yeah, dazzling as ever.

After all the buildup, the ceremony itself was rather short. We took each other's hands and said our promises in front of our family members against the backdrop of the sinking sun— the sky all afire with gold, pink, and orange streaks.

We couldn't have ordered a more beautiful sunset if we'd budgeted it in.

And yet as we were announced husband and wife, there were no rocket-generated shooting stars, though I half expected them.

Shortly thereafter, the party started. Right there. No procession out or any of that formal stuff. Because it was a small, intimate wedding, the chairs were moved to tables that were already set up. And the food was brought in.

We ate, we drank, and we danced. All with our closest loved ones.

It was the best.

I didn't think anyone suspected that the bride and groom were almost too exhausted to enjoy it.

We danced our first dance to "Wonderful! Wonderful!" by Johnny Mathis, repeating those steps to the foxtrot that he'd taught me so long ago on our first date in Amsterdam. It was hard to believe that here we were, three years later. After all we'd been through, we were finally starting our forever. *Together.*

He teased me during that dance. The one that is supposed to be so sweet and emotional, when people dab their eyes and remark on how beautiful the couple is? And then the groom holds the bride close and whispers words of love in her ear...

In my case, it was definitely teasing.

"You've got dark circles under your eyes, Mrs. Drake. Why is that? Were you up all night with some strange man?"

"Why, yes, I was. Emphasis on the *strange.*" He gave me that cocky grin that sent shivers down my spine. "You are too gorgeous for your own good," I said.

"It's definitely for my good. You should have seen the hot piece of ass I scored last night."

"Don't you mean this morning? This has been a *long* day."

"It's not over yet."

The thought made me simultaneously ache with anticipation and with exhaustion.

My wedding bouquet, white roses and white star chrysanthemums accented by silver and gold ribbons and metallic floral ornaments, was quite the prize. All the unattached females in the party gathered around to at least pretend like they wanted to catch it. Despite my best effort to launch it at Jenna, the bundle of flowers bounced off April's head and caught in Kat's hair, where it hung from the side of her long red tresses. She reached up to yank it out, clearly horrified. I assumed she wanted to rid herself of the thing, maybe pass it along to one of the more eligible women.

Much to her growing horror—and everyone else's growing amusement—the more Kat tried to yank the bouquet out of her hair, the more it wound itself around her long hair so that, by the end, she was practically in tears trying to extricate it.

The fates had clearly wanted Kat to catch that bouquet. I'd have to keep my eye on that girl.

Minutes later, upon freeing the garter from my leg—to the tune of various wolf whistles and catcalls—Adam turned his back on his single friends and relatives and tossed the garter over his shoulder.

None of the men seemed even the remotest bit interested in catching that, either. But, hilariously, the garter landed on Jordan's head—despite the fact that he had pointedly closed his eyes and stuffed his hands in his pockets when Adam had thrown it.

When he'd realized what had happened and that it was now sitting on his head, he clearly wanted to punch Adam. And my groom laughed his ass off at his best man.

After cutting the cake—chocolate with raspberry filling, white and gold frosting—we very civilly managed not to cram the slices in each other's face when we fed each other. Then came the toasts—Jordan's, surprisingly, was eloquent and quite civilized.

Adam and I stayed at the reception until the ringing in of the New Year and slipped quietly away minutes afterward. When we left, the party was still going strong without us. Everyone was having a blast, like we'd hoped.

We ducked into an elevator that would take us directly to the honeymoon suite, where the butler had had my items moved this afternoon. Which worked out perfectly, because I had a wedding night surprise in store for Mr. Drake. One I hoped he'd enjoy.

The minute we were alone in the elevator, he pulled me into his arms and kissed me. "So you know, I'm *only* referring to you as Mrs. Drake from now on."

I tilted my head back to gaze into his face, giving him a wide smile. "So I'm the tree and you're peeing on me with your name to mark your territory?"

He winced slightly. "Not quite the way I'd put it. But in a way, yeah...because *finally* you are all mine. Mia even means *mine* in Italian. It's like the universe aligning."

"Or conspiring."

His arm tightened around mine. "I want the world to know it...Mrs. Drake. *Tu sei mia*. You are mine."

"Looks like I'm going to have to find a way to mark *my* territory," I said with a meaningful tap on the wedding ring now gleaming from his left hand.

"I could offer a few suggestions."

"I bet you could."

The doors slid open, right into our suite. And I turned, gasping. All the lights were blazing, and all the entire suite was buried under a snowy blanket. White flowers and petals of every type covered every surface. White petals across the bedspread. White lilies even floated in the infinity pool and hot tub. Like a fresh snowfall in the tropics.

"This is *beautiful*."

He scanned the room, equally in wonder. "*And* a complete surprise—even to me."

"Oh dear, have they managed the impossible? Have they taken Adam Drake by surprise?"

He laughed, unbuttoning his waistcoat and loosening his tie.

"I'm so exhausted. I think I can sleep for a week." I stretched my arms over my head. "Please tell me our honeymoon has lots and lots of sleeping scheduled."

"You'll be able to sleep as much as you want," he said, giving me that knowing smile he always did when he had a secret— which was often. Adam loved his secrets.

"When do I get to find out where we are going?"

"Tomorrow morning, when we leave for...wherever we are going."

I shook my head, laughing, kicking off my shoes. "You know, I'm not even going to try to guess. I've learned my lesson when it comes to you and surprises."

"Except when they involve rockets and payloads of shooting stars?"

I laughed. "Yeah." I sank into the nearest petal-covered chair with a sigh. "I'm *so* tired. So much hot sex all night long..."

Adam toed off his own shoes and left the vest and tie on the nearby dresser before moving over to the bed to sit down on it and stare at me.

"You are gorgeous. Have I told you yet?"

I grinned. "About three hundred and seventy-two times. But that's okay. I like hearing it."

I reached around and unhooked the pearl and diamond choker and matching earrings, setting them on the dresser next to his things.

"I think I should go slip into 'something more comfortable,'" I said, making air quotes.

"I hope it's that naughty nurse's outfit I've been craving." He laughed, unbuttoning his shirt.

I stood. "With the type of patient you are? *Hell no.* That is one fantasy we will *never* be acting out."

He made a face at me. "I wasn't *that* bad."

I grabbed the chic lingerie bag from one of the dresser drawers then headed for the bathroom. "You were the grumpiest of the grumps. No, thank you."

"Never say never, Emilia," he retorted as I shut the bathroom door.

He'd admit, as soon as he saw me, that my choice had been a far better one than a naughty nurse's outfit.

Almost a half-hour later, after I'd removed the wedding dress, freshened up my hair, and figured the contraption out, I reappeared, covered modestly from neck to knee in one of the resort's complimentary bathrobes. Almost all of the lights had been extinguished, except for one. It provided an indirect, ambient lighting that equaled that of lit candles...nice and romantic.

My husband lay across the covers of the bed, wearing nothing but his underwear. He was staring up into the netted canopy, thinking, when I came up to stand in front of him.

His head turned, and he gazed at me expectantly. "When I saw you in that dress today, I thought that I'd never want to see you in anything else. Am I about to change my mind?"

I shrugged demurely, loosening the belt and lowering my robe to the floor so he could see me in the chic Agent Provocateur lingerie. The thing had cost me a small fortune, but hey, only the best for a billionaire's wedding night.

"Holy shit," he muttered, sitting up with wide eyes.

The sparkly ensemble covered nothing at all, in fact. Not that it was really supposed to. It was for purely decorative—and titillating—purposes only. In fact, it was nothing but a series of thin chains holding together coin-sized golden disks in order to imitate a sexy chain mail dress. And it left little to the imagination. I held my arms out and let him have his glimpse.

The cold metal settled against my nipples, causing them to tighten, and though his facial expression revealed nothing, the obvious and immediate swell in his underwear said it all.

I posed prettily. "Now all I need is a giant glowing sword, and I'm all ready to be a first-level character in Dragon Epoch."

Adam rolled onto his side, propping his head up on his hand to study me. His eyes glided over me appreciatively, taking in the small metal disks of my "chain mail" lingerie. The unmistakable glow of lust smoldered in his dark eyes.

Then he sighed loudly. "Oh. I was thinking that with the all-night aerobics we participated in last night, we could take it easy tonight. Maybe cuddle and talk."

I blinked, lowering my arms. *What the...* "Huh?"

He cleared his throat and glanced out the window. "Yeah. We'll tell each other stories and spoon and fall asleep holding hands."

"*For real?*"

He watched my face for a long moment before busting out with laughter.

"Of course not," he said. "God. You're standing right in front of me naked except for that glittery slave girl bikini, looking like you stepped off the set of *Return of the Jedi*." He patted the spot beside him, and I climbed into the bed, settling there. "It's *all* for me. I'm not wasting all that with some spooning, that's for damn sure." He reached out and smoothed a hand up the inside of my bare thigh. "I don't care if I was half dead, I'd still be all over you, explosive spleen or not."

We kissed—he pinned my head back against the pillow ferociously, forcing my mouth open with his. When I came up for air, we were both breathing heavily. "I was worried there for a minute. That didn't sound like you."

He laughed. "I could want to cuddle and spoon..."

I made a face. "Maybe if you were half dead."

We kissed again, this time less urgently. He was trying to figure out how to get his hands up under my chain mail armor.

"If I'm the slave girl, then that makes you Jabba the Hutt."

He did his Jabba laugh. "Mmm. Fresh meat." He squeezed my thigh. "Jabba hungry."

"Now *that* sounds more like you."

As he leaned in to kiss me again, and my hands encircled his neck, I thought about how we hadn't forgotten a thing, how we were falling into the patterns we'd learned when we first started making love. Every movement of ours was like a dance.

Our choreography was practiced, but always fresh. Never tired.

We possessed an elegance branded all our own—legs aligned, parallel lines growing slowly tangled, then perpendicular, then locked together, needy. We intersected at certain vital points, becoming part of each other's geometry, then separated again.

Skin kisses, touching, pressing, kneading against one another. Hands smoothing, grasping, pressing, gripping, releasing. Breathy exhales mingling, inhaled once again. Everything a new mix of my chemistry and his. This wasn't a mere blending of our bodies, the intersection of our sexual organs. We blended of our breath, our sweat, our skin cells. We merged and then separated, different in chemistry, different in body, different in soul.

Every time Adam and I made love, I came away with a new piece of him to carry around with me.

"Okay, that does it. I'm going to be unconscious in five minutes," he muttered after he'd rolled away from me, lying flat on his back, flush from the afterglow of his orgasm. The tangle of my metallic chain mail lingerie now lay in a shiny pool on the floor, all but forgotten. I rolled over, resting my head on his hard chest.

"Did I wear you out already?"

His hand came up to twine through my hair. As the low light glinted off his wedding ring, a thrill zinged through me. Perhaps I liked witnessing my *proof of ownership* as well.

"Only temporarily," he answered. "And mostly because of last night."

We stayed like that for long minutes. His hand relaxed, and his breathing became measured. I lay pillowed on his chest as he slept, his breath tickling my hair. I was tired, too. *So* tired. But I couldn't sleep.

I was a married woman. Someone's wife. *Adam's* wife.

Everything had changed even while *this* felt so familiar, so comforting, so us.

With a finger, I traced the outlines of the muscles on his delicious abdomen, and without realizing it, I was whispering their names. *"External obliques. Pyramidalis. Tendinous inscription."*

My hand traveled lower, toward his navel. *"Umbilicus."*

"What are you doing down there?" he muttered, and it startled me because I thought he'd fallen asleep.

"Oh, nothing."

318 | BRENNA AUBREY

"You're whispering something. What is it?"

I sighed. "It's nothing much. I was...um...taking this opportunity to brush up on my anatomy." I touched the ridge of muscle where his abdomen ended and his hip began, tracing it the entire length. His skin rippled under my touch as if I'd tickled him. "This is the *anterior iliac spine.*" I traced lightly along the skin, over the light dusting of dark hair on his belly to land north of his pubic bone. "This is the *reflected inguinal ligament.*" Which I duly outlined, slowly, firmly. "And this is—"

He grabbed my hand and pressed it to his burgeoning erection. "What's this one called?"

I thought for a moment as I palmed him. Despite his claim of exhaustion, it was already growing firm under my touch. "This one is called...Robocock."

"That's right," he said with a wide grin.

"How many wife points do I get for that?"

"Right now, you get all the wife points. You're a top scorer."

Then he hooked an arm around me and pulled me on top to straddle him, his hands wasting no time to find my breasts, palming them. "Definitely at the top of the leaderboard right now."

"Only for now?"

We managed one more time before we both collapsed in exhaustion. An hour or so later, when I awoke for a few minutes, I realized with a tired smile that we were spooning.

***

Adam was already up, showered, and dressed before I even stirred. Bright light through the open doorway hit me straight in the eyes, and I rubbed them, rolling over.

"Time to get up, sleepyhead," he said from the desk where he, unsurprisingly, sat in front of his laptop, sipping at a mug of coffee. "Happy New Year."

"Are you seriously working? On the first day of our marriage?"

He gave me a benign smile. "Down, girl. I'm tying up the last loose ends before we leave. I'm not even taking the laptop with me. Nor am I taking my phone."

"Oh?" I perked up. "For three weeks? You're going completely without?"

"I went two months without sex, and let me say I'd rather have sex than my cell phone, so this should be cake."

I folded my arms behind my head and settled back against the pillow. "I'll believe it when I see it."

"Which means you are one hundred percent responsible for my 'entertainment.' We have to be up and out of here in an hour, so you'll see it soon."

"And where are we going?"

"You'll find out soon."

I gave a long-suffering sigh as I slipped out of bed and scooped the shiny lingerie from last night off the floor. "I hope there are more where that one came from." Adam nodded to it. "We'll be making good use of them."

I shook my head, depositing the lingerie on the dresser before hitting the bathroom and the shower.

Adam Drake and his mysteries...I guessed I'd known what I was getting into, didn't I?

Chapter 23
Adam

S HE HAD NO IDEA THE AMOUNT OF PLANNING THAT HAD gone into this surprise and why I was unwilling to give it up until the very last minute.

I was sure she was irritated with me, but hopefully, her delight would make up for it.

We raced toward Port Castries, the port of St. Lucia, in a high-speed boat that had taken us from the beach at Emerald Sky. A select group of people from the wedding—our closest friends and family who had wanted to get up early enough to see us off—were with us. Emilia still thought we were headed to the airport.

But as we rounded the last point, the harbor, with all of the white boats and bare masts lined up like soldiers, came into view, and her beautiful brow crinkled into a frown.

Soon, all would become clear. But she turned to me, clearly puzzled behind her dark sunglasses. I reached out and grabbed her hand. Her long, dark hair whipped behind her as we slowed and crept to a stop near one of the docks. The boat driver helped us out one by one, and I led the group to walk toward where the captain told me it would be.

"That looks like your yacht, Adam," Uncle Peter pointed out.

I glanced up at my boat, my hundred-foot yacht that had been taken from our home about three weeks before—"for repairs," I'd told her.

It had actually been taken for a few minor additions and changes and then brought around to the Caribbean, via the Panama Canal, to meet us here.

"Adam's boat doesn't have a name," Kim said. "That one is named *Eloisa.*"

I watched Emilia, who was staring at the boat with an open mouth. On the transom, newly painted in gorgeous script, it read:

Eloisa

Newport Beach

Her hand twitched inside of mine, as if she wanted to pull it free. My hold tightened around hers. I hoped that she appreciated the gesture—that I'd named the boat after her Dragon Epoch character rather than her real name.

She stopped. "What is this? Did you have your boat renamed?"

"It was never named before. Now it is." I stopped beside her.

"Why *Eloisa?*" Kim asked, and I didn't bother to answer. Heath was already explaining. Emilia stared at me with wide eyes behind her sunglasses.

"You had it brought all the way over here? Why?"

I smiled. "For our honeymoon. We're leaving on our own private cruise through the Windward Islands."

"Woo-hoo. Way to go, Mia!" Kat said from behind us.

"At last it's no longer a mystery!" She smirked at Kat. "I have a pretty awesome husband—though I'm sure the itinerary will remain a mystery."

Shaking my head, I filled her in. "We have some bigger ports scheduled, like Dominica and Grenada, but we also have a few privately owned islands and, for a few nights, a deserted island all for us."

"See," Kat jumped in. "He's giving up his secrets."

"Not all of them." I chuckled.

Emilia let out a long-suffering sigh. "Of course not." I brought her hand up to my lips and kissed it. "You like surprises too much."

"Only when I'm the one doing the surprising."

Our friends and family all came on board with us to wish us well while my yacht captain completed a final check before departure—and ran us through a mandatory evacuation drill.

The speedboat that had brought us here would return everyone to the resort, where they would stay a few more days. But first, we all enjoyed champagne and snacks, courtesy of a chef I'd hired for our cruise—as my usual executive chef hadn't been able to commit to the length of our trip. The food—Caribbean fusion canapes, creole-spiced crayfish, shrimp cocktail—was delicious.

With our family all disembarked, we left port while they stood on the pier cheering.

Once they were out of earshot, I pulled her close against me and kissed her gently. That familiar thrill tickled the back of my awareness. But this time it was more acute. Instead of kissing a woman I was powerfully attracted to or my girlfriend or even my fiancée…I was kissing my wife.

Calling her that, even in my head, compounded that exhilarating feeling, turned it into an electric jolt. It was more than physical attraction, more than sexual excitement. I was over the moon and so goddamn lucky that this woman—this amazing, strong, beautiful, brilliant woman—had chosen me to be the man to stand beside her for the rest of our lives.

We'd paid some heavy prices get to this moment. But being here with her, watching that shiny diamond sparkle in the sunlight off her left hand, knowing it was *my* ring she wore, *my* name she bore, *me* whom she had chosen... To be here in this moment after all that was worth any cost it had taken to get us to this point.

And I was certain there was not a happier man on this planet at this moment than me.

She kissed me back, with every bit of enthusiasm I showed her. And when she looked up into my eyes, the pure love I felt shone right back at me. She reached up, smoothing my hair against my head as it ruffled in the wind.

"Well, well, Mr. Drake. Here we are—you and me, alone at last. I can't think of a better honeymoon."

"You'll be sick of me soon."

"Not a chance." Her wide grin parted those kissable lips and revealed her gleaming teeth.

I took her hand, and we relocated to the bridge for an unobstructed, two-hundred-degree view.

"Next stops, Lesser Antilles Archipelago," the captain said. "Any directions?"

I turned to my wife, who was staring out the window, gazing at the wide, deep blue ocean before us. "Mrs. Drake?" I asked.

She turned to me. "Yes?"

"Any direction for the captain?"

She frowned at me for a minute before smiling. "Out there?" she mumbled. "How about thataway? Second star to the right and straight on till morning?"

I shook my head. "It's *your* order. Give whatever you want."

"Okay." She nodded. "Let's go west, then. I've always wanted to sail off into the sunset. And straight into our future."

I pulled her against me, kissing her neck. "As you wish, Mrs. Drake."

Chapter 24
Katya

JEDI BOY: *CRANBERRY—YOUR LAST BUG REPORTS WERE incomplete. I hope you're on the way into the office. I need that shit done yesterday.*

Me: *Just landed. Those reports are SO complete. You have to stop inventing all these excuses just to see me.*

Jedi Boy: *Not everyone can just drop their work to go sun themselves in the Caribbean for weeks.*

Me: *Jealousy looks so unflattering on you.*

Jedi Boy: *You're starting to piss me off.*

Me: *I love you, too, darrrrrrrrrrrling! <3 <3 <3 *smooch**

I looked up and scanned the large room that Heath and I had just entered on our way to baggage claim. Signs everywhere labeled it *Customs and Immigration.*

My roomie—and travel buddy—leaned down with a knowing smirk. "That your team leader again? We just barely landed. Was he stalking the flight info?"

I shrugged. "Probably. He can't run his damn department without me, apparently."

Heath gave me an obnoxious wink. "Maybe it's more than just a work thing. I bet he's been pining away for you."

I shook my head. "I don't buy into your dumb theory about that."

His massive shoulders twitched. "Doesn't matter whether or not you buy into it. Someone who pesters you as much as he does isn't doing it just because of work. He wants you."

"Maybe he just savors the role of *pain in the ass.*"

Heath pointed at a sign that bore both the stars and stripes beside a big red maple leaf. "Over here. Canucks go through the same line as Americans."

"Lucky us." I tucked my cell phone into my back pocket and began digging around in my backpack for my passport as we fell into line.

We wound through long lanes of retractable nylon stanchions that formed a little maze. Around me, I caught scraps of different languages spoken. Spanish mostly, but also Arabic and Chinese. The people speaking these languages appeared every bit as diverse as the languages themselves—women in colorful hijab scarves, men in robes or loose fitting trousers. All looking as exhausted as I felt after their own long flights.

Hearing spoken French, oddly, reminded me of home. No matter where someone lived in Canada, even in the most English of the provinces like my home British Columbia, he could not escape the plush accents of spoken French. Despite all those years I was required to take it in school, however, I still understood hardly a word.

"This place is usually packed. We must have hit a lull," Heath said.

As we walked directly to the passport agent, I kept my head down. I had no idea if they used facial recognition cameras here. And it was probably paranoia on a tin-foil hat crazy kind of level to assume that anyone would be actively hunting for me. But if I was in a database somewhere…

Breathe, Kat. Don't be nervous. I swallowed, trying to ignore the pulse pounding at my throat, drying my mouth. I'd finished my water bottle on the plane and was completely parched. And damn, did I ever have to use the washroom. Could I back out now and run for the toilet? *Breathe, Kat. Don't show your fear.*

Flashing through my brain at light speed was every possible problem that could occur.

No. There would be *no* problems, I assured myself. I shook the tension out of my shoulders. *I've got this.*

There wouldn't be a problem, would there?

Governments didn't communicate that well between themselves, anyway. No way could this passport controller guy have any ideas about what went on in Canada. Americans seldom cared enough to know much of anything about the country just north of them. *So neglect becomes my ally.*

"Ladies first," Heath gestured to the next available passport control officer, and I nudged ahead of him, making a face at his flowery show of chivalry.

"I'll let any ladies around here know. In the meantime, Awesome Gamer Chicks first," I replied, and he snorted.

It would be perfectly fine. Perfectly normal. But if there was nothing to worry about, why was my heart thrumming at the base of my throat as I pushed that little navy blue booklet across the counter toward the man in the booth?

I grinned wide, hoping the toothy smile would help with my plans of distraction.

"Hey, there. How are you?" I piped.

The man, middle-aged with dead eyes, showed no reaction whatsoever. His sausage-like fingers snapped up my passport, and he fumbled to the right page. I waited while he flipped to my picture then held the book in front of him to glance from the picture to my face and back again.

"Name?"

"Katharina Ellis." I made a funny face and posed in profile. "Sorry about the nasty picture. It wasn't exactly my best side."

No reaction. He was already typing the number on my passport into his computer. My fingers—of their own accord—drummed on the counter in front of me. I plopped my free hand on top of them to stop them and shifted from one leg to the other. I tried some yoga calming techniques the moment I recognized that my rapid breathing was causing my chest to rise and fall too quickly. *Breathe in slowly through the nose. Hold breath. Count to three. Let it go through the mouth.*

The man paid no notice, scrutinizing his screen instead. Heath had already passed through his booth and was standing, his American passport clutched in a big hand. He waited for me on the other side. People filed past him to head toward baggage claim.

I caught his eye, and he raised brows at me as if to ask what was going on. I shook my head and shrugged. Were it not for the sign prohibiting cell phones while at the passport control station, I might have pulled out mine to text him.

"How long were you out of the country, Ms. Ellis?"

"Just two weeks. For a friend's wedding." My voice quavered, and I buried the sound in a loud cough.

The man frowned at his computer screen as he typed some more. Was there a problem? What? What did he see on that tiny screen that made him scowl even more than before? That pulse at my throat started to pound. I swallowed through it and resisted the urge to wipe my sweaty palms on my jeans. If I did that, I may as well broadcast to the world that I was a potential fugitive. My nervousness couldn't have been more obvious if I'd tried.

Consoling myself with the thought that it was likely just a new procedure or maybe the system was slow today, I breathed again and continued to chew my thumbnail down to a nub. I watched the officer carefully.

Then he suddenly had a friend standing right next to him. Uh-oh. Since when did Canadians get the full security treatment? We were the cheerful, polite northern neighbors that Yanks liked to poke fun at and we took in stride. No extra security necessary. Except...

This was a new United States of America. Don't give us your tired, your poor, or your huddled masses. We don't need them anymore.

"Ms. Ellis, can you come with me?"

Shit was getting real. Damn it. I *knew* I shouldn't have left the country. But how the hell could I have missed Adam and Mia's wedding? And how could I have told them I couldn't come?

And how to explain to Adam, my boss, that I wasn't even legally working for his company?

My phone buzzed in my pocket. I glanced at Heath, and he had no phone in his hand so it must have been Lucas getting back to me.

I froze, a Canadian deer in the US Immigration headlights. "Ms. Ellis? We have a few questions. Come with me to screening, please?"

My passport officer was now standing as if expecting me to bolt. Where the hell would I go?

Heath walked toward us, and my officer turned, holding up a hand. "Come no farther. You've made your way through control."

Heath's brows crunched, and he held out a hand toward me. "She's my friend. I want to stay with her."

"You're going to have to wait."

"How long will it take?"

"No idea. Go back to baggage claim and wait there. And *don't* come any farther."

I turned to Heath, our eyes met, and I shook my head. The concern in his eyes was clear—his blond brows scrunched together so tightly they looked like one big unibrow.

"Ms. Ellis? *Now*, please."

I jerked back toward the officer. "But my bags."

"You'll need those."

"Can I go get them? Or can he grab them for me?" I gestured to Heath.

"He needs an officer to go with him." My passport controller pressed a button and another, equally dour, bland man showed up in seconds. It's like he was cloning himself.

I turned to Heath, holding up a hand to my ear like a phone, and mouthed, *Call a lawyer.*

"The Canadians?" he replied. He must have meant the Canadian consulate, and a streak of fear shot through me. Shit, *no*, that would be *worse*. I shook my head vigorously, eyes wide. *No consulate,* I mouthed, but he looked puzzled, like he had no clue what I was saying.

Then goon number two grabbed my arm and pulled me toward wherever their torture chamber was located. I wondered how many hours of waterboarding I'd be subjected to before being shipped to Gitmo. *Freaking barbarian Yankees.*

Thank goodness I was good Kat, instead of bad Kat, and bit my tongue. Bad Kat got into so much trouble due to her big mouth. I was in what some might refer to as a semi-barbaric country that still practiced the death penalty and required no mandated maternity leave. Despite its flaws, however, I *did* want to continue living in the States. It took my full concentration to ignore the strains of *O, Canada* which rose in my head, unbidden. *The True North strong and free!*

They led me to a tiny windowless room with two chairs, a table, and a bench. "Wait here."

And they *locked* the door! They fucking locked me in.

Pacing the room only made me dizzy because it was tiny and forced me to walk in minute circles. My mind spun in circles, too. It wouldn't stop racing—wouldn't stop wondering, accusing. Blaming myself.

I should have checked before this to make sure that subpoena hadn't caused a warrant to be issued. Perhaps there had been attempts made to locate me. All this time, I'd been so sure that the Canadian government didn't know where I was. But after this?

I pulled out my phone and quickly texted Heath.

Me: *No Canadian consulate.*
Heath: *Why not? And where the fuck did they take you?*
Me: *I'm in some little cell.*
Heath: *You're in JAIL?*

334 | BRENNA AUBREY

I hurried to type a response when my phone buzzed, once more, but from a different source.

Jedi Boy: *Cranberry, are you on the road yet? I was serious about you needing to get in here.*
Me: *Not now, Lucas!*

The door whipped open, and I almost dropped my phone just as Heath's text popped up.

Heath: *Hold tight, K. I'm calling lawyers now.*

"Ms. Ellis? We'll need to collect your electronic devices."

"*What?*" I immediately shoved my phone in my bra. "You'll have to pry that from my cold dead hands! No one takes my phone."

The officer blinked and straightened. "Do you want entry into the United States of America, Ms. Ellis?"

"Why am I being held?"

He folded his arms across his chest, planting his feet wide apart. "I'm not going to tell you that at this time. Your phone? And your passcode, please."

"You can't search me. I know what your laws say. I have rights."

"We can collect your materials. You are not subject to US law at this time, as you have not been admitted into the country."

His eyes were fixed on my bra—because my phone was in there, but I poked my ample chest out anyway. I knew what my rack did to most weak-hearted men. He jerked his eyes away from my perfect boobs. I folded my arms across my chest.

"Your phone, Ms. Ellis. Or we can have you on a plane back to British Columbia in thirty minutes or less."

A weight dropped in my stomach, knowing I'd likely face a similar team of goons at that airport. And so much more. *Shit. Goddamn it. Fuckity fuck.*

"You aren't going to waterboard me, are you?"

His face darkened. Bad Katya had reared her ugly head. Dammit. My face reddened, and all he did was hold out his hand. Heaving a long, labored sigh, I pulled the phone from my bra.

"It's nice and warm. From touching my bare breast."

The guy rewarded me with a nice red blush before snatching the thing out of my hand and walking to the door. He spun. "Passcode?"

"What are you looking for on that?"

He raised his brows at me. "Code?"

I almost let out a few naughty words about asshole yanks, but refrained, mumbling the code.

Without another word, he was gone. And I was stuck in that damn room. For *hours.*

Without my phone, I had no idea how long it was, because there was no clock in here.

I sat.

I lay across two chairs.

I lay across the table, hands under my head, staring up at the ceiling.

Someone brought me a bottle of water at some point. And let me use the washroom.

No one answered my questions.

I may as well face the music. I was probably on my way back to Vancouver this afternoon. Oh, the look on my family and friends' faces when I showed up after disappearing without even a goodbye the year before.

I rubbed my aching eyes through my lids, regretting for the eightieth time my little trip to the Caribbean. Epic wedding or no, I shouldn't have gone.

Because this had now ruined *everything*.

Suddenly, the door tore open again, and the first passport control guy entered with a man in jeans and a t-shirt, carrying a messenger bag on his shoulder.

"Ms. Ellis," the man said when the officer stopped without a word and looked from one of us to the other. "I'm Sam Wright. Your attorney."

Attorney? God, I hoped that meant *lawyer* in American.

I frowned, opened my mouth, but nothing came out. Suddenly, I was shaking like a leaf in the wind as goon number one stared at me like he was watching my every move.

"Heath Bowman called me."

"Thanks," I croaked.

The officer left us alone, warning that he'd be back shortly with some questions for me. I took in my new attorney from head to toe. He had a husky build, a dark beard covering his face. His khaki pants were baggy, and he wore Birkenstocks over fluffy white socks. And he was young—barely thirty.

"Pardon the lack of lawyerly appearance. It was my day off. I wasn't expecting to conduct any business today." I could forgive him anything but the Birkenstocks. But if he sprang me from detention, even those could be overlooked.

I motioned to the empty chair. "Sorry I don't have much to offer."

"How long have you been in here?"

"I have no idea. Hours. I don't even know what time it is."

He opened up his messenger bag and pulled out a tablet and a packet of papers. "I have a few forms I need you to fill out, but we can take care of that after he comes back in here. I'm going to assume you want to push back on this."

I blinked. "I'm not going back to Canada."

"Well..." His brows twitched together.

"What?" I asked, suddenly swallowing around another big lump.

"On the way in, I managed to obliquely question and get a hint of why they are detaining you. Apparently, you've been working in the US illegally?"

My gut tightened, and I closed my eyes, rubbing my forehead, the headache intensifying. Yeah, that did it. I was in deep shit.

"Why didn't you apply for a work visa?" Sam continued, not even bothering to give me a chance to deny it.

"There are reasons. Uh..." I fidgeted.

"Anything you say to me will be kept in strictest confidence. Attorney-client privilege."

I scratched my eyebrow, suddenly feeling twitchy. "I can't go back to Canada because I don't want them to know where I am."

"Them who? The government or private citizens or...?"

"The police."

He blinked. "Is there a warrant out for your arrest?"

I cleared my throat. It was suddenly difficult to draw the next breath. "I don't know. *Please.* You have to help me. I can't..."

"Did you commit a crime?"

"*No.*" My fists tightened, as if backing up that truth of their own accord.

He sighed, grabbing a pad of paper and scratching some notes. "Are you seeking asylum in the US?"

I almost laughed. From *Canada*? "No."

"Okay, we can get into the details of what is going on with you later, but for now, what I suspect is going to happen is that they are going to admit you into the country and serve you with a notice to appear before an immigration judge."

I blinked. "Okay."

"But if it's true that you've been working in the country without a visa, I'm going to be frank. Your options are few."

"I'll quit the job then." My stomach twisted as if in a vise at the thought of walking away from the best job I'd ever had but...if it meant I got to stay, I'd do it in a heartbeat.

He shook his head, lips thinning. "It's not that easy. There's no way to prove you won't just take another illegal job. You won't be allowed to stay, Katya."

Damn.

"So then what? They kick me out at that point?"

"As I said, your options are limited. But they aren't completely nonexistent." He hesitated, so I nodded eagerly for him to continue. If there was even a shred of hope that I could pull this shitty situation out of the crapper, I'd take it. With gusto.

"Are you in a relationship?"

I frowned, now completely puzzled at his non sequitur question. I opened my mouth to answer, but he held up his hand. "Don't answer me, please. Just consider. If you were, for example, about to marry a legal American citizen, that would be grounds to allow you to stay, provided the deal be sealed legally very soon."

I gulped.

Shit. He wanted me to get *married?*

"And...there's no other way?"

He looked at me. "Given your circumstances? Probably not."

Crap. I had no boyfriend. I'd dated only a few guys since coming to California, and nobody—in any way, shape, or form—that could be construed as seriously. I worked too damn much and didn't get out, and it had been months, really, while I focused on my Twitch TV channel and my other goals for career advancement...

Heath? Could I ask Heath to do it?

"My, um, roommate..."

"Heath?"

"Yeah," I nodded. He'd do it. I knew he would.

"Be careful. Heath is openly gay. It's probably clear from his social media, too." I sat back, surprised that he knew all that about Heath. Before I could ask, he supplied the answer. "Heath is a friend of a friend. That's how I know—and why he called me. Anyway, something like that—a gay man entering into a heterosexual union—would be a dead giveaway that this is a *mariage blanc.*"

A white marriage. Hey, one instance where my limited French actually came through for me.

A marriage of convenience so that I could stay in the US. Where, apparently, they really didn't want me. Was it worth it?

My mind raced. If not Heath, then who? I needed to marry someone, goddamn it!

Sam asked me a few more questions, scribbling notes. The door was yanked open again, and this time, two people I'd never seen before entered. As there were no more empty chairs handy in my tiny little cell, they stood, looking straight at me and ignoring Sam.

One of them held my cell phone in his hand.

I held out my hand. "I want my phone, *please.*"

The two shared a look before he slowly bent to give it to me. I laid it on the table beside me. In doing so, I pressed the home button and the screen lit up with my text updates. There were at least five messages from Lucas, bitching me out for not replying to him.

Dumbass needed to take a chill pill and stop harassing me.

"Ms. Ellis, we've made note of the contacts and messages on your phone and have been able to confirm that you have been employed by a US company without the legal right to work in the United States. How—"

"I'm getting married!" I blurted.

Yeah. Those words came out of my mouth. My voice spoke them. It was definitely my voice. But I had no idea until the second they escaped my lips that that's what I was going to say.

My entire body began to shake.

"You're saying you're engaged? To an American citizen?"

"Yes," I nodded vigorously. "Um yeah, definitely."

The other man grabbed a small pad of paper from his pocket and scooped up Sam's pen. "Can you give us the name of your fiancé please?"

I glanced at my phone again. *My contacts.* I couldn't make up a name—couldn't channel my fourteen-year-old self and magic up a pretend boyfriend. It had to be someone in my contacts.

"Lucas," I blurted again in that faraway voice. "My fiancé's name is Lucas Walker."

ABOUT THE AUTHOR

Brenna Aubrey is a USA TODAY Bestselling Author of contemporary romance stories that center on geek culture.

She has always sought comfort in good books and the long, involved stories she weaves in her head. Brenna is a city girl with a nature-lover's heart. She therefore finds herself out in green open spaces any chance she can get. She's also a mom, teacher, geek girl, Francophile, unabashed video-game addict & eBook hoarder.

She currently resides on the west coast of the US with her husband, two children, and two adorable golden retrievers.
More information available at **www.BrennaAubrey.net**

To sign up for Brenna's email list for release updates, please copy & paste this link into your browser:
http://BrennaAubrey.net/newsletter-signup/

Want to discuss the Gaming The System series with other avid readers? Brenna's reader discussion and social group is located on Facebook
https://www.facebook.com/groups/BrennaAubreyBookGroup/

or Goodreads
https://www.goodreads.com/group/show/180053-brenna-aubrey-books-geekery-gaming.

Made in the USA
Las Vegas, NV
18 June 2021

24990452R00204